A COUNTRY QUANDARY

TALES FROM TOTTENBRIDGE
BOOK 1

VICKI HILTON

1

KITTY

KITTY HELD up the manila folder and tipped the contents onto the smooth, black desk.

"There you go, Stefan. It's all yours." Sheets of paper fell around him like a snowstorm.

Death by a thousand paper cuts.

"Katherine! Don't be so bloody dramatic. Let's talk."

"There's nothing to talk about. I only hope you and your new client will be very happy together. Enjoy the honeymoon period. They'll find out what you're really like soon enough."

Kitty stalked out of the room, her footfalls deliberate and efficient. Heat sprung to her cheeks, and sour bile pooled in her throat. Interns scattered in her wake as she reached her office and leaned against the door that closed behind her. She fought back hot tears. *I won't cry. I won't cry.* Her fists clenched into tight balls.

After six long years at Fenwick and Partners Law firm and countless hours of slog and sacrifice, Kitty's fate had come down to a decision by an "old boys" club she had no way of fighting. She didn't have the right equipment between her legs for a start.

Kitty had spent months cultivating the client, and when they'd requested she take over their account entirely, her boss had 'relocated' her to another team in what he called a parallel move. To her mind, the shift in her role was a demotion, plain and simple.

Unimpressed and full up to the gills with Stefan Watts and his unequal opportunities approach to her career, Kitty took his decision to the partners. No sooner had she rocked the boat then they'd closed ranks around him.

She could stick it out, suck it up, and make the most of things, but she'd had enough of head-butting the glass ceiling. On mutual agreement, she'd just completed her last day. And her last meeting with her jerk of a boss.

Kitty snatched the black-rimmed glasses off her nose and sat down behind her desk, massaging her temples with shaking hands. What would she do now? Her fast track to Senior Associate lay dead and buried. The bland simplicity of her office calmed her racing brain. Its lack of clutter acted like a balm to her chafed pride. A tentative knock broke into her thoughts.

"Yes?"

A flushed woman stood at the door, shifting awkwardly from foot to foot. As one of the newer assistants, Kitty had yet to commit her name to memory. She racked her brain to remember it. Mercifully the rhyme "Abbie gets my Cabbies" sprang to mind. This assistant had been organizing her travel recently.

"Abbie," Kitty said, hoping to hell she'd got her name right.

"Do you need me to do anything?" Abbie approached Kitty like she had a communicable disease, skirting the desk, unsure if Kitty welcomed her presence. "We can tie up loose ends, or I can help you organise your personal effects?"

How does organising an intravenous supply of gin sound?

"Thank you, Abbie, but I'm fine. Stefan can manage the

loose ends. Perhaps you can just order me a cab? I'll be leaving immediately."

The words jarred Kitty to the core. Her time at the company was over, and all her hard work would dissolve into thin air. She'd been right to turn down the new role. After the hours she'd put in to win this client, Stefan couldn't just glide in and take it away from her. She was worth more. If the powers that be couldn't see it, then that would be *their* loss.

As if he heard her thoughts, Stefan materialised at the door, his thin face a picture of concern. Kitty's eyebrows raised, and her lips met in a tight line.

"Thank you, Abbie, that'll be all. I'll be ready in ten," she said.

Abbie nodded and bolted from the room, pale and a bit sweaty. Barely moving out of the way for the flustered woman, Stefan kept his eyes fixed on Kitty as she popped her glasses back on. Ignoring him, she picked up a Sharpie and began to doodle on a pad of bright sticky notes lying on the desk. The door closed behind him with a soft click.

"You didn't do yourself any favours in there, Katherine. So childish," he said, all pretence of concern dissolved. "I think it's probably best that you move on."

Kitty stopped her doodling and put down the pen with white-knuckled fingers. She took a breath and stood to meet Stefan's eyes, looming over him like an Amazonian warrior, her four-inch heels adding to her already significant height.

"You've got to be kidding, Stefan? You pushed me out. But to be clear, you'll regret losing me." *Breathe, Kitty, don't lose control.* "I'm astounded you got away with it!"

Stefan shrugged, an arrogant smirk on his face.

"It comes down to talent, track record, and who you know. Maybe next time...."

"There won't be a next time. I'll never base my career on who my dad went to school with. Who my mum lunches with. And I'll never work with a narcissistic prick like you again."

Kitty opened the bottom drawer of her desk. She grabbed her pristine bag and strode towards the door, stopping to tap Stefan on the lapel of his jacket, making sure she had his attention.

"Good luck," she said, leaving the room with a big smile.

A sick satisfaction swelled in Kitty's chest, and her feet tapped out a regular rhythm on the carpet tiles as if she were walking in time to her own personal theme tune. "Eye of the Tiger" or "These Boots are Made for Walkin'?" Either would work.

Kitty swept out of the lobby and into the lift, settling against the wall with a smirk. How long would it take him to notice?

Her parting gift for her former boss was two-fold. Earlier that day, she had an ally in the IT department change his automatic email signature to:

Stefan Watts, All Round Dick Head

And she'd just left a square of lurid green paper stuck to his jacket lapel, bearing a single word in full caps.

PRICK

2

KITTY

THE TANG of the whisky sour hit Kitty's lips as she crossed her long legs and settled in for another drink. A watched kettle never boils, her mum always said, and she'd been right. Kitty's eyes wandered to the entrance for the hundredth time. According to her watch, the enormous clock that hung on the wall of the hotel bar was running late. She'd mention it to the concierge on her way to bed.

Where had Ronnie got to? It shouldn't take her sister this long to ride the tube across London. Free of her kids for a couple of days, maybe the promise of decent clothes shops and toddler-free changing rooms had distracted her. Quality sister time wasn't something they'd had much of lately, and excitement buzzed in Kitty's stomach. If she ever needed a sisterly pick-me-up, now would be the time.

The polished chrome of the bar glinted harshly in the halogen lights, and Kitty glanced around at tonight's clientele. Familiar faces. She'd spent the best part of a week sitting alongside them. Anonymous bodies in silent solidarity, each glued to their laptops.

Kitty squinted at the bartender, unclear if he'd served her

before. He could've been the same one as last night or someone totally different. They were all easy on the eyes but vanilla enough to blend into the surroundings without distracting anyone from their drinking. This one, though, could make a mean whisky sour.

A bustle at the hotel entrance caught her eye as Ronnie emerged through the huge glass doors, leaving an enthusiastic doorman in her wake. Laden down with expensive-looking bags, her sister charmed and giggled her way across the floor, pulling in everybody's eyes. She envied her vitality. Ronnie drew people like a magnet.

The concierge pointed Kitty out to her sister, who waved enthusiastically before handing her bags to a blushing porter. Ronnie's hug brought a lump to her throat.

"I can't believe I made it!" she said. "How are you? You look amazing, by the way. A life of leisure suits you."

Kitty ran her chewed nails through her three-day old hair. "You lie well, Ronnie, but I'll take the compliment. It's so good to see you," Kitty said as she guided her sister to the barstool beside her and nodded at the bartender.

After ordering another whisky for herself and a gin and tonic for her sister, Kitty took in the glorious creature that was Veronica Cameron. They were polar opposites. Where Ronnie had a petite and dainty figure, tall and clumsy described Kitty perfectly. Ronnie had ashy curls cut in a short bob, while Kitty's thick, dark hair hung in a curtain that reached her waist. Kitty had her mother's dark brown eyes, and Ronnie's were blue. She swore one of them belonged to the postman.

"So, tell me, Sis," Ronnie asked, eyes shining with excitement, "what the hell is going on? Skip over the details about your arsehole boss, but tell me, is there any news on the job front? Got anything lined up yet?"

"Not yet," Kitty sighed. "But it's only been a week. These things can take ages. I want to make sure I find the right job."

One that doesn't come with client theft as a side perk. "I've got good people on the case. As for the arsehole boss, I have a voodoo doll doing its thing in the hotel room. He'll be one ball short of the full package before the next full moon."

Ronnie giggled. "I'd expect nothing less. So, what've you been doing with your free time?"

Watching daytime TV and feeling sorry for myself.

"Oh, you know. I've been to a few galleries and done some shopping."

"Is that it? There've been no wild nights out, no debauched celebration of your temporary freedom with your sexy lawyer friends? I watched *Suits*. I know what goes on in law offices, and I can assure you that's what *I'm* expecting out of this weekend."

"Sorry to disappoint," said Kitty. "I'm a bit out of practice on the partying front."

"Spent too much time at your desk, as usual? You always were a slave to your work."

A sizzle of agitation brewed in Kitty's chest. What the hell was wrong with her wanting to be the best at what she did? Why was it a crime to chain herself to a desk and work like a slave, only to get shafted by the person she thought had her back? Not that she was bitter, obviously.

"Well, that's why I have you here. To show me the error of my ways and to get me drunk and disorderly."

"Cheers to that!" said Ronnie. "Seriously, though, you're living in a hotel, like a movie star! It's a waste not to hit up your little black book for some company."

Kitty huffed. "My little black book is more like a little blank book these days."

Ronnie's eyes narrowed. "How long since you had sex or went on a date even? I never hear about anything juicy going on in your life."

Kitty's heart sank. Not only had her knickers seen little action over the last couple of years, but she could count the number of friends she had on one finger. To say life had been all work, work, work, and more work was an understatement.

"A while," said Kitty, playing with her glass.

"Don't look so glum about it. Just remember what Mum always used to tell you." Ronnie put on a sing-song voice reminiscent of their mother's. "You'd be rather pretty, Katherine, if you would put on a bit of makeup and wear your hair down once in a while."

Kitty groaned and tapped her nail on the black marble bar top. She'd heard those words so often it was surprising her mum hadn't inked them on her forehead as soon as she popped out of the womb.

"Yes, thank you for the reminder." Kitty pulled her hair out of its low ponytail and shook it out. "How is Mum? I bet she's proud as punch that I'm unemployed and technically homeless."

"Oh, you know, barely coping. She's currently knee-deep in re-writes of *The Devil in the Keep*. It's the usual. Untamed Scottish Laird ruins buxom heiress. Pulitzer Prize, watch out!"

Kitty almost spat out her drink with her giggle. Their mum was a prolific historical romance writer. It'd been a curse during their teenage years.

"At least it's a decent hotel. Not the Travelodge at Heathrow Airport. That gives her something to be proud of, surely." Kitty swept an arm around the expansive art deco bar, past marble statues and giant palms whose leaves shuddered gently in the air conditioning.

"Why *are* you living in a hotel in Mayfair?" asked Ronnie, summoning the bartender with a flick of her wrist and an enormous smile. "We'll have the same again," she said to him. "But make it doubles."

"The company owned my apartment. I leased it from them. This is a stopgap until I work out what I'm doing."

"Well, it's a fancy stopgap!"

"I think I've earned it. If I'm going to be on the breadline shortly, I'll do it in style. Plus, I don't want to get a place if I land a job requiring a lot of travel. Do you want something to eat?"

While Ronnie studied the snacks menu, Kitty glanced around the bar, their reflections cast on the mirrors all around them. Her eyes flicked to the right and landed on two young men at the other end, looking far further into their evening than the Cameron sisters.

Kitty's cheeks fired hot under their interested gaze. They were city types, wearing a uniform of neat navy-blue suits and floppy fringed hair. When they noticed her attention, one of them gave her a long slow wink. Kitty froze. This sort of thing didn't happen to her! She'd never been picked up in a hotel bar in her life. Yes, in a conference centre cloakroom and a train carriage, but this was different. This felt grown up.

Kitty leaned into Ronnie, whispering. "Don't look now, but the strippers you hired have arrived," she said, the whisky taking effect.

Ronnie followed Kitty's gaze and grimaced. "I don't like the look of yours much. Any port in a storm, though. Of course, as an old married lady, I only qualify as your chaperone."

"Ronnie, they can't be older than twenty."

She grinned, her impish face lighting up with delight. "Ah, the youth of today, famous for their loose morals. Go get 'em, gorgeous."

As Kitty was about to throw a screwed-up napkin at her sister, the barman arrived, carrying a chilled bottle of champagne.

"Courtesy of the gentlemen along the bar," he said, nodding in the direction of the two men.

If Kitty thought her cheeks were red before, they must be like a fire truck now. The man who'd winked at her earlier licked gently along his lower lip, ending the gesture with a leer.

"We've got to send it back! Please, can we send it back?" Kitty pleaded with the barman, palms growing clammy.

"Calm down, Kitty," said Ronnie, examining the bottle's label. "This is good stuff; we don't want to offend anybody. Besides, it's already open. It would be a waste. Let's invite them over. I think you could do with some fun."

"No, thank you. This isn't my idea of fun."

"Are you crazy? Two *young*, good-looking men bought you a bottle of champagne and no doubt they're up for a good time. What's to say no to?"

Kitty sighed. Ronnie always did this. Railroaded whatever she wanted to do. Took over.

"Honestly, I can leave the three of you to it," Ronnie smirked. "I'll go upstairs to the room and put my rollers in."

Kitty's cheeks worked hard to suppress a smile at the image of her glamourous sister sitting in a fluffy hotel robe with lines of curlers in her hair, like a fifties sitcom housewife.

"Stop! I'm not accepting it. We've got our own drinks," she said.

Ronnie shrugged her shoulders. "Well, *I'm* not going to send it back." She lifted one of the glasses the bartender had poured and mouthed the words 'thank you' to the men whilst nodding towards her sister and adding an eye roll.

"Bloody hell, you are so embarrassing," Kitty squeaked.

"No. I'm taking every opportunity of fun I can get this weekend." She looked at Kitty. "And you need to take an interest in something other than work. You're missing out."

"Now you really do sound like Mum," said Kitty, playing with the edge of a napkin that lay on the polished bar top.

"I hate to break it to you, but your life makes mine look dull, and I have two kids and a mortgage."

Kitty glanced at the men who'd sent over the champagne. She couldn't deny they were cute, but two of them at once? It would be from famine to feast. Was she really ready for that?

She'd skipped her yoga classes for months, so she probably wouldn't be flexible enough for anything more than an evening spent in the missionary position.

The men stood to leave, and with a few quiet words, one of them gave something to the bartender. Kitty turned her back towards them, attempting to look nonchalant.

A few seconds after they'd gone, the bartender brought a folded napkin and placed it in front of her. She picked it up to read the words written inside, her heart skipping a beat.

If you change your mind, I'm staying in room 224

Damn. Ronnie leaned over Kitty's shoulder to read the message. Her eyes grew wide and sparked in mischief.

"You have to go see him! I'll hold the fort. I'll order room service for dinner. I'll do anything, but please go!" Her face took on a serious expression. "Kitty, it's for the greater good. The sooner you get laid, the sooner you can start living like the rest of the world, and we can all stop worrying about you."

Who was worried about her? She was wonderful. Just totally fine!

"It's not my style, Ronnie. Nobody needs to worry about me, but if I want to make senior associate by thirty-five, I don't need any distractions."

Ronnie sighed. "I wouldn't call *him* a distraction. I'd call him a blessing. Oh well. What will we do with the rest of our night if I can't persuade you?"

Kitty stood up, finished her glass of champagne, and picked up the bottle by its neck, turning to leave.

"Sorry to disappoint you, but we'll get all the drunkenness and debauchery done tomorrow. Tonight, I just want to fall asleep in front of Netflix and dribble on my pillow."

3

KITTY

KITTY EMERGED FROM THE BATHROOM, her head throbbing but her body alive with excitement. Ronnie had erupted into the room last night. She'd been shopping and draped her new purchases on every available surface.

Silk curtains and crystal chandeliers battled with dresses and jackets of taffeta and organza, not to mention a motherload of new shoes. Surrounded by the chaos, her sister's sleep-crumpled face still looked glamourous amongst the luxurious pillows. For once, the mess wasn't enough to distract Kitty from her train of thought.

"Hey, Sis! Wake up." Kitty kicked the dainty foot sticking out of the covers. Ronnie scowled, rubbed her eyes, and pulled herself onto her elbows.

"Ow! What's the matter?"

"Nothing's the matter. I just had a call from Aunt Julia." Ronnie sat full upright at the word "Julia."

"Why was Julia calling at...." She checked the digital clock next to the bed. "Seven on a Saturday morning?"

Kitty flopped down on the sateen chaise opposite the bed, avoiding sitting on a pair of Jimmy Choo shoes.

"Did you know she had a hip replacement?"

"Erm, no," Ronnie said. "I haven't spoken to her in years."

"Well, she and I keep in touch."

"You were always much closer to her," said Ronnie.

"She's had a dodgy hip for a while and apparently got a cancellation for an operation. She called to ask if I can help her with her animals until she's more mobile."

Ronnie pulled her fingers through her hair, a small crease in her brow. "What about Jonty? Isn't he around?" Their cousin Jonty lived in the same village as his mum.

"Apparently, he doesn't have the time. Lots of work on or something."

"Okay, so how many animals are we talking about?"

Kitty shifted in her seat. "Quite a few. There's her cat, of course, plus she has a few goats, some chickens, a sheep, and, ahem, a donkey."

"A donkey?" Ronnie scoffed. "Oh, Kitty, really? You can't cope with anything bigger than your average spaniel!"

"I know," she said gloomily. "Donkeys aren't the same as horses, though, are they?" Kitty had a long history with horses. Hated them. And what's more, they hated her.

"I think donkeys have bigger teeth," Ronnie said, laughing.

Kitty's eyes widened, and a shiver ran through her body as she recalled long-buried memories of her time in riding school. The countless falls and bites she'd received still haunted her dreams, but her mum insisted that she continue lessons. She was intent on finding Kitty a hobby.

"What did she say when you told her no?"

"I didn't exactly," Kitty said, chewing her bottom lip.

"Are you mad? Are you sure you're quite the right person to help her? No offence, darling, but you spent most of your teenage years with your nose in a book, and by the look of your skin tone, you've rarely seen daylight for the last five years.

What on earth makes Julia think you'd be any use looking after a bunch of farm animals?"

Wow, thanks for the vote of confidence, Sis.

Although Kitty conceded Ronnie had a point, she didn't like anyone questioning her competence.

"I think you'll find I'm pretty adaptable," she said, arms folding in front of her body.

"But you're such a neat freak! You hate mess, and I know for a fact you have an aversion to mud."

Again, Kitty had to agree. She'd been the only kid on the street who'd brought wet wipes to the park. Ronnie was hitting her stride and climbed out of bed to get sparkling water from the minibar. The pale sun from the window hit her skin, and her cheeks glowed peaches and cream.

"Can you imagine how you'll cope mucking out a bunch of goats or wading elbow-deep in chicken poo?"

The thought of a stinky chicken coop sent a shudder through Kitty. But, as far as she was concerned, her sister had thrown down the gauntlet. She'd show Ronnie she could handle life in the country. Hadn't she spent plenty of time at her aunt's house growing up? And the thought of whiling away a few months in a sleepy village, with pleasant company and time to lick her wounds, sounded appealing. Besides, it was only a matter of time before she'd return to her real life—away from anything with big teeth.

"I think I'll be just fine, thanks," Kitty said, her jaw set tight.

Ronnie raised her eyebrows. "When do they need you by? We still have all the drunk and disorderly stuff to do while I have the chance."

"Well, we better make a start," said Kitty, grabbing a towel from under one of Ronnie's bags. "I said I'd be there tomorrow."

Ronnie tipped back the bottle of water, drinking the entire

thing before eyeing her sister up and down with a smirk on her face.

"I just hope Aunt Julia has a substantial supply of sexy young men waiting for you."

4

KITTY

KITTY DROVE into Tottenbridge late the next afternoon, just as a tempestuous thunderstorm blew over. A vivid rainbow, ignited by the blazing sun, tattooed the slate grey sky. She followed the gentle bend at the end of High Street and approached a charming, thatched-roof pub.

As a youngster, she'd spent many happy hours at The Five Bob. She'd sipped lemonade and caught tadpoles in the pond at the back of the old coaching inn. Nostalgia swept over her as she pulled into the gravelled carpark, heartened to see the words "Off Licence" chalked onto a blackboard outside. *Perfect.* She could get her aunt a bottle of something nice to thank her for the invitation to stay.

After parking, Kitty ducked through a small doorway into the pub. The interior was dark and cool, a pleasure after the muggy air outside. Sturdy oak beams supported a nest of edges and corners, sucking in the light filtering in through the tiny windows. Kitty's pumps tapped on the flagstone floor as she crossed the room, and a deep voice sounded out from somewhere low down behind the bar.

"I'll be with you in a second."

The voice was smooth and husky. Intriguing. Kitty stood on tiptoes and peered over the oak slab of the bar. Two perfectly formed butt cheeks appeared in the shadows as their owner bent over. He wore tight black trousers that left little to the imagination.

The attractions at The Five Bob *had* improved. She'd take sculpted buttocks over tadpoles any day. Wide-eyed and with heat creeping over her face, Kitty lowered her heels silently and pretended to study the wine list, praying that the owner of that beautiful bottom had a gorgeous face to match.

After a few seconds, he emerged, as tall, dark and handsome as she'd prayed he would be. He ran his hands through his slicked-back hair, then placed them on the bar top.

Kitty looked at them, spread out on the wood, and the man coughed as if to get her attention. The noise startled her. *Crap.* What if he thought she'd been checking for a wedding band or a hint at the size of his package? She quickly brought her eyes up to his face, but before she did, she couldn't help but notice he wore no ring on his finger, and his hands were a most satisfactory size.

When their gazes met, the professional look he'd had on his face disappeared instantly. Instead, a devilish smile slowly grew on his lips that had Kitty licking her own. The glint behind his dark eyelashes set a fire in her cheeks like his stare held an invitation to join him on a dark adventure. Cursing her traitorous capillaries, she straightened her shoulders.

"Hello there," the man said.

"Oh! Hello," Kitty replied, feigning surprise at his sudden appearance. "I didn't see you down there. Can I please get something to take out?"

The man drew up close to the bar, his eyes glued to hers.

"What did you have in mind?" he murmured.

Kitty didn't want to admit what she had in mind. With those buttocks, the possibilities were endless.

"I'm not sure. I'm thinking bubbles or perhaps a bottle of gin."

"Well, what's the occasion?" he asked, leaning on the bar, broadening his delicious smile.

"It's a thank-you gift. I'm staying with someone in the village and don't want to turn up empty-handed."

"Perhaps I can help. Who are you staying with, if you don't mind me asking?"

Ignoring every anti-stalker rule she'd ever made for herself, Kitty told him.

"My aunt, Julia Finch."

"Your aunt?" the man asked with a raised eyebrow, moving to take something from out of the fridge behind him.

He handed her a cold bottle of champagne, holding onto its neck a second longer than was necessary, in Kitty's opinion. She looked into his inky eyes, and as she took the bottle, a playful gleam danced there. A fizzing tickled in her chest, and under his scrutiny, she was aware of her glasses and make-up-free face.

"It's on the house," the man said, leaning back on the bar. "Please give Julia my love and best wishes for a speedy recovery."

"And you are?" Kitty asked, clenching her fingers around the chilled glass to stop them from shaking. Why the hell did good-looking men always make her nervous?

"I'm Daniel. Daniel Cunningham. Julia and my mother are old friends."

Daniel, Daniel Cunningham. Double-oh gorgeous and licenced to thrill.

Kitty's lips twitched at her thought, but then she remembered he'd offered to pay for the bottle. If she accepted, wouldn't she then be in his debt? She could easily afford a bottle of champagne on her own, and taking gifts from good-looking men with perfect buttocks was probably a bad idea.

"Thank you for the offer, but I'd prefer to pay myself. I'll pass on your message, though."

"As you like," he said, not even looking slightly phased. "Will you be staying long with your aunt?"

Kitty found her wallet and paid for the champagne.

"I'm here for a while."

His lips twitched at the corners. "Then let me know if it's not to your liking. I'm sure I can help you find exactly what you're looking for."

Kitty's eyes widened, sure there was a hidden meaning in his words, but his smooth smile betrayed nothing. Had she just imagined the flirtatious undertone? Had her sister's words about good-looking men and Tottenbridge seeped into her brain overnight?

Taking a breath, Kitty nodded, smiled, and turned to leave. Her whole body was on fire. It'd been a long time since anyone had made her feel so jittery. So skittish.

She'd taken issue with Ronnie's suggestion that she get laid and live a little, intending to do precisely the opposite. One-night stands weren't her style, and anything more wasn't in her career plan. Still, the tingles of attraction felt good. It was nice to know she was still alive.

Kitty sighed as she got into the car and gunned the engine. She'd better avoid the pub while she was in town.

5

DANIEL

DANIEL WATCHED THE WOMAN LEAVE. He savoured her long, elegant legs and the thick, chestnut hair that swung at her back before realising he hadn't even asked her name. On first impression, she'd underwhelmed him. The glasses she wore were too heavy for her face, and the severe plait did nothing to complement her fine features. But her plump lips were utterly kissable. And though her face was flushed and shiny in the heat of the day, her eyes held a challenge. A hint of hidden desire.

An image of her lying, hair spread out on a pillow beneath him, filled Daniel's mind, and his dick nudged in his trousers. Thoughts of her heavy-lidded eyes staring into his and soft lips whispering his name. *Fuck.* He needed to get a grip. To get laid.

He picked up a glass and helped himself to a shot of whiskey from the array behind the bar, filing thoughts of the stranger for later. He had other fish to fry. Front and centre of his mind was the new schoolteacher in the next village. After a sustained campaign of Cunningham charm, it was only a matter of time before he wore down her defences and she surrendered by falling into his bed. He swirled the ruby liquid around the glass. Why didn't the idea fill him with as much satisfaction as it had before Julia's niece walked into his pub?

"Who was that, Tiger?" Daniel turned to face the buxom redhead who managed his bistro, a suggestive smirk painted on her pink lips. She carried a pile of menus in her arms and had a pen tucked behind one ear. "Not your usual type," she said, the twang of her Australian accent familiar and soothing.

"Au contraire, Amber. I have many types."

She cocked a brow. "I'm well aware of that, and I'd overlook a quick flirtation, but I know that gleam in your eye usually means trouble."

Daniel's grin spread, and he pondered her, tipping his head to one side.

"How long have you been standing there?"

"Long enough to see the warning signs. Should I be the one to sound the alarm? Ring the church bells and warn any newcomers to arm themselves with a chastity belt?"

A chuckle escaped Daniel's lips. Amber never failed to make him laugh.

"I can always rely on your subtlety. I don't recall *you* ever resorting to a chastity belt. From memory, your drawbridge was down, and your portcullis was up." His lips curled, remembering the summer they'd met and the affair that followed.

"True, but we're both older and wiser now, aren't we?"

Daniel smiled ruefully. Amber was one of his biggest regrets and biggest comforts. Although they'd enjoyed a brief fling, she was always there. She was always happy to provide a bit of light relief in his otherwise predictable life. She never judged him and had lied for him on several occasions. And, best of all, she ran his bistro and pub like clockwork, leaving him free to pursue other, less wholesome hobbies.

"Tragically, yes," Daniel said, gently roughing up her hair. "You're immune to my charms these days. Though, I'm not sure

I can say the same." Daniel swept his eyes over Amber's ample chest, and she rolled her eyes.

"Whilst I appreciate the compliment, think again, darling. Once bitten, twice shy, remember?"

"Only once? I recall a lot more biting than that."

Amber winced. "Ouch. Okay, boss. Back to work. Here are the updated menus," she said, handing him the collection she had clutched at her chest. "I'll open the bistro."

6

KITTY

Kitty pulled up outside Rose Cottage. Its sturdy, white plaster walls and thick thatch roof were the scene of a thousand jigsaw puzzles. Memories of summers long gone flooded back. Often shipped off to spend the long holidays with her aunt, Kitty loved escaping the pressure of her overbearing mum.

Flashbacks of making forts in haystacks, gathering blackberries and fishing for minnows in the river filled her mind. Kitty smiled. How simple life had been back then. She had no intense drive in her gut to succeed and no thoughts outside of what adventures the next day would bring.

Kitty picked up the champagne and stepped out of her pristine Audi, and the steamy, earthy after-rain smell filled her nostrils. She smoothed down her skirt and checked that her hair was still in place. Before she could knock at the rose-rimmed door, it opened, and her cousin Jonty stood at the threshold with a huge grin.

“Hello, Kitty-Kat,” he called. Kitty threw him an exaggerated eye roll at the nickname. It had been years since she’d heard it. Jonty snickered. “We’ll have no insubordination, thank you. You’re here to work, Cinders.”

"Well, I see you've changed very little, Jonty," Kitty said, a smirk on her lips.

"Apart from the receding hairline and the developing paunch." He laughed, rubbing his pot belly. "Come in, and I'll show you to the kitchens."

Kitty followed Jonty into the cottage. Its interior was a collection of hodgepodge passageways and rooms. The low beams above her head made her feel like Alice after she'd sampled the "Eat Me" cake in Wonderland. Surfaces cluttered with trinkets and picture frames fought for space, and a worrying amount of cat fur coated the soft furnishings and gathered in the corners.

He led her to the kitchen. It was the heart of the house. Modern and tidy, and thankfully a decent coffee machine was perched on the countertop. French doors opened onto the patio, and the sweeping view of the fields, stretching out before the garden, took her breath away. She'd spent far too long in the concrete jungle.

Outside, under the shade of an enormous umbrella, Kitty spotted her Aunt Julia. She sat in a garden recliner, positioned to take in the view. With her eyes closed and her blonde curls pinned up, she looked a little older than Kitty remembered.

"Mum's having a nap. It was all I could do to stop her from spring-cleaning the whole place for your arrival. I'm afraid I had to make up your bed, so I apologise in advance for my appalling hospital corners."

Kitty smiled. "How's your mum doing?" she asked.

"She's okay. Getting more mobile, but the real battle is stopping her from doing too much and getting sore and tired."

"I *can* hear you." Her aunt's sing-song voice emerged from outside. Jonty winked at Kitty.

"She's in a bit of pain, but I've hidden all the gin bottles. I can't trust her not to self-medicate."

"Honestly!" Julia's laugh tinkled through the muggy air.

"Depriving a recovering patient access to decent amounts of alcohol is against the Geneva Convention. I've checked. Now come out here and let me see you, Kitty. It's been too long."

The air was sticky after the rain. As Kitty followed her aunt's voice onto the patio, a bead of perspiration trickled down her back. Maybe a pencil skirt and shirt weren't the best outfit choice.

"Hi, Aunt Julia." Kitty leaned down to give her a kiss on her soft cheek.

She eyed her niece up and down. "Well, look at you. Didn't you grow tall, darling?"

Yes, I know. Kitty smiled, half expecting her aunt to ask if she got nosebleeds at her altitude. It wouldn't be the first time.

"Please, none of the formalities here. If you call me Julia, I'll promise not to call you Kitty-Kat." Her infectious smile reminded Kitty of water fights in the sun, evening chocolate binges and endless games of gin rummy. It was a smile that warmed her heart.

"Thank you so much for your invitation. I'm sure Dad filled you in on the drama," Kitty said, grateful Aunt Julia had dropped the subject of her height. Kitty's dad, she'd discovered, had been the one to call Julia and let her know that she might be at a loose end for a couple of months.

"He told me enough. It sounds like you've had an eventful time. But I'm glad you're here, darling. We've so much to catch up on, and a bit of female company will be welcome." She gestured towards Jonty with mock aggravation. "Son, can you settle Kitty in and show her the ropes with the animals? I'll make a start on dinner."

"No, you won't, Mum. You'll sit still and rest. Holly made a shepherd's pie and salad. Can you at least trust me with that?"

"Who's Holly?" Kitty asked.

"My future daughter-in-law. Before the end of the century, if you please, Jonathan," said Julia. "I want to look half decent in the wedding photos."

"No pressure then," Kitty winked at her cousin.

"Indeed. Come on, Cuz, I'll show you to your room."

Kitty collected her bags from the car and followed Jonty upstairs to the same room she used to stay in as a young girl. It was all angles above her, as the exposed beams crisscrossed like a giant game of Kerplunk. The lack of fur signalled a cat-free zone, and Kitty was glad to see that Julia had added a small ensuite. But as she'd aged and got taller, everything seemed smaller. Eyeing the minuscule shower cubicle, she considered getting a panic button installed. Small showers and long limbs were never a good combination and led to some fantastic bruises.

"Watch your head up here. We can't afford the lawsuit," Jonty said when he noticed Kitty ducking under the eaves.

"Enough of the 'tall' jokes, please. It's a cross I've learned to bear over the years. Besides, I don't like your chances of negotiating a settlement against me."

After dropping her luggage, Jonty took Kitty to the paddocks. He showed her the animal pens and the sheds where they slept and the lean-to containing food, hay, and general supplies. As they looked in on the goats, Kitty found their thick, musky odour overwhelming, and she struggled not to gag. She might have to Google gas masks after dinner.

In the close air of the shed, the trickle of sweat from earlier had turned into a torrent, and her shirt was now stuck to her back like cling wrap. A wave of nausea swept over her.

"Where are the instructions?" Kitty scanned the general chaos on the shelves of the lean-to. Unlabelled boxes and packets of pellets lay everywhere.

"Erm, I don't think animals come with instructions. I've just been winging it. They're all still breathing."

Jonty ran through a list of daily chores, and Kitty found a

pen on the side to take notes. There was nowhere to write anything down, so she used the back of her hand. She screwed up her eyes, trying to make sense of the tins and boxes stacked in every available space. At least she'd have something to keep her busy tomorrow.

Satisfied she had a handle on things, Kitty stepped out of the shed without looking, plopping straight into a large, muddy puddle left behind by the rain. Ankle deep, her beautiful red pumps transformed into a boggy brown shade, and her heart sank. They'd cost her a fortune.

Horrified at the carnage, she battled not to show weakness in front of her cousin. To show weakness was not in Kitty's rule book. She hated being laughed at—by anyone.

From the look on his face, Jonty struggled to suppress a snicker, and Kitty's brow furrowed. *Shit! Don't think of the price. Don't think of the price,* she repeated in her head. He must think she was so stupid. If she couldn't even get her footwear right, how would she keep a bunch of animals alive? Jaw set, Kitty ignored her cousin and headed back to the cottage, sloshing along in her ruined shoes.

She peeled off her pumps outside the door, saying a silent prayer of mourning to Saint Crispin, the patron saint of shoemakers, as she popped them into the bin. *If I part with my shoes, please protect me from harm at the hands of anything four-legged.* Their loss was the first sacrifice to the gods of the countryside. Kitty hoped it would be the last.

Looking down at her feet, mud from the puddle had pooled between her toes, staining them a dingy beige. *Delightful.*

"There's a hose over there." Jonty pointed to the corner of the house. "Looks like you might need it."

With a grimace, Kitty hobbled down the path, cursing the pebbles digging into her skin. It was a far cry from the plush carpet of her apartment or the smooth streets of the city. But what had she expected? She'd signed up for this. Coming to the country was her own choice.

FOLLOWING a dinner full of laughter and reminiscing, Julia went to bed. Kitty offered to wash up, and after shutting the chicken coop, Jonty poured them both a glass of wine. They sat on the patio in the still evening air as crickets strummed in the fields. Kitty's gaze was caught by the emerging stars reflected in the violet sky.

"I'd forgotten how beautiful it is here," she said.

"I can't seem to leave," said Jonty. "This village is like the Hotel California. I hope you don't think me rude, but I have to ask. What happened at Fenwick? You were working with Stefan Watts?"

"You know Stefan?"

Jonty nodded. "We worked together when I'd just finished my law degree. He was an ambitious bastard as far as I can remember."

Kitty gave a wry smile. The legal world was incestuous. Everybody knew everybody else's business.

"Ambitious is his middle name. That's what I used to like about him. He was inspiring. He could be brutal, but he brought me in on some great deals."

"How long was he your boss?"

Kitty fingered the outside of her glass, swallowing down bitter words. "Too long. He got his pound of flesh, though. I don't think I saw blue sky for months at a time."

"So, what happened?"

Kitty sighed. Talking about it still twisted a knife in her gut. "He found a way to remove me from a client I'd just landed. He wanted the glory and the billable hours. Unfortunately, the new role he found for me was way below my pay grade."

"That's not right," said Jonty, scowling.

Kitty shrugged, tucking her newly cleaned feet underneath herself on the bench. "I made a complaint the next day. But he got in first. The old boys' network ground into gear. To them, I was a fly in the ointment, and at the end of the day, one of us had to go. Fenwick decided that would be me."

"That's terrible," said Jonty, rubbing his forehead.

"I know, right? I dread to think what he said about me, but they offered me an 'honourable' exit. The chance to resign, references and recommendations, etcetera. I can't work for another law firm for three months."

"Meaning you're at a loose end, and that's why you agreed to look after Mum's brood."

"Meaning I have three months to find a shit-hot job and get back in the game. I don't like to sit around. I need to keep moving." In fact, she hadn't stopped moving since she'd qualified. Without the ability to quell the insatiable burn of ambition inside her, she'd likely go mad in Tottenbridge.

"Do you want to go back to the lion's den?" asked Jonty, his voice hushed.

"What else am I going to do? I can't abandon all I've worked for. My entire career, my reputation, my contacts? I'm not cut out for anything else."

Jonty smiled. "I don't believe that. But I get where you're coming from. Better the devil you know than the devil you don't? Look, get a good night's sleep. I'm working tomorrow, but I was hoping you would help me in the evening?"

"On a case?" Family law was Jonty's specialisation.

Jonty sucked a breath in through his teeth. "Not exactly. You see, I'm still a bit of a geek. It's trivia night at the pub tomorrow, and my team, *The Con-quiz-tadors,* could do with some help."

Kitty giggled. "You need me for trivia?"

"You're incredibly clever, and it'll be a perfect opportunity to meet the crew. Besides, Holly would love another woman on board. She feels the pressure in the makeup and fashion rounds."

Open-mouthed, Kitty threw a cushion at his chest. Thank goodness he was only joking. She had no idea about makeup and fashion. She hadn't read a magazine that wasn't a legal publication for years.

"And I suppose that leaves you men with asking for directions and following flat pack furniture instructions?" she said, a challenge in her voice.

Jonty snickered. "I'm not sure flat pack furniture is something that comes up often in trivia, but touché! Seriously though, it'll be lovely to have you on the team, even if it's for one night. Plus, Josh was looking forward to catching up with you again."

"Who?"

"Josh. You remember Josh? Tottenbridge's answer to Huckleberry Finn?" Kitty's brows drew together.

"Don't tell me you don't remember Josh? He remembers *you*. You used to tag along with us when you stayed during the holidays. Blond kid, good at everything. He taught you to fish."

Kitty trawled through her memories. Perhaps she did remember Josh. Not for fishing or being like Huckleberry Finn, but for carrying her piggyback across the fields one afternoon when she'd smashed her toe against a rock. He'd carried her for what felt like miles and taken her to see his dad, the local vet. His dad had cleaned and dressed her crushed nail and taken her back to Julia's house in his dusty old Land Rover. Josh had made her a daisy chain to cheer her up. That was the last time she'd seen him.

"I think I *do* remember him. I remember his dad, at least."

"His dad died a while back. Josh is the local vet now."

"That's sad. And what is Josh's specialised subject for trivia? Fishing? Raft building?"

"Being late," said Jonty.

7

KITTY

KITTY FOLLOWED Jonty through the door of The Five Bob. A buzz of conversation hung in the air, and its steady hum was punctuated with bursts of laughter. Well, so much for avoiding the pub. Her efforts had lasted precisely thirty-one hours. There was nothing like a bit of willpower.

Even in flats, she was taller than most people. Seeing how conspicuous she was, Kitty slumped her shoulders to reduce her size. With a huff of breath, she eyed the crowd at the bar. Would Daniel Cunningham be working tonight? Her thoughts had drifted to him during the day as she'd grappled with organising Julia's sheds. The memory of his pert buttocks behind the counter was far more appealing than stacking and labelling animal feed. Was it a coincidence she'd put on a little mascara and lip gloss tonight?

They stood at the bar while Jonty ordered drinks, and despite her best efforts not to, Kitty cast her eyes around, looking for Daniel. Like a teenager at her first school dance, she fiddled with the ends of her hair, weaving the strands between jittery fingers. Jonty handed her a pint of cider, and Kitty took a satisfying sip, the cool, crisp liquid fizzing on her tongue.

Then she spotted him. Her stomach lurched, and her fingers gripped the glass tight. Daniel's tall, dark figure cut through the crowd, heading towards them, eyes glued to her. Hot pressure seared her chest and taking in his handsome profile under her dark lashes, she wished she'd at least worn a skirt.

Daniel drew up to her and Jonty, a gleaming smile on his face. He was close enough that the heat of his body radiated through his shirt, kissing the bare skin of her arms. Kitty's teeth gripped her bottom lip. In the crowd's buzz, Jonty was trying to say something to her, but she couldn't hear. The minute Daniel spoke, however, his voice cut through the noise, and her head turned toward him like a heat-seeking missile.

"Feeling vulnerable this evening, Jonathan?" Daniel asked.

"Sorry?" replied Jonty.

"Resorting to some new talent in your team." He nodded towards Kitty, who was mortified to suddenly be the centre of attention. Perhaps her new specialist subject should be feeling awkward.

Jonty guffawed. "Got to give the others a run for their money, you know. This is our new secret weapon."

Daniel smiled and turned his eyes to Kitty, offering her his hand in greeting. She took it, his warm palm wrapping around hers perfectly.

"Jonty's forgotten his manners this evening, so I'll introduce myself. Daniel Cunningham," he said with an almost imperceptible wink. "And you are?"

"Katherine. Kitty."

"My cousin," Jonty said, stepping towards Daniel.

"Ah, your cousin. Come to look after Julia, I believe? Mum keeps me up to date on all the gossip."

He wasn't going to mention their meeting then.

"Enchanted," Daniel said, his eyes drilling into her. "Can I get you another drink? Load you up with booze to grease the old brain cells. Amber can bring it to your table."

Daniel gestured towards a pretty woman with fiery hair, who stood behind the bar, a surly pout on her lips. If Helen of Troy's face launched a thousand ships, Amber of Tottenbridge's face might sour a thousand milkshakes. She looked like she'd rather slip her a shot of bleach.

"I'll think more clearly without too much cider," said Kitty. Daniel leaned into her and whispered, his warm breath grazing her ear.

"I had you down as more of a champagne lover than a cider drinker anyway," he said, finally referring to their meeting the other day.

She looked up into his eyes, and heat fired in Kitty's cheeks before he straightened up and addressed them all again.

"Well, good luck. I'll be expecting great things from you this evening, Katherine," Daniel said, and with a flick of his eyebrows, he left them with a dazzling smile.

Kitty let out the breath she'd been holding. "Who the hell is Daniel Cunningham?" she asked as she followed Jonty to a large wooden table at one end of the room.

"His family owns the pub, and he manages it for them. He's a bit of a player."

Kitty's eyes widened. Of course, he was. Nobody that good-looking could be anything else.

They arrived at the table where Holly waited, surrounded by answer sheets and pens. She'd written their team's name at the top of every sheet and sat flipping a beer mat idly, waiting for the quiz to start. Holly and Kitty met earlier at Rose Cottage and bonded over a cup of tea, one too many cookies, and a shared love of teasing Jonty. Two more old school friends joined them shortly before the quiz began.

The first rounds passed, with each team jostling for supremacy, needling each other with friendly banter. When one of Jonty's heckles hit a nerve with another contestant, a crumpled piece of paper sailed through the air, almost landing in Kitty's glass. She found their intense commitment to a trivia night hilarious. However, her competitive streak emerged after a few more drinks, and she battled with the rest of them.

Neck and neck with the team at the next table, the excitement was almost enough to take her attention off Daniel Cunningham. Almost. His eyes were on her all evening. After the amount of cider she'd drunk, Kitty abandoned her blushing and found his steady gaze and lazy smirk intriguing instead of disconcerting.

Across the pub, his playful eyes taunted her, drawing her in like a black hole. She hadn't seriously considered sex for ages, and Daniel made her think of sex. She also considered that a one-night stand wasn't on her to-do list, and everything about Daniel Cunningham screamed one-night stand. Kitty had bigger fish to fry than the local playboy, but still, there was nothing wrong with a bit of window shopping.

When the emcee announced it was time for the final rounds, Holly held up an answer sheet covered in pictures of celebrities dead and alive.

"I hope Josh gets here in time," she said.

Kitty had almost forgotten about him. "Why Josh?" she asked.

"He's good at the famous face round."

Kitty shrugged. It was a good enough reason. "I assumed he wasn't coming. There isn't much point now," she said, looking at her watch.

"No, he's on his way. Josh is *always* late. He had a call out, but he'll be here to save the day and take the glory, no doubt."

Kitty grinned. From her memory, she pictured the lanky blond boy running over the fields towards the pub, a blue cape billowing in the wind, and a sausage dog cradled under one arm. Super Vet!

She didn't recognise many of the so-called famous faces on the sheet but wrote Shirley Temple under the one picture she *was* sure of. The other images swum before her eyes, and Kitty pushed her glasses up to the top of her head. That'd be the heat of the room and the three pints of cider she'd drunk.

To rein in her dancing vision, she focussed on the edges of the crisp beer mats and the scratches of a hundred years etched into the heavy table. She wavered so much that her loosened fingers dropped her pen, sliding it down her lap and tumbling into the darkness of the floor. With a loud 'tut,' she bent down to retrieve it. No mean feat for a woman just shy of six feet tall.

As Kitty disappeared, crouched under the table, laughing voices erupted overhead, and an extra pair of feet appeared. Bent over, her hand groped to find the pen in the dark, and blood rushed to her head, causing a fresh wave of dizziness.

Labelled the world's clumsiest woman by her mum and sister, Kitty lived up to her reputation. She came back up from under the table, smashing her forehead into the edge of its solid oak top and crushing her glasses. A loud 'crack' rang in her ears, and a collective gasp went up around her. Kitty's hands flew to her face, and she closed her eyes, bowing her head at the sharpness of the pain.

"Shit! Are you okay?" a low, husky voice asked.

"Yes. No, not really. I'll be okay in a minute. I'm just waiting for the stars to clear." With visions of bluebirds circling around her head Looney Tunes style, Kitty smiled.

"Hold still," the voice said. A solid hand gripped her arm, and another untangled the broken glasses from her hair.

"There you go. No blood. Sit tight, and I'll get you some ice."

"Good thinking, Doctor," Holly said.

Doctor? Kitty bit down on her bottom lip. Wasn't a vet a doctor? If that voice was Josh's, she wanted to see the rest of him. He didn't sound like someone who hung out in a blue cape, brandishing sausage dogs. His voice was warm honey, sugar and spice, and all things nice.

The quiz continued around her, and under an assault of excessive fussing, Kitty assured Holly she was fine and to get back to winning. Alone in her thoughts, she peeked around to find her rescuer. Only one figure stood at the bar. Although blurry, without her glasses, the man was tall, with a broad back and golden blond hair. *Damn.* That was Josh?

Kitty stayed still in her seat and closed her eyes again, waiting for the pain and dizziness to settle. As she did, a crisp, clean smell of shower gel reached her nostrils, followed by the heat of a body sliding into the seat beside her. She breathed him in. *Holy crap*, he smelled good.

"I have the ice, but it's melting fast," the silky voice said, sending a tingle to her knickers. That voice could melt all the ice in the Arctic, let alone in the pub.

Kitty winced at the sharp sting at her hairline but soon settled into its soothing numbness.

"How does that feel?"

"It feels incredible." Her breath hitched. "I mean, it feels great. No, I mean, it feels better," Kitty babbled, pleading with herself to calm down.

Heat rushed to her cheeks, and she put her hand up to hold the bundle of cubes, brushing his skin as their fingers passed. She opened her eyes, and Josh's face swam into semi-focus. Soft, smiling blue eyes greeted her, crinkled at the corners, and fringed by fair lashes. His tanned skin, brown from being outdoors, stretched over cheekbones that could slice bread, and his blond hair, cut short, framed his face like a halo.

Kitty smiled. Not Huckleberry Finn. More like Huckleberry Sin.

"How embarrassing. I'm so sorry," she said with a grimace.

"Don't worry. I have this effect on most women. Five minutes with me, and they start head-butting furniture."

Kitty laughed. As the quiz continued around them, her hand reached out to her glasses, the remains of which Josh'd placed on the table.

"They're a write-off," he said. "I'm assuming you can still see something without them?"

"Yes, just about. I have contacts at home. I only wear these to make myself look smarter at trivia nights." Kitty fell into his smile as his fingers reached up to her forehead.

"Is it okay to touch you?" he asked.

"Oh, yes, please," Kitty said without thinking. *Shit!* That hardly sounded PG. It was a reasonable question from a medical professional, and she'd made it sound like something from *365 Days*.

Josh's eyebrows raised. "Your head, I mean. After all, we hardly know each other."

His low chuckle swept over her, curling her toes. She nodded, mortified. And as his hand hovered over her skin, an involuntary shiver ran through her body. Not an internal shiver. Not even a small, becoming shudder, but a full-blown jelly wobble. Kitty sucked in a breath pleading with her body to behave. Katherine Cameron, ice queen and mistress of self-control, was in danger of making a total fool of herself.

"I'm sorry, it's just sore."

"We'll need to be careful you're not going into shock," he said, laughing. "I'm Josh, by the way. You might remember me."

Kitty winced internally. Had Jonty told him she hadn't had a clue who he was?

"Nice to meet you again, as grownups. I'm Kitty."

Josh smiled, his blue eyes sparkling in the pub lights.

"The last time I saw you, you were bleeding out in my dad's consulting room. I hope your toe survived into adulthood?"

Perhaps he was laughing with her, perhaps *at* her. But Kitty, who always took herself too seriously, didn't mind. His eyes were still on her head. This close to him, the light freckles that peppered his nose reminded Kitty of an eggshell.

"I'd hold back on the ice," Josh said. "The skin on your forehead is quite thin. It can burn."

Josh dropped his fingers and brushed away a strand of long hair that had escaped Kitty's ponytail. As their skin touched, their eyes met, and she fought an overwhelming urge to turn her face into his palm.

A cheer went up at the table, startling them both. Their team had won the penultimate round and was now within striking distance of the leaders.

"It's all up to you now, Josh," Holly said as she pushed the answer sheet for the Famous Faces round towards him.

"I'm no help on this one, so I'll check the damage instead," Kitty said, pointing at her head. "Let's hope I can make it to the bathroom without bumping into anything else."

"I'm pretty sure the table didn't mind," Josh grinned.

8

DANIEL

AT THE BAR, Daniel toyed with a glass of whisky, watching Kitty and Josh. Their gentle flirting wasn't lost on him, and the smile they'd exchanged as she walked away wasn't entirely innocent.

Daniel sighed. He had a bit of competition. He was irritated that it was Joshua Fox. Half the females in the village had mooned over Tottenbridge's answer to Thor at one time or another. Josh was never interested in any of them. Even Amber indulged in a fleeting crush a year ago. It was a total waste, in Daniel's opinion.

When Kitty emerged from the bathroom, his eyes flew to her. She stopped at the side of the room while her team erupted in euphoric delight as the emcee announced their victory.

All smiles, Jonty waved over at his cousin. She stuck up a thumb at him and turned towards the bar. Daniel stiffened to attention. With Josh sniffing around, he'd need to turn the charm up to eleven.

"At least Jonty can go to bed happy," he said when Kitty arrived at the bar, looking worse for wear. A sizeable bump sat in her hairline already. She turned back to her cousin, but following her eyes, Daniel suspected it was Josh she was more interested in. He was deep in conversation with Jonty's girlfriend.

"Our handsome vet saves the day again," Daniel said.

Kitty's head swung around at his comment.

"Everyone's good-looking without my glasses." she snickered, sitting on a stool at the bar. "It overrides the fact that I can barely tell where I'm going."

"Then there's hope for me yet. What can I get for you?"

Kitty smiled. "I don't know. My head's thumping, and the noise is getting to me. I assume you saw me throw myself at the table?"

"As long as you don't throw yourself at any other men, I'm not worried."

Kitty's eyes widened to the size of hubcaps.

"Too corny?" he asked. She nodded, fighting a smile. "I should update my material," he said.

"And I should go home."

"No, don't do that. We haven't chatted. Have a drink with me, for medicinal reasons, of course."

A thoughtful look passed over her face before Kitty hung the strap of her bag over the bar stool. It was a good sign that she wasn't about to run for the hills or straight into Josh's arms. Satisfied, Daniel's eyes travelled up to her forehead.

"I hope you won't sue me, by the way." Daniel pointed to her head. "I would've come over, but you were in such wonderful hands." He gestured to Josh, who was on his feet at the side of the room, checking his phone. "How's it feeling?"

"Pretty sore. I'm going to channel Darth Maul for a while," she said, referring to the bright pink lump forming.

Daniel grinned. "Do you know Joshua?" he asked, trying to keep the edge out of his voice.

"A little, I suppose. I used to come and stay here with my aunt as a kid, and we played together."

"I see."

Daniel contemplated Kitty as she continued to glance over at her table. She was beautiful without her glasses and even with a giant lump sprouting from her forehead. Having sealed the deal with the schoolteacher last night, Daniel now considered himself at a loose end between the sheets. Never one to hang about after a conquest, this new arrival in town tempted him. She was intelligent, different to his usual type, and only in town for a short time. As far as he was concerned, there was no downside.

"I have something to help you feel better," he said. "Stay there."

Daniel disappeared around the back of the bar, running smack bang into a flushed Amber carrying a tray of empty drinks and a surly sneer.

"Watch out!" she said, then noticing Kitty sitting by the bar, she tipped her head to the side, eyebrows raised. "She's back then."

Delight flared in Daniel's chest. Was that jealousy in her voice? Daniel loved to play with Amber, who he suspected still harboured a healthy crush on him.

"Indeed she is and in need of my help. I'm about to swoop in and rescue the fair maiden." He reached around Amber and picked up a bottle.

"Don't forget to oil your suit of armour, then," she said, a pout forming on her pink lips. "You wouldn't want it to squeak."

"Bitterness doesn't suit you, Amber."

"Oh, I'm not bitter. I'm just worried about her safety." She winked at him and headed off to the other end of the bar, red curls bouncing at her back.

When Daniel returned, Kitty was still staring at Josh. He was standing, talking on the phone, with a serious face. Before long, he hung up, had a quick word in Jonty's ear, and left.

Before Kitty registered any response to his departure,

Daniel put a bottle of brandy down on the bar and set about organising two ice-filled glasses.

"I usually provide a barrel of brandy and a fluffy St Bernard for injured customers, but she's having a night off. Animal Welfare has been on the phone again about her work hours."

Kitty's throaty laugh stirred his groin.

"To new acquaintances and sore heads," Daniel said, offering her the glass.

"To sore heads," she repeated, taking a sip of the drink. "Oh, that's good."

"We aim to please. Now, tell me how you came to be roped into Tottenbridge's answer to *The Weakest Link*? You don't strike me as the trivia type."

"It's a long story."

"I've got all night." Daniel raised an eyebrow and gazed deep into her eyes, running his hand along the smooth top of the bar. They were bigger without her glasses, framed by perfect brows and long, dark lashes.

"I'm not sure *I* do," said Kitty. "I need my bed. My head is killing me, I'm half blind, and I've got to get up early to feed a paddock full of hungry goats."

It was Daniel's turn to laugh. "Why don't you let me walk you home? It'll only take a few minutes and give you some fresh air. I can even give you a fireman's lift if you collapse from a concussion."

Kitty's head tilted to the side. "Why the hell not?" she said. "Give me a couple of minutes to say goodbye to Jonty."

Nervous that her cousin may say something less than flattering about him, Daniel kept his eyes on her as she headed towards her table. Kitty approached her cousin and whispered in his ear. Jonty's jaw clenched, and his eyes narrowed as he threw Daniel a suspicious glance.

Getting protective cousin vibes, Daniel returned his look with a cherubic smile. Kitty and Jonty spoke for a few more seconds, and then a burst of triumph filled Daniel's chest as she turned around and headed back towards him.

When she arrived at the bar, Daniel found it hard to wipe the smile off his face. Things were looking up.

"Everything okay?" he asked. Kitty looked way too relaxed. Way too nonchalant.

"Sure. I was just getting a few pointers on feeding the chickens in the morning."

She was lying. Jonty wouldn't willingly let his cousin within twenty metres of Daniel without a chaperone. Most men in the village would feel the same way. He chuckled. Kitty must be persuasive.

"Are you sure Jonty trusts you with me?" said Daniel.

"I'm a big girl. I can take care of myself."

"Oh, I don't doubt it, Katherine," he said, finishing his drink.

"Please, call me Kitty," she said.

He pulled his lips together. "You see, I prefer Katherine. If that's okay with you?"

Kitty shrugged and slid down the stool to the floor. "Whatever works for you, Daniel."

"Music to my ears," he said. "Let's go."

9

JOSH

JOSH HEADED to the urgent call out he'd got at the pub, his sturdy truck negotiating the ruts and runnels of a parched field in the dark. He'd hated to leave trivia night so early without the opportunity to say goodbye to Kitty.

The corners of his mouth lifted. She was the star of his fondest childhood memories. Kitty—the mystical creature who turned up every summer—spreading smiles and fun, only to disappear again as school started. He looked forward to every visit, and to say he'd admired her was an understatement.

She was his first boyhood crush. Of course, she would never have known. But as she ran wild with him and Jonty, always armed with a pack of tissues, she'd wormed her way into his young heart.

They'd both changed, but tonight, the years had peeled away. Kitty's carefree spirit was missing at first. Josh always pictured her with a glow in her cheeks and unruly, tousled hair flying around her shoulders as she ran. Smash to the head notwithstanding, Kitty was pale and shy tonight. But then she smiled at him. Her face softened, and old feelings raced back, crashing into his chest.

Memories of his youthful crush raced in his head. The first time they'd fished in the river together, she'd tucked her skirt into her knickers, and his blush lasted for hours. The time they'd played Chinese whispers in the haystacks, her breath tickled his skin as she leaned in and giggled in his ear.

They were memories he'd kept locked up tight. Life was easy back then.

There was still something about Kitty, though. Something that made him want to get to know her again, to spend time with her. He'd hinted as much to Jonty when she'd left the table. His friend hadn't shut it down precisely. Still, after giving Josh a rundown of her recent past, he'd suggested Kitty needed some space to breathe.

"It's just nice to see her again, that's all. I'd forgotten how sweet she is," he'd told him.

Jonty's words still swirled around his head, battling for supremacy with the memory of Kitty's smile.

"I love you, Josh, but the last thing Kitty needs are complications."

10

KITTY

She and Daniel left the lights of the pub and walked down the quiet, tree-lined lane. The canopy closed high over them like building thunder clouds, obliterating the moon that hung heavy in the sky. The air was sticky and sweet, and instead of the traffic noise of the city, all she heard was a steady humming of insects.

Kitty glanced at Daniel in the darkness. He was the absolute opposite of Josh, with his dark eyes, olive skin, and artfully styled hair. He probably spent more time perfecting it than Kitty spent on her entire body. The corners of her mouth twitched upward as she pictured him in the mirror, pouting at his reflection, teasing every strand to perfection.

For some reason, she felt guilty about leaving the pub with him. She'd only met Josh for about twenty minutes, but there'd been something about him. A spark of attraction between them. At least, she thought there had been. But after they'd won the quiz, he'd disappeared without saying goodbye. And then Daniel had been there, all good looks and expensive brandy. Was she really that easily swayed?

"I need to confess something," Daniel said. His husky tone

set Kitty's senses on high alert, and fingers of sensation tickled at her neck.

What the hell was she thinking of, walking in the dark with this virtual stranger? A man who her cousin had described as a player. Kitty was sure he hadn't meant Scrabble. A bit of fresh air had seemed like a good idea, but she'd be lying if she said she hadn't thought about how fast she could run in her sandals.

A tight giggle escaped her lips. "I assume that if you're going to murder me and bury my body in a field, you wouldn't announce it."

The corners of Daniel's mouth ticked up. "Nothing so dark. I brought provisions." He held up a metallic hip flask. "In case of emergencies, of course."

Okay, so now add alcohol into the mix, not to mention a woozy head. What could go wrong? Daniel walked in step with Kitty, his body close. Each time their arms brushed, a static charge sparked in her body. Some of his hair had escaped its careful styling, and loose strands draped over his forehead, casting shadows over his sharp cheekbones. Kitty let out a slow breath.

Stylish, self-assured and no doubt in demand, Daniel oozed sexiness and brimmed with confidence. Kitty wasn't stupid. His offer to walk her home wasn't due to a sense of civic duty. From how he'd looked at her tonight, it was quite the opposite. Satisfaction tingled in her chest at the thought, but the aftertaste of mistrust was impossible to ignore, along with the nagging question of why he was even here with her.

Sexy, handsome men didn't come on to Kitty. *Nobody* came on to Kitty. Not that she ever tried to give off the 'I'm desperate for a shag' vibe. With her work schedule, she could barely muster the "Do you want to meet for a drink?" vibe. She was aware, though, that her colleagues laughingly called her The Ice Queen.

They emerged out of the lane and onto High Street. Kitty recognised the cafe, bakery, general store, and antique centre housed in beautiful old buildings. At the end, the road forked around the village green, with its small playground and duck pond.

"I remember coming to play here as a kid," she said, smiling.

With a mischievous grin spreading across his face, Daniel took Kitty's hand and guided her across the deserted street that fringed the grass. The heat of his soft skin infused with hers as their fingers intertwined.

"Let's relive your childhood," he said. "Though, a few things may have changed."

It all looked the same, as far as Kitty could tell. The darkness made it hard to focus on anything. "Like what?" she asked.

"You haven't heard of the demon ducks of Tottenbridge, then? It was probably before your time. Rumour has it that one of them escaped the flock and stumbled across a discarded pot of anabolic steroids."

Kitty snorted a laugh. "Excuse me?"

"I know it sounds far-fetched, but there really is no other explanation."

"For what?"

"For the mutation. Our normal-sized, mild-mannered mallards became vicious and grew to the size of Labradors. They can be quite terrifying, but I think ducks sleep at night, so we should be safe. Unless, of course, you're carrying any wheat products. I've heard it said they've a dog-like sense of smell and have chased people down the street for a few crusts of bread."

Kitty smiled. "Well, thanks for the warning. I'll make sure I keep my carb consumption to a minimum."

Daniel pulled her up to the kerb, and they stood at the edge of the green. Dew formed a scattering of jewels on the grass, and the lure of the cool droplets was too much for Kitty to resist. She removed her hand from his, bending down to take off her sandals. Daniel joined her, pulling off his shoes and socks.

"You're going to be a bad influence on me," he said. "I hope you won't suggest we skinny dip in the pond. We'd traumatise the wildlife."

Kitty's mind flashed back to schoolgirl memories of a brooding Colin Firth portraying Mr Darcy as he emerged from the pond at Pemberley, sodden white shirt plastered to his toned torso. She took a breath. Daniel would make a fine stunt double, but in the interests of keeping her toes and her virtue intact, she probably shouldn't suggest it.

Kitty chuckled as they walked towards an old swing in the middle of the green.

"What?" he said. "I hope you're not laughing at the poor ducks. It's not their fault. They don't know when to say no." He paused. "It's something I can relate to."

Kitty's heart fluttered a beat as his eyes glinted in the darkness. They came to the playground and put their shoes down on the grass.

Kitty sat on a swing and rocked gently back and forth. Her head spun from the bump, and she checked her momentum with her bare feet, easing the motion to the slightest sway. Silence settled between them before Daniel sat on the next swing. His eyes were on her the whole time.

"So, tell me, Katherine. Aside from Julia's new hip, what brings you to our humble village?"

Kitty huffed. "My sister says I need to live a little," she replied.

"Interesting."

Daniel unscrewed the top of the hip flask and offered it to Kitty. She took it, enjoying the residual heat of his pockets on its smooth, metallic sides. When she tipped it up, the liquid inside hit the back of her throat like a freight train, and she swallowed hard to avoid choking. She didn't want to come across as an amateur.

"Not as interesting as you might think. I'm not a complicated person," said Kitty.

"My kind of woman. But if you need to live a little, why are you in Tottenbridge? It's hardly Monte Carlo."

Kitty gave Daniel a brief rundown of how she'd lost her job and why Julia had invited her to stay.

"And that is how I found myself in your pub tonight, smashing up your furniture," Kitty said finally.

Daniel shook his head slowly. "Well, just so you know, you can bump into my table any time, but the guy you worked with sounds like a complete dick. It's a shitty situation. He should get some kind of payback."

"Oh, he will. We'll meet over a boardroom table one day, and I'll remove his fingernails one by one, metaphorically, of course. Then I'll slowly grind him to a pulp."

Daniel chuckled. "Remind me never to cross you."

He drank from the flask, then handed it back to Kitty, brushing his fingers over hers ever so slightly. A tingle crept up her arm.

"So, after three months, what's next?" he asked.

"I'm waiting to hear about some opportunities. I can't kick my heels in the country forever."

"You're a city girl, then?"

Kitty smiled. "I am. And I took Julia's offer under false pretences." She took a drink but, this time, held onto the flask. "I hate mud, flies, and getting dirt under my nails. Everything animal-related smells awful, and I've discovered goats are evil! I'm not sure what I was thinking."

Daniel laughed out loud, his voice piercing the stillness. "It's the rectangular eyes, isn't it?"

Kitty giggled.

"Do you know what I think?" Daniel said as he stood and walked around the back of her swing.

He took a chain in each hand and pushed her gently, the swing creaking above her. The hairs on the back of Kitty's neck stood up, and she was so very aware of his closeness. Of the languid way that he moved. Like a tiger stalking prey. She held a breath.

"I think you need some distraction while you're here."

The held breath sat in her throat. "What would you suggest?" she asked quietly.

"Well..."

Daniel's voice trailed off, and he moved around to the front of the swing set and leaned on its frame. His tall, trim figure, silhouetted in the streetlight's glow, reminded Kitty of a film noir antihero. She reached out to hand him back the flask, and he took it, eyes on hers and a dark, delicious smile on his mouth.

"I'm going to seduce you."

Kitty's stomach lurched, and a fizzy heat crept through her body. Had he really just said that? Out loud? She opened her mouth to speak, but Daniel continued to talk, screwing the lid back onto the hip flask.

"I think I'm just what you need. A handsome, single man, ready to help you live a little, just like your sister suggested. I could fulfil your every desire."

He cocked one of his eyebrows high, and Kitty's cheeks burned like a furnace.

"View it as a holiday romance. One wild fling before you settle back to a life of undervalued over-achievement. What do you think?"

Kitty wasn't sure *what* she thought. Despite her logical brain screaming for dear life, temptation nibbled at its edges. Daniel Cunningham was hands down the sexiest man she'd ever met. And he was offering to seduce her. Like it was a choice.

But perhaps it was. She never did this sort of thing, never allowed herself to get distracted from her goals by offers of no strings attached sex from men in the dark. Maybe she deserved some fun. Ronnie's voice rocked into her head, pleas for Kitty to get laid and put everyone out of their misery.

It'd be a physical thing, that's all. And what was wrong with a bit of insta-lust? Kitty's chest rose and fell, keeping time with the arguments swimming inside her head.

But Daniel's suggestion was crazy, and she'd be mad to think it would end well. She couldn't jump into bed with the first gorgeous stranger she met. That sort of thing only happened in books.

Kitty looked up at Daniel's shadowed face, meeting his gaze. Her head thumped, and she put her hand up to the lump on her forehead, the pain snapping her back to reality.

It was time to get real. She wasn't about to get involved with anyone, no matter how no-strings the offer was. She needed to stay focused on getting a new job. Get through the next couple of months and concentrate on keeping a bunch of farm animals alive. Not get into trouble!

Kitty stood up and grabbed her abandoned shoes, turning to face Daniel.

"I'm not here for a holiday romance, Daniel. I'd rather keep my head in the game, not on your pillow. And not in the gutter either."

Daniel smiled and shook his head. "I don't give up that easily, Katherine," he said.

Why was she not surprised?

"Please, call me Kitty. It's like you're my teacher or my boss if you call me Katherine."

"Would you like that?" he murmured. "Unfulfilled fantasies, perhaps?"

Kitty pressed her lips together, fighting the nudge low down in her tummy that his voice and words had caused.

Daniel continued. "I still prefer Katherine. Perhaps your name is fulfilling some secret fantasy for *me*, but I guess you'll never know, seeing as you won't join me on my pillows or in the gutter."

Daniel winked at her. Did he not have an off switch?

Kitty huffed. "I'm not sure I want to hang out with sewer rats. Bad choice of words. Sorry," she said, shaking her head. "I'm tired."

"Oh no, it's appropriate. I like to get dirty."

With a lazy smile, he picked up his socks and shoes, took her hand, and led Kitty across the green toward Rose Cottage. The cool tarmac of the road soothed her racing thoughts, and they walked the rest of the way in idle chit-chat.

When they arrived, he paused at the shiny car parked outside on the street.

"Nice wheels," he said. "Unless Julia's been shopping, this must be yours. Perhaps being a workaholic has its perks."

Kitty nudged him in the ribs. Despite turning his offer down, it didn't mean they couldn't still be friends. He unlocked the gate and opened it for her, but as she stepped through, he didn't follow.

"Come in for a drink?" Kitty asked out of politeness. It was what one normally asked at the door, wasn't it? All she really wanted was her bed, though.

"If you're trying to get into my trousers, we could just take care of that on the doorstep," he said, his voice husky and his eyebrows raised skyward.

Kitty's mouth dropped, and Daniel laughed.

"Relax. I need to get back. Amber hates to lock up alone."

"Amber?"

"You met her earlier. Redhead. Gives me a lot of lip."

Kitty recalled the surly-faced lady behind the bar.

"She's my right-hand woman. Makes me look good and frees me up to drink the profits and charm any beautiful women who wander into my pub."

Kitty rolled her eyes, and Daniel leaned on the gatepost.

"Speaking of which, come and join me for a drink sometime? We can map out your plan for global domination together." A cheeky twinkle danced in his eyes, and Kitty found herself accepting his offer.

"Why not?" she said, shrugging her shoulders.

"Good. There's no escape now. I know where you live," Daniel stood up straight, putting one hand in his pocket. "It was lovely to meet you properly, but now I think you need to get to bed. It's going to take a lot of beauty sleep to tame this beast."

Kitty's eyes widened, and her heart skipped in her chest. Was he talking about himself? She opened her mouth to speak, but before she could, he kissed the tip of his index finger and touched it to her bruise. It was a tender gesture after all his bravado and flirting.

The corners of her mouth curled. "Good night, Daniel," she said.

Kitty turned towards the cottage and headed up the steps. After finding the key in her bag, she looked back to see Daniel Cunningham walking down the road, still barefoot, whistling in the moonlight.

11

KITTY

Kitty woke early with the groggiest body in recorded history. The cockerel screeched his morning greeting, and her forehead throbbed as if she'd clashed with a sledgehammer instead of a table edge. Perhaps the pounding at her temples was a fitting reward for clumsiness and late-night brandy drinking with handsome strangers. It would serve as a reminder not to go off script in the future.

After she'd arrived home last night, Kitty checked her emails, desperate for job news. Apart from the three ads for vibrators and one for support underwear, her inbox was empty.

Now awake, she recalled her adventures last night. Her meeting with the tabletop, then Josh, and finally, her late-night walk with Daniel. Had she made the wrong decision about his proposition? He was very persuasive, and how often did gorgeous men come knocking at her door offering no strings attached flings?

The cockerel crowed for a second time, and Kitty stumbled over to the bathroom in the half light of dawn. She examined her head in the mirror. The golf-ball sized bruise was an absolute corker. Its purple hue already yellowing at the edges.

Kitty brushed her teeth with one hand and rummaged around in her sparse make-up bag for her concealer. Why she was bothering she didn't know. It wasn't as if the goats would notice.

She threw on a smart pair of jeans, a pale blue shirt, and some glittery flip-flops. The shirt was part of a business suit. She didn't want to ruin it, so she kept a few buttons undone at the bottom and tied the leftover 'tails' into a knot. She crept through the house to the kitchen, not wanting to wake Julia or the cats. That would mean conversation, and she wasn't sure she could string a sentence together yet.

After three large glasses of water, a steaming cup of coffee and two paracetamols, Kitty headed down to the animals. The chaos of the sheds irritated her yesterday, so she'd organised the supplies. Now, scrubbed and cleaned, labelled, and regimented, Kitty was happy. It was neat enough for a photo spread in *Vogue Living–Farm Edition,* if there even was such a thing.

A visit to the chickens was first on her list. Kitty was surprised to find she didn't mind chickens. Not only were they useful, but they were friendly and didn't smell as bad as she'd expected. She wished she could say the same for their coop, though. It stunk to high heaven, but she collected six warm eggs that morning, fighting the urge to dry retch.

Next, Kitty moved on to Jill, the donkey, who'd left a nice parcel of poo in the corner. She skirted around the beast to shovel it away, flinching with each noise and movement the animal made. Jill's unpredictability and strength worried her. If she got knocked over or kicked, she wouldn't put it past the old donkey to trample on her for good measure. She'd probably break bones.

With shaking hands, Kitty steadied her breath as she put on the leading bridle and took Jill outside. Stepping out onto the path, she glanced down at her feet. They were already filthy, covered in sawdust and tiny, sharp bits of hay. It was pointless hosing them down. They'd be caked in mud and dirt again in no time.

After depositing Jill safely in the paddock, Kitty checked on the goats. Getting them down to join their donkey friend was daunting. She'd already fostered a healthy dislike for them after they'd spent the previous afternoon butting her in the bottom and nagging her for food. And this morning, when Kitty opened the door to their shed, they crowded around her, buffeting each other in gleeful anarchy.

She'd written a list of the goat's names and a short description of each on a whiteboard hanging near the door. When she checked them off, one by one, she noticed that Dora, Julia's favourite, was nowhere to be seen. There was a tick next to her name on the board, so she *had* put her to bed last night. Where was she now?

A fierce burn rose in Kitty's chest. When she arrived, she probably left the door ajar, and Dora could've slipped out of the shed into the garden. Kitty wracked her brains, but she couldn't remember whether she'd closed the gate after Daniel left last night. *Shit!* Cursing her stupidity, she prayed the goat hadn't gone far and would happily be munching roses in the flower bed.

After bustling the remaining goats down to the paddock, Kitty began the search, but Dora was nowhere to be found around Rose Cottage. Kitty looked up at Julia's bedroom window. Her curtains were drawn, so hopefully, she was still in bed, blissfully unaware.

Burning hot and breathless, Kitty ran around the side of the house to the front, and her heart dropped when she saw that the front gate was wide open. She cursed herself for getting so tipsy and distracted last night. Jonty's words had been very clear during his guided tour the other day: *Life in the countryside – rule number one...always close the gate.*

Kitty stood in the lane checking in both directions, hoping

to spot the goat's sturdy rump as she made her escape. But nothing. If Dora had turned right, there would've been plenty of gardens to visit for a free meal. If she'd gone left, there was too much ground to cover alone. She'd have to call Jonty to help.

A fan of choosing the path of least resistance or least judgement from her cousin, Kitty turned right towards the village. She searched every front garden on her way but found no Dora. However, relief swelled in her chest as further down the lane, Kitty saw potential evidence the goat may have passed by.

A few decapitated sunflowers lined the front of one garden. And the vegetable stall outside another was trashed, with half-munched potatoes and carrots littering the ground. She made a mental note to put some money in the stall's honesty box when she had Dora home, then moved on.

The lane soon joined the village green, the scene of last night's intrigue with Daniel. There was no sign of Dora on the dewy grass, so Kitty continued onto High Street. Almost halfway up, something large and tan jostled around on the grass outside the village store. It *had* to be Dora.

With Kitty's heart thumping hard and fast, she picked up the pace, attempting to run in her dew-coated flip-flops. Her feet were smothered in grass clippings, and she slipped and slid against the rubber. As she got closer, Kitty could tell it *was* Dora. What other goats were likely to be out picking up a weekend paper? She was in front of the shop, attempting to devour the advertising board outside, yellow teeth grinding against the wood.

She approached slowly, but her heart sank. In her haste, she'd forgotten to bring anything to lead the goat back to Rose Cottage with. Her only option was to grab her pointed little horns and wrestle her home. The chances of doing it on her own were slim to none. She'd have to call Jonty. Kitty ran her hands over her pockets, finding them empty. She'd left her phone on the side.

"Shit, damn, and bollocks!"

Kitty's exasperated cry rang out in the still of the sleepy village, and hot tears stung her eyes.

12

JOSH

JOSH WAS PICKING up a bag of croissants from the Bakery when he heard a cry. Curious, he stepped out the door to see a frantic woman hanging onto the horns of a wriggling goat. She was trying to wrestle it from the wooden board it was chewing on. He couldn't help but chuckle; it wasn't the sort of thing you normally saw on a Sunday morning in Tottenbridge.

The woman was all arms and legs. The long hair tied on the top of her head threatened to escape, and her shirt was filthy. Barefoot, she'd abandoned a pair of flip-flops on the side and was hanging on for dear life, swearing like a sailor. Taking in her sweaty face, pink from exertion, Josh spotted a purple bruise on her forehead, and his stomach lurched.

Kitty!

A smile grew on his lips as he watched her battle with the goat. She looked adorable, with her face like thunder and her long hair medusa-like in its dishevelled bun. Bent over to hold onto the animal's horns, the filthy shirt she wore rode up, revealing the creamy skin at her waist. Josh took a breath. He was tempted to pull up a chair. He could sit and watch her all day, but that would be cruel. She needed help. He dropped his bag of croissants on the ground and moved towards her.

"Whoa, back up," he said, his voice fighting with a loud grunt of frustration from Kitty.

She didn't hear him, and the tussle between her and the goat escalated. The beast was infuriated by any attempt to hold her horns and head. Kitty tried in vain to pull her away, but as the animal gave one final, violent shake, she lost her grip and flew backwards onto the grass, landing with a thump on her bottom.

"Fuck!" she yelled.

The object of Kitty's efforts immediately reattached herself to the board, and Josh ran towards his old friend, crouching next to her. She was fine. Up close, her bruise looked angry and tender. She'd tried to cover it up, but its purple mass shone through. Her cheeks were shiny and flushed, and she had a huge smudge of mud across her right cheek.

Josh struggled hard to suppress a smile, and Kitty's eyes flashed a million swear words at him. It was his final undoing, and unable to contain it any longer, his chuckle became a full-on belly laugh. The resulting look of fury on Kitty's face made it even worse, and when he offered her his hand, she ignored it.

"Stop laughing," she said. "It's not funny!"

Her request had no effect, and Kitty's face took on a vicious look.

"Isn't there a chihuahua waiting for you to give them an enema or something?" she growled.

Josh doubled over, holding his aching sides while Kitty slumped down, defeated, in the grass. But as his amusement subsided, so did the fury on her face. The corners of her own mouth twitched, and she covered her face with her hands, shoulders shaking. For a terrible moment, Josh thought she might be crying, but her giggles confirmed it was tears of laughter.

After Kitty collected herself, Josh offered her his hand. Again. She took it this time, and he hauled her up.

"Bloody goats," she mumbled, wiping her eyes. "I hate them."

Josh smiled. "Listen, you aren't the only one who's fallen out with a goat."

He lifted his white T-shirt to reveal a livid pink scar just above the waistband of his jeans.

"Must have been painful," Kitty mumbled, looking away quickly.

"It was. Goat horns are bloody sharp. And..." he turned to where her goat was still chomping into the sandwich board, "It's time to return you back to Rose Cottage, young lady."

"Me or the goat?" asked Kitty.

13

KITTY

Kitty brushed off the front of her jeans and turned round to do the same with her bum. She caught Josh watching her, and the smile on his face had her heart skipping a beat. He looked as if he'd like to help. Instead, he handed her his croissants and sprinted into the village store. She followed his broad back with her eyes, savouring the way the muscles underneath his T-shirt jostled for supremacy. Her teeth gripped her bottom lip.

When Kitty first saw Josh smirking at her as she sat on the dirty ground, rage filled her chest. And then he'd laughed at her. Like she was silly and useless. Her brow had creased, and every swear word she knew had run through her head at the sight.

But then, when he hadn't stopped, and she'd run out of curses, she'd taken in his face. His golden skin that stretched over his high cheekbones, the soft glow in his cheeks, and the gorgeous crinkles at the corners of his blue eyes. She'd noticed them last night too.

It was hard to stay cross at someone so spectacular-looking, particularly when they were offering you a helping hand.

Josh returned from the store with a pack of corn chips and a sheepish smile as if he'd overheard her thoughts.

"These should do the trick," he said, opening the bag and waving it near Dora's nose. Her head immediately picked up, and she disengaged her teeth from the sign. Josh fed her a couple of corn chips, tempting her a few feet at a time down the road.

"Not only do they have nasty horns," he said, "but they have powerful jaws and teeth built for grinding. Plenty of hands get mangled by goats. I consider myself lucky to have only been speared so far."

Kitty turned her wide eyes to him, recalling the scar at his waistband. If that was lucky, she'd hate to see what the alternative was. Kitty had tried to appear concerned when he'd shown her, but all she could think about was tracing the puckered skin with her fingertips. She'd shivered and looked away instead. It was hardly an appropriate thought to be having so near the village church. *And* on a Sunday.

"Getting her home is going to be tricky, isn't it?" she asked.

"Potentially," Josh said, patting Dora's tan and brown neck. "We need to make sure we're done before the chip bag is empty."

Josh's grin did nothing to calm Kitty's shaking hands. But not wanting to look too much like a helpless damsel, she volunteered to oversee the corn chips while Josh took a careful but gentle hold of Dora's nearest horn. The three of them struggled back to Rose Cottage with only a few more sunflowers being beheaded.

Together, they led Dora to the paddock, shut her in and stood together, leaning on the gate. A warm breeze rustled through the trees while bees danced on the flowers. Josh shifted his weight against the wood, and the bright sun lit his skin. Every muscle carved into his forearms went straight to

Kitty's core, lighting a little burn between her legs. Trust her to be a sucker for a solid forearm.

A silver band circled his wrist, its metallic hardness glinting in the sun.

"This is pretty," Kitty said, reaching out to it. Josh's head turned as if her touch had startled him. "Sorry." she breathed. "It's just nice, that's all."

The corners of his lips curled, "It's a gift from my niece," he said.

"How old is she?"

"Four. Just about to start school. She's crazy. You'd get on."

He winked at her and looked back at the paddock. His eyes scanned the animals inside. It was a friendly gesture, nothing more, and Kitty's thoughts flew back to Daniel. His winking had felt entirely different. Dark and tempting.

"I still love goats," Josh said. "Even if one got me. Each one has a distinct personality."

Kitty snickered, "I'm not sure Julia's goats vary much between pushy and vindictive."

"They look happy enough. You must be doing something right," Josh absentmindedly turned the silver bracelet at his wrist, a cheeky grin on his face.

"Excuse me! I think I can keep some goats alive for a few days," Kitty answered, returning his smile.

He snickered and ran his fingers through his hair. "How is it all going? Not too overwhelming?"

Kitty's immediate thought was that Jonty had been on the phone with Josh, telling him how she wasn't coping. It'd been the shoes and the puddle story, no doubt, and now the Dora debacle had given him even more ammunition.

"No, it's fine," Kitty said, unsure if it was Josh or herself she was trying to convince. "It's just an exercise in organisation. Come on, I'll show you."

She walked Josh towards the cottage and showed him to the supplies shed. Once inside, he stood, mouth agape.

"I wouldn't recognise it," he said. "I've been here before when Julia's had a sick animal, but I don't remember it looking like this."

Kitty stood back and admired the order she'd created in the cramped space. Each animal type had its own section with food and medicine supplies. She'd written up detailed care instructions. Like the goats, she'd named each animal and included an identifying description, even the chickens. *They* had their own chart noting the number of eggs laid each day. The shed was spotless, and not one spiderweb clung to its wooden corners.

"It's like a giant filing system," Josh said, smiling. "This would be great for my sister. She's pulling her hair out most days."

"I didn't realise you had a sister. I don't remember her."

Josh shrugged. "Thea didn't hang out with me much. She was too busy helping my dad save all the local waifs and strays. Not much has changed. She runs a small animal sanctuary out of our farm."

Josh and Kitty closed the shed and walked back through the garden to Rose Cottage.

"Thank you so much for your help with Dora," Kitty said, chewing on her bottom lip. "I'd never be able to face Julia if I'd lost her."

"No problem. I can give you my number in case you need anything."

Her cheeks flared hot. She could think of plenty of things Josh could help her with. But instead of listing them, she just nodded and thanked him.

"I don't suppose you want to stay for a coffee?" she asked, playing with the hair at her nape. "I mean, you're probably busy. Chihuahuas and stuff...."

Josh looked back at Kitty, eyes a little wide for her liking.

Was he going to cut and run now his goat-rescuing duties were over? "I'm never going to turn down caffeine," he said. "We can eat the croissants, though they may be squashed by now."

Damn, he was staying for coffee. Kitty hoped she'd remembered to turn the dishwasher on last night. Julia's coffee was so strong that if not, the dregs of yesterday's brew would've welded onto the bottom of the cups by now.

They went inside, and Josh sat at the kitchen table while Kitty surreptitiously checked the clean cups' status and fired up the coffee machine. Mercifully, four pristine cups sat in the washer.

"So, tell me more about your sister's place," she said. "What sort of animals does she rescue?"

"Similar to Julia's, plus rabbits and guinea pigs, a ton of geese, ducks and chickens, a few sheep, some goats, two pigs, and two beautiful horses. With all of that to cope with, she's desperate for help. She relies on volunteers and donations. It's a tough gig but a labour of love for her."

"Just awful," Kitty said as she poured the coffee. She'd caught sight of her warped reflection in the chrome toaster. Her face was a cross between a gargoyle and the sea hag from *The Little Mermaid.*

"Do you like horses?" Josh asked. "You should come and ride them. They always need exercising."

Kitty's blood ran cold, and she stopped pouring the coffee.

"I wouldn't be much use," she said. "I've blanked out every riding lesson I ever had."

"What do you mean?"

Kitty brought over the mugs and popped them down on the dining table. She pulled the band out of her hair, and it tumbled around her shoulders. How could she word this without blowing her pretence at being in control of Julia's hobby farm?

"I'm not entirely at home with animals. In fact, the big ones terrify me."

Josh tipped his head to one side, and his brow furrowed. "I'd never have guessed that. I can usually tell when folk aren't 'animal people.' You don't give off that vibe at all. From what I remember, you have a big heart. Animals can sense that."

Kitty was just about to confess that most animals shied away from her like she was rat bait, but instead, Josh leaned over and extracted a twig from her hair. She blinked twice under his smiling eyes, and then a reliable smoulder hit her cheeks. *Damn*, Tottenbridge and blushing. There must be something in the water. Perhaps it was the same thing that had infected the ducks.

Kitty laughed under her breath, recalling her reflection in the toaster. "I must look like I was dragged through a hedge backwards."

"You still look lovely," Josh's said, his soft blue eyes sweeping over her, lingering a little too long at her forehead. *Crap,* she still had that ungodly bruise. She brought her fingers up to touch it.

"Even sporting a purple lump?"

Josh smiled. "The colour suits you."

Kitty rolled her eyes internally. Couldn't he just draw the line at being talented, caring, *and* gorgeous? Must he add swoon-worthy to the list?

"You still wear your hair long," Josh said, eyeing the dark strands that skirted just above her waist.

She'd always wanted long hair as a kid, but her mum had cut it short in an unflattering bob. As a result, Kitty spent her younger years being mercilessly teased for it. She was taunted for looking like a boy and called "matchstick" on account of being so tall with a rounded haircut. Kitty hated school. As soon as she was old enough to make decisions about her own hair, she'd grown it. The last time she'd measured, it was twenty-six inches long. Kitty one—Valerie Cameron nil.

She grabbed the length and twisted it over one shoulder. "It's kind of like my superpower. I can't bring myself to cut it, but it gets in the way, so I tie it back, mostly."

"You should wear it down more often," Josh said. "It's beautiful."

Kitty bit her lip, waiting for the Rapunzel jokes to follow, but none came.

"I have an offer for you," Josh said, instead. "If you agree to visit Thea and give her some organisation tips, I'll help refresh your riding skills, and I promise to be gentle with you. I can't say the same for my niece, though. One look at your hair, and she'll be chasing you around with a plastic hairbrush and her Barbie clips."

The cheeky gleam in his eyes couldn't cancel out the wave of nausea that crashed over her. The thought of sitting on a horse was terrifying. Kitty didn't want to make a fool of herself, but she didn't want to come across as a wimp either. Not with Josh. At least if she agreed to help his sister, it could be an opportunity to spend more time with him. Get to know him again.

"Okay, I'll go to see your sister," she said, taking a large sip of the very strong coffee she'd made.

Before she could lock in a time, Julia hobbled into the kitchen, one hand on her walking stick and the other carrying her giant tabby cat, Herod.

"Joshua! What on earth are you doing here?" she said.

Kitty looked at Josh with wide eyes, pleading for him to not mention this morning's misadventure with Dora. Giving an almost imperceptible nod, he stood and gave her aunt a big hug.

"Morning Julia, how are you feeling? I'm checking in with Kitty, making sure she has everything she needs."

Breathing a perceptible sigh of relief, Kitty beamed. Like a knight in shining armour with the most heavenly forearms she'd ever seen, he'd rescued her. Covered up for her. As Josh sat back down, Julia threw Kitty an approving smile.

"I can report she's in control of everything," Josh said. "The animals love her. You're lucky to have such a capable assistant on board."

Under the table, Kitty nudged his foot in quiet conspiracy, and he glanced over, giving her a wink that made her heart melt.

A warm glow swelled in Kitty's chest as the three of them sat and drank coffee together. The conversation, full of laughter, flowed easily. And for the first time, it hit her that she wasn't stuck behind a desk and stressed to the max. Even if Dora the explorer goat had caused her thirty minutes of grief, she wouldn't change a thing that had happened.

Even Herod, who usually enjoyed taking unprovoked swipes at Kitty, purred on Julia's lap. Josh entertained them with stories of close shaves and sticky situations with all manner of animals, and Kitty was content to watch her old friend's handsome face. The idea of climbing up on a horse with him was suddenly appealing.

After a short while, Josh's phone buzzed on the kitchen table. He checked the message, and a slight frown appeared between his blond brows. He ran a hand through his hair.

"I'm sorry, I have to go," he said, moving his chair out from under the table.

Kitty stood to see him out, and as they walked to the front door, she thanked him for his help with Dora and for his discretion with Julia.

"All in a day's work," he said. "And don't worry, your secret's safe with me."

Josh was about to leave but paused before stepping down onto the garden path.

"By the way, I don't give enemas to Chihuahuas, Kitty. I'm a farm vet."

He gave her one more jaw-dropping smile and left.

As she wandered back into the kitchen to join Julia, Kitty picked up the dirty mugs.

"What's a farm vet?"

14

KITTY

THE DAYS at Rose Cottage wore on in a familiar rhythm. Kitty would wake up, grab coffee, and head out to the animals. She maintained a healthy dislike of the goats. She hadn't yet considered forgiving Dora for the indignity of the other morning.

Her thoughts often drifted to Josh when she was alone with the animals. Kitty came up with a million questions to ask him. Even though she had his number, she was too shy to contact him first. He was probably busy overseeing sheep getting tick baths or whatever else a farm vet did. Kitty had Googled his job, and it didn't sound like fluffy bunnies and kittens. Quite the opposite.

Forced to submit to relaxation, she spent her afternoons lying in the garden in her string bikini, re-reading her mum's novels. It turned out that Julia had a healthy collection.

That morning, Kitty and Julia sat together drinking coffee on the patio, the bright morning sun already searing them.

"I feel it's time I re-entered the world of the living," Julia said, pushing back her chair. There's a wine tasting for the Women's Club this afternoon. It's at the Five Bob."

The Women's Club was a social organisation for ladies of a certain age. Based on Julia's stories, the club revolved chiefly around cake baking and flower arranging.

"Wine tasting?" Kitty asked.

"Oh yes. We get up to all sorts at the W.C. It's not all fetes and cake stalls. Some of those women are wild," Julia said, with a glint in her eye.

"How wild are we talking?" Knowing her ability to party, Kitty was surprised Julia hadn't gone bonkers cooped up on her own.

"Last time we had a function at the pub, I spotted two ladies on High Street. One was taking the other home in a wheelbarrow."

Kitty pictured two elderly spinsters weaving down the road, the one in the barrow brandishing a bottle of wine and a fat cigar. She giggled.

"Don't worry, I'll behave," said Julia. "I can't drink too much because of my painkillers."

Kitty put her coffee cup down on the wooden table in front of her. "Who's taking you?" she asked, secretly looking forward to some alone time. She'd got to a rather juicy bit in her mum's book, *The Scottish Scoundrel,* that deserved a more thorough reading. From memory, that book had been one of Kitty's primary sources for her early sex education.

"I was hoping *you'd* take me," replied Julia as she tickled Herod's ears.

Kitty's stomach dropped. An afternoon at The Five Bob meant a very high likelihood of running into Daniel Cunningham. The thought filled her with a mixture of excitement and terror. She hadn't seen or heard from him since their moonlit stroll, but she had thought of him. More often than she would have liked.

"Not one of your friends?" Kitty said, praying her aunt

would find another chaperone. Julia sighed. "Nobody is expecting me, and I'd like to make an entrance. Please, darling. We'll only be out for a little while."

Kitty reluctantly agreed, telling herself she was accompanying her aunt to be helpful and not as an excuse to see Daniel again.

After much primping and preening on Julia's part, they left the house together for the slow walk down the lane. Kitty offered to drive, but Julia insisted on walking, saying Jonty could take them home later.

She'd selected a flamboyant, flamingo pink trouser suit and sun hat dressed in fabric peonies. Kitty adored her over-the-top style, envious of her confidence to carry it off.

She herself drew quite a contrast. She wore a utilitarian pair of green slacks, a white shirt, and green espadrilles. She'd pulled her hair back into a high ponytail, and it swung heavily behind her like a pendulum. After receiving a consignment of contact lenses in the post, Kitty was enjoying life without her glasses. The goats would probably have eaten them by now, anyway.

Progress was hot, slow, and steady, and although the two of them chit-chatted about anything and everything, by the time they reached the bakery, Julia was tired. They decided to stop for a coffee and sat at a table outside on the street, ordering two cappuccinos with scones, jam, and cream. The checked tablecloth billowed in the scorching breeze, and a vase of delicate poppies wilted in the sun. Kitty hoped her mascara was still intact and not halfway down her cheeks.

"So, give me an update. What's been going on in your world?" asked Julia.

Kitty sighed. "I'm getting radio silence from the headhunters. Nothing. I'm unsure if I should be nervous or offended."

Julia reached out and patted the back of Kitty's hand. "It's only been a couple of weeks. Give it time, darling. The perfect opportunity is waiting just around the corner, I'm sure of it."

Kitty wasn't convinced she could adopt Julia's optimistic approach. Used to getting results fast, the search for her ideal role was proving to be anything but. The coffee arrived, and the rich aroma enveloped her nostrils, its familiar smell calming her. She'd make some more calls this afternoon.

The village was its usual quiet self, but a low throbbing reached Kitty's ears, and she scanned the street. In the distance, she spotted a muddy SUV coming towards them, its engine breaking the silence. When the car drew level, it pulled up alongside the kerb. The tinted window rolled down, and a blonde head stuck out. It had thick, curly ears and a very long tongue. And a silky voice followed it.

"Wendy! Get out of the way," it pleaded.

Josh! Kitty's heart skipped, and she stood up, walking towards the car, leaving Julia open-mouthed.

"Get down!" Josh said. His tone was more insistent but was shortly followed by a burst of laughter. "Oh, for God's sake, this is hopeless!"

An enormous dog greeted Kitty as she walked up to the window. Fearless, she lifted her hands to its head. It had the biggest grin and the softest curls she'd ever felt.

"Hello there," said Kitty, twisting long ears around her fingers. A dog of this size would normally worry her, but after a few licks, it settled back into the passenger seat with a 'whump'.

Kitty scrubbed at her cheeks, laughing, while Josh winced.

"I'm sorry for the face wash, but she loves cappuccinos. Normally, I'd prefer a formal introduction, but someone seems to have other ideas." Josh reached over and gave the top of the dog's head a scratch. His eyes shone.

"This is Wendy, my entourage. Wendy, this is Kitty, my old friend."

Ouch. He'd called her a friend. Kitty wasn't sure why it bothered her so much. Ignoring the gnawing in her gut, she grinned and gave the dog's ears another tickle.

"She's lovely!"

"Don't let her hear you say that. She's already chewed my socks this morning."

"Well," Kitty said, addressing Wendy, "I'm sure they were delicious."

Josh eyed her with mock suspicion. "I'm going to have to watch you two. I'm glad we saw you. Wendy's been meaning to give you a formal invitation to visit the farm. She gives a great guided tour, leaving you coated in fur as a souvenir."

Crap! Kitty had been so preoccupied with herself and her job search that she hadn't popped in to see Thea yet.

"I'm sorry. Job hunting has side-tracked me, not to mention the stress of keeping Julia on the straight and narrow."

Josh's eyes lit up with laughter. "You have your work cut out. Your aunt is a handful."

"I heard that," Julia said from her seat at the table.

"Then you'll know I speak from experience," Josh shouted out the window. "Don't say I didn't warn you, Kitty."

She cocked a brow. "I wish I'd known that before I'd agreed to escort her to the pub!"

"What's going on at the pub?" he asked.

"Just a debauched meeting of the W.C.," said Julia. "Why don't you join us? I'm sure the ladies would appreciate seeing your handsome face."

Josh grinned. Why hadn't she noticed he had dimples before?

"Not this time," he called, then lowered his voice to address Kitty. "Duty calls. Don't forget Wendy's invite. And keep your wits about you this afternoon. Those ladies get up to all sorts."

Kitty nodded, enjoying the sight of his bulging triceps as he gripped the steering wheel. "I promise I'll pop by soon."

"Make sure you do," Josh said, gunning the engine and pulling away with a wave.

Kitty watched his car disappear down the road, excitement fizzing in her gut. When he was out of sight, she turned to Julia, who had the biggest smile on her face.

"Katherine Cameron, you're blushing!" she said.

Kitty's mouth gaped. "I'm not. It's just hot!" she said, her hands touching her fiery cheeks.

Julia dipped her finger in the pot of cream in front of her and licked its tip. "Joshua is rather dreamy, though," she giggled. "Don't look so shocked, young lady. I may be old, but I'm not blind. Such a lovely young man, too. I can't understand why he hasn't been snapped up."

Kitty couldn't understand it either.

"So dedicated to those animals. Just like his father," Julia said, misty-eyed. "Now *there* was a good-looking man."

Kitty snickered, and with a dramatic sigh, Julia glanced at her watch. "Look at the time! We really must get to the pub. I want to get a good seat next to our host."

"Who's the host?" asked Kitty. Fledgling butterflies tested their wings low down in her tummy. Like they were preparing to hear one name in particular.

"Daniel Cunningham," replied Julia. Kitty's stomach flipped over, sending those butterflies into a flurry. Of course, he was the host. The way her luck was going, fate wouldn't have it any other way.

"His family owns the pub," said Julia, picking up her walking stick and fuchsia pink parasol. "*There's* another good-looking man who should have married years ago."

One side of her mouth lifted. She could never imagine Daniel being married. "Are you sure you're not too tired?" Kitty offered. "We could head back, you know."

"No. If I'm going to exhaust myself, I'd better make it worthwhile," Julia said, getting to her feet with difficulty. "Come along and meet Daniel. I'm sure you two youngsters will get along like a house on fire."

Kitty swallowed hard.

15

DANIEL

DANIEL CURSED the God Bacchus as he rethought his decision to host the wine-tasting event for the Tottenbridge Women's Club. Several overdressed and over-made-up women tittered around him as he stood at the bar, trying not to choke on their various perfumes. Crepey chests and red lips fought for supremacy, and Daniel was seriously concerned he might be swallowed whole in the feeding frenzy.

He had a crushing hangover from a poker game the night before and had forgotten this event until he'd had a panicked phone call from Patricia Gore, the organiser. With his head about to explode, they'd had a ten-minute conversation about whether the three wheels of cheese he'd ordered would go with her homemade quince paste.

Daniel took a breath and reached for the half-drunk glass of brandy he'd left on the bar. Perhaps the hair of the dog and a second wind would get him through the afternoon unscathed.

Just as he'd knocked back the last of the dark liquid, the old wooden pub door swung open and encased in a shaft of sunlight, Julia arrived, wearing a ridiculous hat. The corners of his mouth lifted slightly. She looked like a flamingo.

Daniel was just about to go and say hello, when from behind Julia, Kitty appeared. She peeped around her aunt as if checking the lay of the land, and her fingers played with the end of her ponytail. Daniel grinned. Things were looking up.

"Excuse me, ladies," he said to the surrounding W.C. members, "but our guest of honour has just arrived."

Daniel swept the gaggle of ladies away as he strode towards Julia, placing an arm around her shoulder and guiding her to a seat at the head of the table.

"Julia! It's so lovely to see you. How are you? I'm assuming you're on the mend, and you'll soon be tap dancing on the bar again, just like the good old days." Kitty's eyes met Daniel's, and the smile she gave him confirmed her appreciation of the fuss he was making of her aunt. Brownie points for him.

"And who's this?" he asked, giving a subtle wink to Kitty.

"This is my niece, Kitty," said Julia. "She's come to help me until I'm back on my feet. She's a lawyer, you know. Very successful and single," Julia said with emphasis.

The furious look and the blush her words brought to Kitty's face were delightful. Daniel wanted nothing more than to kiss the pink from her cheeks.

"Then, as a successful, single lawyer, we'll have to take special care of Katherine while she's here. Give her a warm Tottenbridge welcome." Daniel wiggled his eyebrows at Kitty, and her rosy-hued cheeks flared even hotter to match Julia's outfit.

"Katherine? Have you two met already?" she asked.

"Just in passing," Daniel said. "Your niece has been getting friendly with the furniture lately. How's the head, Bruiser?"

She pulled a face, and Daniel snickered.

"Well, it looks much better. Much less lumpy. I'll call off the St. Bernard and keg of brandy I ordered."

Daniel turned to Julia again, helping to settle her in the seat at the head of the large wooden table. "I've been telling

Katherine that she should find a little distraction while she's in Tottenbridge. A hobby. What do you say, Julia?"

Kitty's eyes narrowed, and she looked as if she was about to strangle him. The thought of her being just a little cross with him had his dick nudging at his fly.

"Oh, absolutely," said Julia. "I've been saying that too much work and no play has made Kitty a little too serious."

"Then let's begin loosening her up this afternoon," he said with a wink.

Kitty glared at him, a pout on her lips, and Daniel wondered how long it would be before she bit back at his teasing her? He wanted her to bite back. To bare her teeth a little. Hell, that wasn't the only thing he wanted her to bare. He'd thought about his proposition to her at the village green and the way she'd turned him down. Daniel wasn't used to being refused. He intended to change her mind.

"Okay, let's get started, ladies. Please take a seat, and we'll begin," Daniel said to the hive of women who buzzed around the bar. He sat Kitty next to Julia at his side and leaned down to whisper in her ear. "You look amazing, by the way. I promise not to get you *too* drunk."

Her wide-eyed look was exactly what he'd hoped for, and with a smirk, Daniel cleared his throat.

"Okay, ladies, for our first tasting this afternoon, we'll start with a pure, virginal white." He cast a look at Kitty before continuing. "But don't let that deceive you. This sauvignon blanc is a little firecracker."

As he spoke, one of his bar staff poured the guests a small glass of wine, and Daniel followed suit for himself and Julia. But when it came to Kitty, he gave her a full glass, catching her attention. She raised a single eyebrow but didn't say a word. She still wasn't ready to bite back, then.

Once everyone was ready, he proceeded with his tasting notes, holding court and his audience's rapt interest.

"This wine, whilst on the surface appears unassuming, has hidden depths. Note the beautiful body on the first taste. The flavour that curls around the tongue. Though young, fruity, and fresh, its finish is one of lingering sophistication that leaves one wanting more."

He delivered every single word to Kitty, her gorgeous discomfort driving him on. Her seduction would be fun. Daniel relished the rising colour on her face as the women clucked and chattered, sipped their wine, and picked over the cheese boards.

She looked everywhere else in the room but at him. Simply willing her to glance over was having no effect. He wanted to play. To banter. And she was either too shy or too stubborn. He hoped it was the latter. More fun that way. He was going to have to up his game. He quietly made some notes on a napkin. After a few minutes, he tapped his glass with a knife to quiet the chatter.

"Lovely ladies of the W.C.," he said, holding up a bottle of red. "If I could have your attention. I would like to welcome an honourary member this afternoon. I believe you all know Julia Finch has recently undergone a hip replacement." There were murmurs and nods around the table. Julia blushed graciously at their well wishes. "You may not know, however, that her niece Katherine is in town to help with her convalescence."

Further muttering of approval rolled through the gathered ladies as Daniel warmed to his subject.

"Katherine would have us believe she's a lowly corporate lawyer, but I know she wouldn't mind me divulging her genuine passion, seeing as we're amongst friends." Kitty's eyes grew to saucers as everyone turned to look at her. "Katherine is, in fact, a celebrated star of amateur theatre, having been recently nominated for the Dame Judith Dentures award for Rising Talent."

The whisperings of the ladies grew to full-on chatter, and

the furious look that Kitty threw him hardened his dick. Christ, he needed to get her into bed.

"I was wondering, Katherine, if you wouldn't mind demonstrating your craft by reading the tasting notes for the next wine."

Cries of approval and encouragement rang out, and Daniel held out the napkin he'd written on. "Please?" he asked, his wolfish smile growing by the second.

Kitty turned a violent crimson and took a couple of deep breaths, the shape of her small breasts obvious through the thin shirt. Her eyes darted to his, and he met them with what he considered his most smouldering look. He'd practised it since he was a teenager when he'd realised his looks could get him what he wanted.

Kitty fisted the napkin on her plate, her teeth chewing on her bottom lip. For a long beat she stared at her glass, but eventually, she placed a hand on the table and rose slowly. Imaginary fingers curled around Daniel's balls, and he smiled. She was going to take his bait. Take a bite. Kitty straightened to her full height and stared right at him, a defiant look in her eyes.

"Thank you, Donovan," she began, a saccharin-sweet smile on her lips. "It would be my pleasure. I only hope I can do your words justice."

As he handed Kitty his hastily scribbled notes, he winked. She'd purposely used an incorrect name for him. It was a nibble if not a full bite. A small firing shot, but a promise of things to come, he hoped. He liked a woman who didn't give in to him too easily.

Kitty cleared her throat as Daniel poured her an even larger glass this time. Again, she didn't protest.

"This second wine is dark and smooth," she began. "It's described here as tall, bold, and strong, with gentle, earthy notes, providing a cheeky flourish on the back palette.

However, some would define it as an overly confident, young pretender with a definite hint of cheese."

She was teasing *him*, now. Describing him in her own words. And he loved it.

Kitty continued. "I think you'll find it's full of overblown and unnecessary complexities that can leave a rather disappointing burn in the gullet. I'll allow you to decide for yourselves, but I'd suggest the best way to approach this wine is to knock it back soundly."

Daniel took a breath at her final words as Kitty drained her glass in one go, slamming it down on the table when she'd finished. Amidst applause from the women of the W.C., the triumph on her face lit Daniel's fuse, and he fought the urge to carry her off to the cellars and bang her brains out.

"Touché," he mouthed with a grin, and Kitty's eyes flared before she sat back down.

The afternoon continued in the same pattern. Daniel would pour Kitty a bigger glass than everyone else and then introduce the wine in ever more risqué language. Kitty drank every single one. Daniel could hardly believe nobody noticed his sex-laced commentary, but most of the women hung on his every word. Not unused to female attention, he played it up even more.

As the event wound down, Daniel could see how drunk Kitty was. Hell, even *he* was tipsy. Who knew the W.C. could be so much fun? Her eyes were unfocused, and she was wobbling a little as she stood and headed towards the bathroom.

"Ladies," he said, standing himself. "Thank you for coming today. I hope you learned a little something about our beautiful British wines. Now, excuse me, I have a little business to attend to."

When he caught up with Kitty, she looked flushed and was weaving towards the bar unsteadily. Daniel hooked an arm under hers and led her to a bar stool where she could sit.

Perhaps he'd gone a little too far. She'd have a shocking hangover tomorrow.

"I need to call a cab," she said, slurring her words and having trouble focusing on him.

Daniel huffed a laugh. "This isn't the big city, you know. A tractor ride is the closest thing you'll get to a cab."

"Can I get a wheelbarrow then?" she asked, a ridiculous giggle escaping her lips.

Daniel levelled his gaze at her. "Katherine, I believe you're drunk."

"I'm *definitely* drunk," she said, giving him a wavering thumbs up. "My sister would say it's been far too long, and I have you to thank for breaking my drought. You've been very naughty today. You're a bad influence, Daniel Cunningham."

Daniel smiled and lowered his voice to a husky purr.

"I can be as bad as you want. And I think you want me to be wicked."

Kitty licked her lips and dragged her eyes up to meet his. She leaned closer, and Daniel's heart sped up as he felt a stirring in his jeans. Was it really going to be this easy?

His eyes raked over her flushed face and full lips, longing to claim them. If he made a move, he was sure she'd kiss him, but this wasn't the way he wanted it. Not a drunken snog in his pub. He wanted to seduce her. To dazzle her with his charm. He wanted her to desire him in the cold light of day with no booze involved. There was no triumph in anything less.

"I know I'm going to regret this," he said, taking her arms and gently guiding her body back to upright, "but I won't take advantage of you. You probably won't remember most of this afternoon, but I hope you remember how much you want to kiss me right now. If you do, hold that thought, and I promise we'll revisit it."

"I need to call a cab," Kitty slurred again, clearly oblivious to what he'd just said.

Daniel sighed. "Right-o," he said. "Let's find Julia and call your cousin to take you home."

Kitty leaned into him again.

"Did I tell you? You're a bad influence, Daniel Cunningham," she said, aiming a pointed finger at his chest and missing completely.

"Oh, I know," he said. "And you're absolutely gorgeous."

AFTER THE W.C. ladies cleared the pub, Daniel stood behind the bar, polishing glasses. Tired and deflated, he regretted leaving Kitty for another day. Why didn't he just let her kiss him? They could be back at his place now. Putting a smile on both of their faces.

Amber bustled in from the bistro, carrying napkins and half a bottle of wine. Her fiery curls caught the bright lights of the bar as she put her cargo down and reached over to take out two glasses.

"You survived then?" she asked, pouring them each a glass of the leftover shiraz.

"Just about. Those women are so demanding."

"When did that ever bother you?" she smirked. "I thought you prided yourself on being ready to please." Daniel's eyebrow shot up. "Did I see your new special friend drinking up a storm earlier?" she asked.

Daniel snickered. "She was assisting me with the tasting notes," he said.

"Was that all she was assisting with?"

"Unfortunately, yes," he said, putting down the polishing cloth and examining the clusters of freckles on her cheeks. "I'm afraid her reluctance to succumb to my charms is providing stiffer competition than I'd usually face."

Amber's nose crinkled as her fingers played with the edge of a bar mat.

"That doesn't sound good. She looked wasted when I saw her. Surely that'd loosen her up a bit?"

"I don't want her loosened up in that way. I want to do the loosening myself. If I have to rely on getting women drunk, I may as well give up and join a convent."

"A convent is for nuns," Amber said, smirking.

"I know, but I'd still need something to look at. Man cannot live on red alone." He took a gulp of this drink.

"Why do you care so much, Tiger? It's not like you to mope about a girl."

Daniel scowled. "Christ, I don't know. There's something about her, but I can't pin it down," he admitted.

Amber laughed. "Maybe it's because you want to pin *her* down, and she won't be pinned."

"The only pinning down I want to do isn't for polite conversation," he said, his lips curling.

"Surprise, surprise." Amber rested an elbow on the bar. "Look, why are you trying so hard? It's not your style. Like you've always told me, the ladies come to you. Not the other way around, remember?"

Daniel paused. "Maybe she's different."

"Different, how?"

"She's smart and sexy and earns enough money to keep me in brandy and petticoats for the rest of my life."

Amber rolled her eyes and finished her glass.

"Well, I wish you'd get on with it or get over it. Your love life exhausts me, Daniel."

16

JOSH

JOSH WALKED into Small Oaks Farm. Each brick and dusty corner held the happiest and saddest memories. His sister and his niece lived here now, and he'd avoided her repeated pleas to move back in. His work hours were crazy, and his late-night call-outs could disturb the peace in the house.

Who was he kidding? The real reason he declined her offer was more selfish. Josh didn't want to get swept up in Thea's whirlwind life. Drop in, be the doting uncle, then exit back to his little cottage. That's how he liked it.

There was no sign of Thea, so Josh headed to her office. She'd set it up in an old storeroom at the back of the house, and the chaos inside sent his head spinning. There wasn't a spare space on any surface. Paperwork coated every desk. *It's organised chaos,* Thea always said, but just looking at it drained him. With envy, he recalled the organisation that Kitty had brought to Julia's shed.

"Are you in here somewhere, T?" he shouted, poking his head out the door into the hallway.

"Coming!" Thea's distant voice sang out.

While he waited, Josh sat down at her desk and played with

a stapler. He'd thought of Kitty all morning. When he'd seen her with Julia at the cafe, he'd wanted nothing more than to stop and join them. She'd taken to Wendy instantly. Why it pleased him so much, he couldn't say. Or wouldn't. The corners of his mouth turned up as he recalled the smile she'd left him with at the car. That same smile still made his heart beat a little bit faster.

"What's got you looking so happy?" Thea asked, disturbing his thoughts.

She stood before him, boots caked in mud and arms full of cat treat bags.

"Do you think you could wear any more spiderwebs?" he asked, pulling sticky strands out of her hair.

She dropped the bags on the nearest desk, scattering papers all around.

"I like them. Their grey gives me an air of authority." Thea's eyes narrowed. "What's up, little brother? I wasn't expecting to see you until later."

"I had a few minutes between appointments, and I wanted to check in with you about Crackle's foot, plus tell you about your new secret weapon."

Thea bit into an apple that was left on the side. Crackle was one of the many cats that called the farm their home.

"Her foot is better, thanks to you. I still don't know where she got it caught, though." She took another bite, chewing loudly. "So, tell me, what is my new secret weapon? Have you dug up a generous new donor? One with bottomless pockets?"

Josh shook his head. "Jonty's cousin is in town, staying with Julia. She used to visit them for the holidays as a kid. You might remember her."

"Oh! How's Julia doing?" asked Thea.

"She's doing better now that Kitty's here."

"Who on earth is Kitty?" Thea asked, mid munch.

Josh rolled his eyes. "She's Jonty's cousin. Come to help Julia with her animals."

"Oh, I see!" Thea nodded, taking another massive bite out of the apple. "What's that got to do with me?"

Josh picked up the stapler again, its smooth plastic sides shining in the fluorescent light overhead. "She's overhauled Julia's place. Her animal sheds were a bit of a mess. It was fine for Julia since she knows where everything is, but for anyone else, it was a shit show."

"Overhauled how?" asked Thea. "What's her background? Animal husbandry?"

"No animal background at all. She's a corporate lawyer. Never even owned a hamster, but she's doing great with the animals and is bloody organised."

Thea eyed her brother thoughtfully. "Why would she be *my* secret weapon?"

"She took the chaos of Julia's place, researched, organised and regimented the whole setup. It's running like a military operation now."

Thea giggled. "Does she have the goats standing at attention on the paddock at dawn?"

Josh huffed. "You may laugh, but this place is a shit show, too. I know you're running single-handed now, but you could use a little of Kitty's magic, I think."

Thea sighed. "I know it's a mess, but keeping this place going on my own with a four-year-old is full on. I'll catch up with my tail when Ammy starts school."

"But why wait?" Josh said. "Kitty's here for a couple of months and has free time."

Thea looked around at the office and wrinkled her nose.

"I suppose if I ran off with Brad Pitt tomorrow, you'd struggle, and I haven't seen my hole puncher for weeks. So, she's organised. What else should I know about her?"

Josh snorted with laughter. "She's self-admittedly pedantic, a neat freak, and definitely quirky, but for all of that, she's warm, funny, and bloody smart." And on his mind, way more than he'd like to admit.

"She sounds...er...interesting."

Josh scowled at his sister.

"What? You haven't painted a very flattering picture."

"She's great, T. You'd like her."

Thea narrowed her eyes and surveyed her brother. "Are you sure *you* don't like her?" she asked. "You never talk about women. You live like a monk."

Josh's cheeks lit hot.

"I barely know her," he lied, unwilling to admit to his boyhood crush, let alone his current one. "Besides, I don't have time for anything outside of work. Three girls in my life are enough."

"Sounds to me like you're trying to talk yourself out of something. You have time for a girlfriend, Josh, but you avoid it. Your walls need to come down someday. Me, Ammy, and Wendy aren't always going to be enough. You need an adult, romantic relationship."

Josh stood, put his hands in his pockets and looked down at his boots. She was right.

"I know you hate to talk about it," said Thea. "But I worry about you. Your Saturday night fun is playing Legos with Ammy,"

Josh had to laugh at that.

"That's not my little brother," she continued, her voice softening. "You were the life of every party. It's time to live again."

"Back off, please," he said, his brow furrowed.

Thea spoke gently, walking to where he stood and placing a hand on his shoulder. "I know your heart got broken, but it happens to everyone, and it's been three years."

His gut wrenched at her words. True, his heart was

damaged, but it was nothing to the heartbreak she'd been through. She was the one who needed help mending.

He stepped in and gave his sister a tight hug. "We're quite a pair, aren't we?"

She pulled away from him and nodded. "But we'll survive," she said with a sigh. After a beat, the corners of her mouth twitched. "Okay. I admit defeat. I'm struggling here, so please bring your secret weapon to survey the damage."

"She's already agreed to pop by, so be on your best behaviour," he said, extracting himself from Thea's arms and heading out the door. "See you later, Sis."

Josh walked back across the yard to his cottage, reflecting on Thea's words. He *was* lonely. A loopy mongrel could only provide so much company. It wasn't as if he hadn't tried to dip his toe back in the dating game, but it always left him empty, as if his heart wasn't in it.

He walked through a gap in the stone wall bordering his house. It was his mum's art studio, which he later converted into a one-bedroom cottage. His mum had coped with her lonely life as a farm vet's wife by surrounding herself with hobbies and then with children. She'd loved his dad, but as a kid, Josh was aware of her spending many hours alone, keeping things going at home. When his father retired, her relief was evident.

He stared across the rolling fields. Gnarled trees dotted the landscape, standing to attention like dilapidated scarecrows. The high-pressure demands of his job meant long hours and isolation. Being a farm vet left him with little energy for anything else. Who would want to share that life with him?

17

KITTY

"YES!" Kitty screamed, throwing her phone into the air. "About bloody time!"

She texted Jonty and her sister with a massive grin on her face.

Kitty: Bingo! I've got an opportunity at Wilbur Blake! They want me to head their energy team. OMG, this is amazing! Just had to tell someone. Interviews, here I come! XOX

The funk of the last fortnight lifted. She'd worried nobody wanted to hire her, and now a top-tier firm was interested. Excitement bubbled in Kitty's chest. Things were looking up! She had a chance to get her life back. She couldn't wait to tell Josh.

Full of renewed optimism, it was time for Kitty to address her wardrobe issues. Her clothes were a disaster. She'd ruined three pairs of designer jeans, her favourite shirt, and her flip-flops were wearing thinner and thinner. She could almost feel each blade of grass and pebble through their dissolving rubber.

Kitty threw on some smart trousers and a T-shirt, then headed to the kitchen, where Julia listened to the radio at top volume. She stopped to drop a kiss on Herod's head as he guarded the coffee machine on the counter. When she walked in, she turned the radio down to a tolerable decibel.

"I'm going clothes shopping. Do you want to come?" Kitty asked Julia, who sat at the table, reading the paper.

"No, thank you, darling. It's too hot for shopping, and I've yet to wear half my wardrobe."

Kitty laughed. Julia had a vast walk-in dressing room upstairs that'd put Carrie Bradshaw to shame. Herod and Kitty shared hot, buttered toast as she told Julia about the job.

"It's such an amazing opportunity. I'd head up my own bloody division!"

"It sounds fabulous, darling. We'd miss you, but I suppose we can't hold on to you forever."

Kitty grinned. "I'll come to visit more often. Get some of that work-life balance I hear about. I'm going to drop in to see Josh's sister on my way back from town. He promised me riding lessons if I gave her a hand at the farm."

Julia's carefully tweezed eyebrows raised. "But you hate horses."

But she didn't hate Josh. And she was willing to get back in the saddle if *he* was holding her reins.

18

KITTY

KITTY SHOPPED up a storm in the sticky heat of town. When she was finally satisfied, she set off back to Tottenbridge to drop in on Thea at Small Oaks Sanctuary.

The drive flew by, and Kitty left the windows down, belting out her favourite playlist the entire way. She couldn't do this in London. Any journey she took in the city was short, and she'd choke on the fumes if she dared to open the window.

Arriving at the other end of the village from Rose Cottage, the sturdy farmhouse of Small Oaks Farm loomed in the distance. Butterflies stirred in Kitty's stomach. The memory of her bleeding toe was so clear now. How could she have forgotten about Josh? It wouldn't be so easy to forget about him now.

Kitty pulled up outside the farm. The only living thing that stirred was a giant tortoiseshell cat lounging in the sun. As if finding her unimportant, it put its head back on its paws and shut its eyes.

The yard was smaller than she remembered. A horseshoe of old stone buildings skirted a cobbled square. Buckets and brooms lay against any available wall. Kitty walked towards the front door of the farmhouse and knocked.

The door was hanging open, and after getting no response, she knocked harder and shouted.

"Hello!"

"Crap!" a woman said as a loud thump rang out. "Come on in."

Kitty headed through the open front door into the cool depths of the house.

"I'm in the kitchen. Walk past the stairs and come straight through," said the disembodied voice.

She picked her way through a cluttered hallway. Mangled Barbie dolls littered the floor amongst upended picture books, pens, and pencils.

"Sorry for the mess!" the voice said as if reading her mind.

Kitty ventured down the hallway, skirting the side of the stairs. Old family photos hung in a line on the wall. She passed them slowly, unable to resist the urge to look. The first picture was of two golden-haired children riding giant horses. She recognised Josh. This was the boy she remembered. His face glowed with happiness. The girl on the other horse must be Thea. Kitty looked towards the door and, certain she was alone, continued to examine the pictures.

The next photo was of the two children fishing in a river. Josh held a fishing net and a jam jar while Thea hugged an old greyhound. Further down, the pictures changed. The golden-haired children had grown up, still wearing the same smiles. Josh was a teenager, running through a cornfield, a black Labrador at his feet. His joyous face caused the corners of Kitty's mouth to turn up. Thea was in the next picture with a kind-looking, dark-haired man. She wore white and had flowers in her hair. Further on, a photo showed her and the man holding a tiny baby, cradling it between their bodies. Josh's niece.

The next picture showed Josh holding a little girl on a pony. Shirtless and barefoot, Kitty could see every muscle in his chest and stomach. Her breath hitched as she fought the urge to inspect any closer, a blush reaching her cheeks. *Damn,* she hadn't realised he'd look like *that* underneath his clothes.

In the last picture, Josh wore fluffy bunny ears and carried the little girl on his shoulders. Kitty smiled. The love, evident in the photos, tugged at her heart. She only had pictures of early birthday parties and opening presents around the Christmas tree. Nothing like these. No wonder Josh stayed near his family.

Kitty reached the end of the hall and entered the tiny kitchen.

"Hang on a minute," came the voice.

Crockery, papers, and saucepans lined the countertops, and frothy net curtains hung at the windows. Long legs poked out from the cupboard under the sink, their booted feet wiggling. The drain made a dull clunking noise and the owner of the legs emerged. It was the golden-haired woman in the photos. *Thea.* When she stood up, she was almost the same height as Kitty.

"Sorry for the lack of a welcome. There was something wrong with the sink. Somehow a pair of Barbie shoes fell down the drain and got stuck in the pipe. I'm Thea Fox. How can I help you?"

Kitty laughed. "Barbie shoes down the drain? I can see how that might be a problem. I'm Kitty, Jonty's cousin. I think your brother might have mentioned me?"

After a beat, Thea grinned. "Oh, my goodness, yes! He has! He told me about the military operation you've introduced to Julia's," she said, flicking the kettle onto boil.

"Oh lord, that makes me sound weird," murmured Kitty.

"It's surprising what my brother finds exciting." She raised an eyebrow in jest.

"He wanted your opinion on this place."

Had Josh wanted her opinion? What on earth would she

know about running an animal sanctuary? Thea beckoned Kitty to sit down, which she did, being careful to avoid a decapitated Buzz Lightyear toy.

"Sorry. I'd say Buzz is a casualty of Wendy."

Thea busied herself making a pot of tea, and small talk progressed to the two of them putting the world to rights. Kitty liked Thea Fox. She was down-to-earth, practical, and hilarious. Devoted to her daughter, the sanctuary, and her brother, the natural optimism she exuded was refreshing after the cold cynicism of her work colleagues.

Thea gave Kitty a run-down on the workings of the sanctuary and offered to show her around.

"Come on, I'll give you the grand tour," Thea said as she made another cup of tea.

Taking their drinks, she showed Kitty around the farm. Most of the animal accommodations were old, including the stone stables and outhouses. There was a large duck pond at the end of the yard and three large paddocks containing horses, a few sheep and, much to Kitty's annoyance, a small herd of goats. An old barn housed a couple of pigs and a purpose-built rabbit and guinea pig enclosure. The rest of the buildings contained supplies and food. Chaos reigned, just as Josh had described.

"I know where everything belongs," Thea said, "but trying to describe it to other people is the problem. I have a young girl, Belinda, who comes in a few mornings a week. She wants to be a vet, but I do most of the work myself."

Kitty ran a hand through her hair, wondering if it would be rude for her to stamp the mud off her shoes yet. "How the hell do you get it all done?"

"Joshie helps where he can. He does most of my vet work for free."

Kitty's heart glowed at her words. Josh was Dr Doolittle mixed with Mother Theresa.

Thea's tour ended on the other side of the farmhouse. This was where Josh's practice had a small office, and an enormous vegetable garden grew rampant.

"Josh grows all our veggies. He stops us all from getting scurvy," Thea laughed.

Kitty smiled. Was there nothing he couldn't do? Turn pond water to gin? Bring about world peace one Chihuahua at a time?

She spotted a small building set at the back of the house. Its large windows were fringed in wisteria, and a riot of wildflowers grew in the courtyard at the front. A large dog bowl sat next to the doormat, painted with a big "W." The little house had to be Josh's place.

"That's his cottage," said Thea nodding towards the building. "I wish he still lived in the house with us, but I guess at thirty-two, he wants his space."

Kitty snickered to herself. She couldn't imagine living on the same patch of land as Ronnie and her kids. It would likely end up in a family divorce court. They could never spend more than a few days together without fighting.

"This operation is a massive undertaking," said Kitty as they walked back to the farmhouse.

"Yeah, it's pretty exhausting, but I love it." Thea paused and took a gulp of the cold tea she was still carrying. "It was my husband Phil's idea. His baby. I've always been around animals, and I got swept up in his passion. We opened the place together. He passed away, though. Cancer."

Thea's words trailed off, and she looked down at her mug. Kitty swallowed hard. The poor thing.

"So, I can't let it go," Thea continued. "I need to make it work. For his sake and for Amelia's. She's our daughter."

Kitty thought of the angelic blonde girl sitting on Josh's shoulders in the photo, and her heart lurched. Thea could really do with a break. "It sounds like you could do with some help," she said.

"Is it that obvious?" said Thea with a wry smile.

"Look," said Kitty, glancing around the yard. "I'm here for a couple of months. I'm happy to lend a hand and take some pressure off."

Thea grimaced. "Aren't you busy with Julia's animals?"

"It's fine. Her animals don't take too much time now that everything is organized, and I get bored with nothing to do. Full disclosure, though—a potential job has come up. There'll be a few interviews taking my time."

"That's exciting. Josh told me you were brilliant."

Kitty smiled to herself, her cheeks aching with the effort to keep her grin low-key. It was nice to meet a man who admired her OCD brain. Usually, people found her pedantic tendencies annoying.

They arrived back at the house, and Thea showed Kitty through to the chaotic office. Her head reeled at the clutter, and as she sat at one desk, her fingers itched to sort through the pile of papers in front of her.

"I'm thrilled to help with the animals, but would you think me rude if I offered to help you with all this, too?" Kitty pointed at the stack of paperwork.

"Oh, my goodness, be my guest," Thea said with a look of relief on her face.

Kitty was about to offer a plan of attack for the out-of-control paperwork when a little girl ran into the office. She held a naked and shorn Barbie in one hand and a peanut butter sandwich in the other.

"Mummy!" she cried. "Peppa Pig has finished. I've got nothing to do now."

She noticed Kitty. "Who's this?" she asked.

"This is Joshie's friend, Kitty. She's helping Mummy out for a bit."

The little girl appraised her.

"She's got very long legs. Like Barbie," she said, waving her doll in the air.

Kitty smiled. She'd never in her life thought she'd be compared to a Barbie doll.

The girl took a bite of her sandwich, her head tilted to one side as she chewed. After what felt like minutes, her impish face erupted into a big grin.

"I like her," she said, hopping onto Kitty's lap, covering her trousers with sticky fingerprints.

Kitty cringed inside, freezing like a statue. She disliked kids almost as much as horses. They were unpredictable, noisy, and perpetually needed a good wash. As she sat with the little girl on her lap, all she could think about was laundering her clothes as soon as she got home.

The phone rang, and with a wave of her hand, Thea turned away to answer.

"My name's Amelia," the little girl said. "You can call me Ammy,"

"Hi, Ammy. My name's Katherine, but you can call me Kitty."

"I know," she said, raising her gummy fingers in the air. Kitty watched them, wide-eyed, praying that Ammy wouldn't touch her hair. She'd treated herself to a blowout in town.

"Are you going to marry my uncle?" the little girl asked innocently.

Kitty almost spat out her tea. She opened her mouth, gulping at the air like a beached fish.

"Bugger!" Thea said as she put the phone down.

"What's wrong, Mummy? Did you forget to pay the bank again?" Thea blushed a deep red as Ammy picked apart her sandwich, having abandoned her Barbie in Kitty's lap.

"The babysitter cancelled. Has a migraine. Dammit!"

Thea leafed through a contacts book on the desk, leaving a trail of muddy fingerprints on every page.

"Kitty can look after me," Ammy said.

Thea's eyes turned to Kitty. She took one look at her and shook her head.

"It's okay. I'll see who else I can dig up."

Kitty's brow creased. What was wrong with her babysitting for Ammy? Did she look that hopeless? She had to confess it was probably a good judgement on Thea's part, but she hated being deemed inadequate at anything.

"I don't mind," she offered. "I have two nieces of my own." Who she never saw.

Thea looked to where Kitty sat, Amelia settling back in her lap.

"I don't like to ask, but there's an important function. I'm going to get a big donation. Joshie told me he was working late tonight and couldn't help.

"It's fine. I love kids," Kitty said, wondering if Thea could see right through her lie. What was she doing? She didn't know how to entertain a four-year-old.

"Oh my gosh, that would be amazing," said Thea. "Thank you so much. I'll pay you, of course,"

"Please, no. Consider it a donation."

19

KITTY

KITTY ARRIVED BACK at the sanctuary later that evening. The night was hot and humid, and the front door was wide open again. She shouted into the hallway.

"Hi. It's Kitty,"

A distant voice replied, "Come in!"

Kitty stepped into the house and headed to the kitchen. The dishes in the sink were washed and put away, and fresh flowers sat in a vase on the kitchen table, adding a sweet, heady scent to the room.

First down the stairs was Ammy. She was fresh out of the bath, smelling of soap and shampoo. She looked adorable in a pair of Peppa Pig pyjamas and fluffy slippers, her tangle of blonde hair tamed and tucked behind her ears.

"Hi," said Kitty. "I love your pyjamas."

"Who do you like best? Peppa or George?"

Kitty made a great show of considering her question. "I think I like Daddy Pig the best. He makes me laugh the most and has the loudest grunt."

Kitty had checked up on the show when she'd got home

earlier. In all her legal dealings, she'd learned that a little research went a long way with a tricky client.

Ammy's face broke into a smile, and Thea entered the room, still hooking an earring through one lobe.

"Mummy looks like a fairy," Amelia giggled.

"Thank you, darling," said Thea, popping a kiss on her daughter's head and turning to Kitty. "Ammy's had a bath and her dinner. She'll nag you for snacks, so she can have some crisps and an apple. Bedtime is 7:30, 8pm at the latest."

Ammy wailed and stomped her foot.

"No arguments, young lady." Thea raised an eyebrow at her daughter.

"It's okay," said Kitty. "I'll deal with it. You get going." Kitty ushered Thea out of the room and down the hallway. "You look lovely, by the way."

"Thank you. I appreciate your help." Thea smiled as she picked up her bag at the door. "I won't be late."

When Thea left, Kitty wrangled the grizzling girl to the table to do some painting. Unable to find brushes, they used their fingers, and Ammy announced they would paint a picture of her uncle. Kitty fought a smile as she put together his likeness. She smudged him with a golden tan, big blue splodges for eyes, a wide smile, and a mess of blond hair.

"He needs a body," said Ammy. Kitty glanced over to see an excellent picture of Josh on the little girl's paper. Ammy's was better than hers!

Kitty set about drawing Josh a body. Based on the photograph she'd seen in the hall, how could she ever do him justice? Was it possible to create a six-pack with some watercolours and an index finger? Kitty quickly ran out of space on the paper, so she had to make Josh's body relatively small. There was no room for his legs, so she painted them long and loopy, wrapping around the page. She finished it with some enormous boots. Amelia thought the picture was hilarious.

"His legs are all bendy!" she squealed with laughter.

After completing another couple of pictures each, Kitty was itching to get Ammy tucked in bed. She wanted to do some research for the new job on her phone.

She was about to begin negotiations when there was a quiet knock. Kitty turned around and saw Josh standing at the kitchen door, holding a bottle of wine and wearing one of his trademark grins. Wendy followed him, heading straight to Ammy, wagging her tail.

"This looks cosy," he said.

"Joshie!" screamed Ammy, running up to her uncle and flinging herself up to meet his free arm. He pulled her up as if she weighed nothing, and she snuggled into his neck, giving him the biggest hug.

Kitty turned away to hide the heat in her face at his unexpected arrival. When he'd appeared at the door, her stomach had done a double flip, and now her body fizzed with energy. Why hadn't she worn more mascara? As she busied herself putting away the paper and paints, she focussed on steadying her quick breath. If she didn't stop breathing so fast, he'd think she was hyperventilating.

"This is Wendy, Joshie's doggie," Amelia said with pride.

"Kitty and Wendy have already met," Josh said as he placed Ammy on the ground. "What did I miss?"

"We've done some painting. We did pictures of you."

Josh's eyebrows raised. "I hope you captured my rugged good looks," he said with a smirk at Kitty.

She turned away, fire in her cheeks.

"Kitty gave you bendy legs!" Ammy shouted, roaring with laughter.

Her mouth dropped in mock horror. If it wasn't enough for Thea to not trust her babysitting abilities, now her daughter was calling into question her artistic talents. "It wasn't my fault! I didn't know we were aiming for accuracy.

Mine's more abstract," she said, folding her arms around her middle.

Ammy delivered their pictures to Josh, who examined them carefully and then diplomatically declared them joint winners.

"What do we win?" she shouted in delight.

"You win an extra episode of *Peppa Pig* before bed, and Kitty wins a glass of wine."

Ammy disappeared into the sitting room to the TV, and Josh gestured for Kitty to sit down. He poured them both a drink and joined her at the table.

"Thank you so much for helping Thea out. I didn't know what time I'd be home."

"No problem. I can go now if you like?" Kitty said, desperate for him to say no.

Josh paused, playing with a felt tip pen lying on the table, spinning it round and round. "Please stay. Ammy seems to enjoy your company."

His eyes drew level with hers. Soft blue. They subtly changed between blue and green depending on the light. Or maybe their colour was dictated by his mood. Not that she'd thought much about his eyes, of course. But she had to admit, she'd rather Josh enjoyed her company instead of his niece. Kitty took another sip of the rich red wine, recalling the glory of the body beneath his clothes.

"Besides, it would be nice not to drink alone," he said, eyes still on hers. Kitty chewed on her lip, wondering how loaded his statement was.

"How was your day?" she asked, fidgeting with the fringe of the tablecloth.

"Pretty busy. It seems like yours was more eventful, though."

Kitty smiled. "Yes. Thea showed me around."

"And before you knew it, she roped you into babysitting?" Josh asked, taking a sip of his wine. She shrugged her shoulders.

"I feel like a fraud. I've little experience with kids. My sister keeps me away from my nieces." Or was it she who avoided her nieces? "She thinks I'm incapable of surviving. Having said that, kids remind me of goats."

Josh snickered. "Without the horns, though."

Kitty's mind went straight to the scar at Josh's waistband, and her cheeks went into blush overdrive all over again.

Ammy took this moment to storm back in, announcing that *Peppa Pig* had finished.

"Well, it must be time for you to go to bed then," Josh said.

The little girl had other ideas, and in between grumbles and outright tears, Josh negotiated the price of a drama-free bedtime, agreeing to one game of Twister. It'd been so long since Kitty had played, she wasn't sure she remembered the rules. She didn't enjoy gyms, and the nearest thing to exercise she got was going to and from the coffee machine at work.

Ammy announced that there would be a 'twist' to Twister. She'd be the one spinning the arrow, and the adults would be the ones playing. Kitty's heart skittered in her chest. What the hell? Scrabbling around on the floor wasn't exactly dignified, and what if she slipped a disc or, more likely, pulled a muscle? How would she feel about asking Josh for a rubdown? Kitty huffed a breath. At least she'd decided to throw her denim shorts on before she left Rose Cottage.

"Thank goodness I didn't wear a skirt," she said without thinking.

Both Josh and Ammy stared at her like she'd sprouted another head. Had that just come out of her mouth? Before Kitty had time to blush, though, Ammy spoke.

"You could do it in your knickers," she suggested with an innocent smile.

Josh and Kitty looked at each other. The corners of his mouth trembled to suppress laughter, and his eyes shone with amusement. *Out of the mouths of babes and children.*

Josh was unphased by the whole idea of Twister, apparently. As Ammy unboxed the game, Kitty couldn't remember the plastic playing sheet being so small. Both she and Josh were tall. How the hell would they both fit on the mat?

Wendy had taken up a watchful residence on the sofa, and as the game started, all Kitty could do was hope that her knees didn't give out. The first few spins were easy, but things unravelled when Amelia was on to the fourth.

"Left hand green," she ordered.

Josh, who was in a squat with one hand behind him, had to put his other hand down and ended up in a crab-like tabletop pose. Standing far too close for comfort, Kitty couldn't help but notice his T-shirt had ridden up, and his bronzed, toned stomach was on full display. Her mouth suddenly ran dry. Abs like his weren't something she saw every day, and boy, where could she sign up for a subscription? Kitty was trying so hard not to stare that she forgot to take her turn.

"Come on!" said Ammy.

"Yes, sorry," Kitty mumbled breathily, wishing her shorts weren't quite so tiny. The only place she could put her hand down was on the other side of Josh, which meant she'd be bent double over him.

They were going to make a giant X-shape of awkwardness together, but there was nothing else for it. It was her turn, after all. Kitty moved her hand across and over Josh's body, giving him way more space than was strictly necessary. Still, the heat of his skin radiated through her thin T-shirt, and their eyes met as she balanced above him. His were full of mischief.

"I'm pretty sure I saw this in the Kama Sutra," he said.

"What's that?" asked Ammy.

"It's a puzzle book, especially for adults," he replied.

The way his eyes bore into Kitty sent a tingle across her skin. Instead of the crippling embarrassment she felt, he acted like the situation was hilarious. All she could think about was how close their hips were, not to mention their... *Stop it!* She needed to focus on staying upright, not the proximity of his package.

"I believe you're blushing, Kitty," Josh said, his eyes full of mischief.

"I'm not!" she said, with emphasis. "It's all the blood rushing to my head! Please hurry and spin the wheel, Ammy. I might pass out if we stay like this."

"Right hand red!" she shouted, her impish face grinning.

"Seriously?" said Josh. "That's a physical impossibility."

Aha! A chink of weakness in his superhuman Twister strength, perhaps. Maybe those abs couldn't do the impossible.

"Ha! Maybe your experience with Kama Sutra puzzles will help," Kitty said, one eyebrow raised in triumph.

She had the easiest choice. She only had to move one of her hands to the next dot. Josh needed to twist under her to make his turn, but Kitty's entire upper body was in his way. He attempted to make the move three times, retreating to his starting position after each try.

"Come on, buddy, is that all you've got?" she said, sensing victory was near.

Josh narrowed his eyes and, with a look of determination, launched himself in a half twist underneath her, ending up on his back in a crumpled heap across the game board.

Kitty giggled. "I wish I could have seen that in slow motion," she said, staring down at him with a grin of pure delight.

"My uncle normally wins. He's strong, even if he has bendy legs."

Kitty admired Josh's arms as they lay above his head. His thick biceps escaped the sleeves of his T-shirt, and her tongue flicked out to wet her bottom lip. She wondered how his arms would feel wrapped around her.

"I told you I got his legs right," Kitty said and was about to get up when Josh lifted his hands to the sides of her waist and tickled her.

Immediately, Kitty went down on top of him, screaming and cackling all the way. Her reaction to being tickled was a mix of horror and uncontrolled laughter. All the noise was too much for Wendy, and she launched off the sofa to check if they were okay, licking their faces and barking at the top of her lungs.

"Get her off!" Kitty screamed in laughter. "It's disgusting!"

She tried in vain to push Wendy away and, in desperation, burrowed her face into Josh's chest to escape the onslaught. His arms were around her in a moment, and their warm skin touched. His embrace was safe and strong, and a wave of goosebumps danced over her skin where his fingertips rested. While he shielded her from Wendy's overzealous tongue, Kitty relaxed against him, enjoying the feel of his firm body under hers and the fresh scent of his hot skin. What she wouldn't give to stay in his arms all night.

Josh commanded Wendy to back off, then lowered his head to whisper in Kitty's ear. "Are you okay? She can get a bit overexcited."

Wendy wasn't the only one.

Josh's breath touched the skin behind her ear, and her nipples hardened against him. Time to climb off before he noticed. Reluctantly leaving the warmth of his chest, she rolled off Josh, and they both lay on their backs, sobbing with laughter.

"My face aches!" Kitty said.

Not wanting to be left out, Ammy ran over and launched into Josh like a missile. He hugged her tight, eyes closed. His golden lashes brushed his cheeks, and his mouth, soft and full, formed a contented smile. He was beautiful. Kitty rolled away, feeling like an intruder, and climbed onto the sofa to join a sheepish Wendy.

"Okay, missy," said Josh to Ammy, "time to get to bed."

Amelia protested with a half-hearted cry, but Josh bundled her up and carried her, rugby ball style, under his arm.

"Say goodnight and thank you to Kitty," he said, pausing at the door.

"Good night, Kitty. Thank poo." The little girl gave her a toothy grin, amused at her play on words.

"Thank poo, too," Kitty smiled back. "Sleep well."

Amidst thumping floorboards and shrieks of laughter from overhead, Kitty packed away the Twister game. She couldn't remember when she'd laughed so much. After a few minutes, everything went quiet upstairs, and Kitty couldn't help wishing it was *her* who Josh was tucking into bed. With a sigh, she found her half-finished glass of wine and took a healthy slug.

"Reprobate," came a familiar, honeyed voice as Josh appeared at the door.

"Reprobate?" she asked. "I need all help I can get. Twister was never my strong point. Though, on the back of tonight's win, I may take it up again."

"Then I demand a rematch, so you best get training," he said, joining her and refilling their glasses.

Kitty followed Josh through to the sitting room, and they flopped down together on Thea's well-loved couch. The room was small, cosy, and as cluttered as the rest of the house, with an enormous fireplace at one end. Josh handed over her glass and raised his in a toast.

"To Twister."

"To Twister and the Kama Sutra," Kitty said, clinking her glass against his with a clear chime.

Josh smiled. "You hungry?" he asked. "Thea has some Dairy Milk in the fridge. Refrigerating chocolate is sacrilege in my opinion but it's essential in a heatwave."

"No thanks. I'm a Snickers kind of girl. They're my kryptonite."

"Interesting," he said, his eyes drifting across her face. "Hold still."

Josh lifted his hand and brushed his thumb against the line of her cheek. At the intense look in his eyes, Kitty's breath caught, and her heart almost beat out of her chest.

"I've been wanting to do that for an hour."

"What?" she asked, eyes wide.

"You had a paint smudge."

Kitty's face warmed, and she brought her palm up to her cheek.

"Oh great," she said. "I must look like a chimney sweep."

Josh's eyes crinkled. "You look perfect."

A burn filled her chest, and racing blood roared in her ears. He'd said she looked perfect. Plain old Kitty. Kitty, who nobody really glanced at, looked perfect?

Josh shifted on the sofa and cleared his throat, running a hand through his hair. "Any news on the job front?"

Kitty's insides thumped back down to earth, and she attempted a smile instead of bursting into a scream of frustration. She didn't want to talk about the new job. She wanted to revel in her "perfection".

"I had an email this morning about a great role. I don't want to jinx it, but I think it could be the one. It'll be busy, with lots of travel, but I'm sure I can handle it." Josh listened as Kitty told him the details. "I'm so happy. It's the sort of role I've always wanted."

"Then I hope it all works out for you," he said quietly. "Thank you again for agreeing to help Thea, while you're still here."

Kitty plumped up the cushion she leaned on. "My pleasure, but do you mind me asking, what happened to Thea's husband?"

Josh sighed. "Phil had aggressive bone cancer. They gave

him two years to live, but he only lasted eighteen months. It was brutal."

After he spoke, he clamped his jaw tight and looked at his glass of wine. "That's terrible," Kitty whispered, tears pricking at the corners of her eyes. "It must have been so tough for Thea and Ammy. How has she coped? Thank goodness she has you."

"It's been rough, but kids are resilient. We talk about her dad a lot. Thea takes things in her stride, but don't let that fool you. Every day is a battle for her."

Kitty nodded. "Ammy will grow up without a dad. That's so sad."

"Do you want kids?" Josh asked, turning to her.

Whoa, where had that question come from? They'd only just had their first Twister game. It was hardly time to talk about babies. "I don't know. Maybe one day, but kids don't seem to like me much."

"Ammy likes you," he said. "She didn't stop talking about you when I put her to bed."

"Really?" said Kitty, surprised at how pleased she was to win the little girl's approval.

"I think you're going to have a little shadow there."

She smiled at the idea. "Anyway, to have kids, one has to have a sex life," she said, immediately regretting it, a burn rushing to her face. "TMI?" she asked, cringing.

Josh laughed. "No, I think that's the way it happens."

"What made you want to be a farm vet?" Kitty asked, desperate to change the subject. "I mean, I read the James Herriot books when I was younger, and it doesn't seem very glamourous."

Josh rubbed the light covering of stubble at his jaw. "It's not. It was my dad. I idolised him, and I wanted to follow in his footsteps. Unfortunately, I inherited his practice *and* his single-minded approach to the job. I'm afraid I don't find time for much else."

"No sex life for you either, then."

This time it was Josh's turn to blush, his cheeks matching the colour of the overstuffed sofa cushions. Kitty's body was warm and heavy with wine, and as Wendy snored between them, Josh eyed her with a thoughtful look.

"It's nice to have you here, in Tottenbridge. I wasn't sure what to expect when Jonty said you were coming. When we last met, you were a gangly tomboy, and now look at you."

"Gangly?" she asked. What did he mean by gangly?

"Sorry, terrible choice of words. What I meant to say is that you are a pleasant surprise. I wish we'd kept in touch."

Kitty's face dropped. The conversation was going from bad to worse. First, he'd called her gangly, and now he'd called her pleasant. Pleasant was how you described a walk in the country or a garden party. She was practically drooling over him, and he called her pleasant.

"Oh shit, that came out all wrong, too," Josh said, stumbling over his words. "What I meant to say is that...."

"Hello!" a hushed voice greeted them as Thea emerged into the sitting room. "Oh, Joshie. I didn't know you were here."

He stood up and gave his sister a hug and a kiss. Wendy also got to her fluffy feet and nuzzled Thea's outstretched hands.

"I came over to supervise. I heard on the grapevine that Kitty was a bit of a hustler at Uno, so I couldn't leave her and Ammy alone. I wouldn't put it past your daughter to gamble the farm away."

Kitty busied herself straightening the cushions on the sofa but couldn't help smiling at his joke. "Did you have a good evening?" she asked.

Thea dug into her bag and brought out a cheque. She held it between her fingers with a big grin on her face.

"That's fantastic! That should keep the donkeys in carrots for a while. Look, I should head off. I need to be up early," said Kitty.

"Well, you can't drive. You've had wine, and this village has no straight roads," Josh said.

"I can walk."

"Or you can let me walk you back?"

Her heart jumped at the suggestion.

"Don't worry, Joshie," said Thea, "I'll run Kitty back. You have an early start too."

"I'm fine, really," she said, willing Josh to repeat his offer.

"No, it's okay, it's no bother. I won't be long, Josh," Thea said cheerfully.

Kitty stood up and met his eyes. Their vivid blue was unreadable, but he reached out and touched her arm as she walked past him to follow Thea.

"Kitty," he said.

She turned toward him.

"I meant to say earlier that I think you're amazing, and I'm glad you're back, even if it's only for a short time."

The corners of her lips curled. "I hear you're only after my military precision. Thea told me as much."

A look of guilt crossed Josh's face.

"It's okay," she said, "I take it as a compliment, and if it's any consolation, I think you turned out alright too. Thanks for tonight. I haven't laughed as much in ages."

"Me too," he breathed. "Good night."

20

KITTY

THE FOLLOWING DAY, Kitty woke at the rooster's shrill crow. She was fond of him now and would miss his morning alarm when she headed back to London. After feeding the animals, she returned to the house to cook eggs for herself and Julia, brewing two steaming coffees. Just how they liked it.

The sun was up, promising another hot day ahead, and Kitty heard her aunt stir upstairs.

"You ready for breakfast, Julia?" she called out.

With a yawn, Kitty walked to the door to fetch the newspaper from outside. It was anyone's guess where she'd find it today. The delivery boy flung it into a different bush each morning.

"Yes, please," shouted Julia down the stairs.

Kitty opened the front door. The newspaper sat neatly on the step, and alongside it was a small package. She picked it up and carefully unwrapped the brown paper. A small bunch of wildflowers lay inside, along with a Snickers bar and a note that read:

Welcome back to the village. Wendy xo.

21

KITTY

Kitty passed the next few days in a hot haze. England was enjoying a historic heatwave that showed no signs of ending. The sun parched the earth, forming large cracks in the fields. On a more practical note, though, the relentless humidity was playing havoc with her hair.

Kitty had helped Thea at Small Oaks each day since babysitting, but so far, she hadn't seen Josh. When she subtly steered their conversation around to find out how he was, Thea told her how busy he'd been and that she hadn't seen him either. It was maddening.

After the evening they'd shared and the gift he'd left, she didn't understand the radio silence. But she had to stop thinking about him. The first round of job interviews went surprisingly well, considering her mind was entirely distracted by frustration and saucy fantasies of what might happen if they ever played Twister again.

There was no such problem with Daniel. Thinking of Daniel was exciting. He peppered Kitty with texts, and they chatted late into the night twice. Daniel was a simple creature.

If Kitty ignored his corny chat-up lines, she found him charming and amusing company.

He'd attempted to initiate her in sexting, which ended in fits of giggles when he sent her a "stick pic." It was a picture of his naked torso, with a large branch strategically covering his groin.

That morning, Kitty rose early, organised Julia's animals for the hot day ahead and headed to Small Oaks. She'd begun arriving earlier and earlier, using the excuse of the weather, but really hoping to bump into Josh before he left for work.

Each day, she made progress in organising. There were empty spaces on the desks now, and she'd created a proper filing system for the reams of paperwork once littering the surfaces.

Kitty stood, studying the day's chores on the notice board, trying to work out which task would get her geographically nearest to Josh's cottage. Thea came in, grasping a cup of coffee, hair wild like Medusa's.

"Morning, boss," said Kitty.

"Oh, thank goodness you're early," Thea said. "I've organised the food and water for the rabbits and guineas, but I need to collect some feed and bedding donations. Can you man the fort while I'm gone?"

"Sure can."

"Great. I fed the moggies. They're camped out in the house. It's going to be stinking hot today. Amelia's with Pamela, so they shouldn't bother you." Thea's childminder was a bloody godsend but wasn't interested in helping with the animals.

"Okay then, off you go. I've got the rest covered.".

"Thanks, Kitty, you're amazing. Belinda will be in a later, so leave the stables to her. The horses are in the paddock already. Josh took Madonna out for a ride at the crack of dawn." Kitty's ears pricked up, and her heart skipped.

"Why so early?" she asked. And more importantly, why

didn't he ask her? She was still waiting for the promised riding lesson.

"Why does Joshie do anything?" snorted Thea. "Perhaps he wanted her exercised before it got too hot."

Kitty bunched her hands into fists. Exactly. She had to stop looking for hidden meaning in everything. Josh was just a nice guy, grateful she was helping his sister. That he was gorgeous and kind had nothing to do with it. Still, it felt like he was avoiding her, and Kitty didn't like it.

"I won't be long," said Thea, heading out the door.

The morning was Kitty's favourite time of day at the sanctuary. It was still and peaceful, and hearing the birdsong put a spring in her step. Unfortunately, it wasn't working today, and as she set to her tasks, Kitty spent most of her time ruminating on "Mr Hot and Cold."

The birds at the pond were her first port of call. The heat was sweltering already, and as Kitty wiped the sweat off her brow, the thought of jumping into the green water wasn't entirely unpleasant. Though still nervous about the geese, the pond gave her a fantastic view of Josh's cottage. Not that she cared, but if Josh was at home or working in the yard, she'd glimpse him.

Kitty cast her eyes around one final time. No sign of him. With a sigh, her shoulders slumped. What had her life come to? This time last month she'd been a high-flying corporate powerhouse. Now she was caked in dust and stalking the local vet!

22

JOSH

Josh pulled up outside his surgery with a sigh. He'd had a tough morning, euthanising several sheep attacked by a fox. He turned off the engine and walked to his cottage, planning to make a strong coffee.

As he stood at his kitchen window, leaning against the counter, his mind drifted to Kitty. Why the hell had he suggested she help Thea? It was the worst thing he could've done. The possibility of seeing her every day was torment. He had the biggest crush on her. She was leaving town soon, and there was every chance she'd leave him heartbroken if he didn't keep his feelings in check.

It had been such a long time since he'd had feelings for anyone. About anyone. His life was solitary, and he rarely let others into it. Thea always gave him a hard time, but nobody had made it through his walls. Until Kitty arrived.

Glancing out of the window, something caught Josh's eye down at the pond. He picked up his mug and wandered outside into the courtyard. The sight that greeted him made his heart lurch and the corners of his mouth twitch. A bedraggled Kitty stood at the water, fending off an army of angry geese.

Sweaty and flushed, she was holding a bucket, dressed in tiny shorts and a pair of old, oversized wellies. Her ponytail swung around her, and she was shouting obscenities at one enormous bird, kneeing it away as it chased her in circles.

He chuckled. The sight was hilarious and so sexy. Josh sucked in his bottom lip. Her legs, long and brown, were lithe and toned, and her small, high breasts strained at her top as she jostled the goose away. Josh took a breath, and his dick stirred in his pants.

With a groan, he turned away. Her looking so bloody adorable was the last thing he needed to see. Since he'd left the Snickers bar for Kitty, he'd purposely stayed away from her. The last few days were an exercise in convincing himself he shouldn't get involved.

She'd made it clear her career would always be her focus. They were too similar in that respect. Although he wasn't sure, he hoped the attraction might be mutual. But what if he was wrong? The thought of making a fool of himself brought burning bile to his throat.

Josh glanced down at his white knuckles as they grasped the handle of his mug. He needed to focus on himself. Get through the weeks until Kitty left to go back to London. With a nod, he was about to walk back inside but looked over his shoulder to check on her one last time.

As he did, he almost dropped his coffee mug. Kitty had abandoned her bucket and picked up the old blue hose, turning it on herself. She held it over her head, and water cascaded over her body, coursing down her olive skin. Her tight crop top was plastered to her body, and her nipples were hardened by the cold of the water. *Fuck.* The sight was absolute torture. She looked magnificent. And if his dick had stirred earlier, now it was growing more solid by the second. He had to get inside. Get his mind off her body.

After thumbing through a magazine on livestock farming

and checking his phone eight times, Josh could no longer contain his need. He had to find Kitty, even if it was just to say hello.

He headed across the farmyard, looking for her. After a fruitless search outside, he went to the stone barn housing the pigs. If she were there, would she talk to him? He'd hardly given her any encouragement of late. He shook his head, his heart thundering as loud as his work boots on the cobbles. It didn't matter. Just seeing her would be enough.

He gently pushed open the door to the barn, and there she was, bent over the pig's gate. Droplets of perspiration snaked between her shoulder blades, and her cotton shorts clung to her like a second skin. Josh's dick threatened to re-harden, and he cursed his body for its poor timing. He leaned up against the stone wall of the barn, enjoying the touch of cool rock on his skin.

"Good morning, beautiful boy," Kitty cooed to the pig, giving him a scratch.

"Good morning," said Josh, a grin on his face.

Kitty spun around, eyes wide. When she saw Josh, her body relaxed, but it didn't stop her from throwing a discarded glove in his direction.

"Bloody hell Josh, you frightened the life out of me."

She didn't look happy. What was he expecting, though? How would he feel if she'd spent the majority of a week avoiding him?

"How are you?" he asked. "I haven't seen you for a few days."

Kitty's brows furrowed. "Oh, has it been that long? I hadn't noticed," she said, hands on her hips.

Josh flinched.

"I'm great, thanks," Kitty said. "Jeffrey is great company."

Did the lady protest too much? Josh smirked. "I'm sure he

is. He's always been a bit of a ladies' man. Shame he wasn't on hand to scrub your back down at the pond, though."

Kitty's eyes opened wide, and the colour in her cheeks heightened. Perhaps he shouldn't have said anything, but he couldn't resist. She looked at him like a petulant toddler. How he wanted to kiss those pouting lips.

"I'm sorry. That was uncalled for," he said, wondering if he should just confess that she was slowly driving him insane. "Do you want a hand?" he asked, stepping into the middle of the barn.

"Pardon?"

"Jeffrey. Do you want a hand with him? My way of saying sorry for my appalling manners. I'm sorry I haven't been to see you. It's been a tough week."

Kitty gave him a wan smile. "Thanks. He's the least of my worries, though. It's Jemima that seems to have it in for me." she said, gesturing to the pig in the next-door stall.

"Maybe she's jealous of you?"

Kitty turned to look at the pig with a snicker. "She's bearing a grudge for something. Can you help me get her down to the pen at the other end? Jeffrey will follow her."

They worked together to encourage Jemima into the new stall, and just as she'd said, Jeffrey followed her. The movements of Kitty's long, supple limbs taunted Josh, and it was an effort to keep his eyes off her bottom as she pushed the stubborn pig along. His mind flew back to their game of Twister and the feeling of her body against him when he pulled her down on top of him. He'd sealed his fate with that one action. After that point, he couldn't avoid his feelings any longer. But he'd have to worship her from afar, just like when they were kids.

After putting the pigs in the new stall, Kitty slid the heavy metal bolt across its door and turned to Josh.

"Thanks. I don't suppose you have time to help me clean

the poo they left behind?" She cocked a dark eyebrow. "I'll let you use my lucky spade."

Her grin caught him off guard. Perhaps she wasn't so mad at him after all.

"Josh wiped his hands on the front of his jeans. "It's tempting, but I can't. I'm on the road today. I wanted to check in on you, though." Josh paused and shifted his weight. "How are your interviews going?" he asked.

Kitty shuffled her feet around the straw on the floor.

"They're going great. I'm three in so far. The firm wants me to spend a few days with them next week."

Josh's heart lurched, and his heart rate sped up. Its racing was a reminder that he would lose her soon. She looked so beautiful, lit up by a shaft of sunlight making its way through a loose patch of tiling.

"Can you be free tomorrow?" he asked, rushing his words. "I wondered if it would be a good day to ride along with me? Show you what I do." He paused. "Only if you're interested, of course."

Kitty's eyes locked onto his, and perspiration sprung at his top lip. She was hesitating.

"I'm not sure, Josh. I'll check with Thea," she said, wiping away a strand of dark hair that had escaped her ponytail and now clung to her neck.

"Don't worry about Thea. She'll be fine with it. She may struggle without her new wing woman, but it won't be a problem."

Josh's eyes travelled down to Phil's oversized wellies. "You may need to rethink your footwear, though."

"Ha! Yes. It'll take bigger feet than mine to fill these boots."

Josh smiled. "Leave Thea to me. I'll come and pick you up at six forty-five. Can you be ready?"

"After a long beat, Kitty spoke. "Okay," she said, giving Josh the most hope he'd had in a while.

23

KITTY

KITTY ARRIVED HOME weary and sweaty. Dog tired, the promise of the day with Josh had kept her going. He'd avoided her all week, plain and simple, no matter what excuse he'd come up with. It hurt, and she had no idea why, but he was her friend. She'd give him the benefit of the doubt. Something about him pulled at her, a need for his approval. A need to be near him.

Julia's tinkling laugh carried on the breeze from the back of the house, interrupting her thoughts. A low, lilting baritone joined it. Intrigued, Kitty followed the voices to find Daniel and Julia sitting on the patio, demolishing a giant pitcher of Pimms. Daniel's eyes hung on her as she stepped into the sun, and the corners of his mouth turned up.

"Kitty! You're back! I was wondering when you'd finish," Julia said. "Daniel came to keep me company. We've been waiting for you." Julia gazed over at him, her eyes shining with adoration.

Daniel Cunningham had worked his magic again. He gave Kitty a conspiratorial wink, and she couldn't help but smile. His eyes contained the cheekiest gleam. He was aware of his effect on Julia. Relentless in charming everyone around him, but damn, she'd forgotten how sexy he was.

"Hello there," he said, standing to greet her with a kiss on her cheek. The warmth of his body blended with hers and beckoned her to sink into him. Soft stubble grazed her skin, and the woody, spicy scent of his cologne tickled her nose. Kitty stiffened. He smelled amazing, and she probably stunk of pig poo.

"It's good to see you in person, Daniel," she said, moving away from him. "How've you been? Did you manage to get the splinters out?" She was referring to his 'stick pic'. She'd saved it to her camera roll and looked at it if she ever needed a giggle.

Daniel's eyes crinkled, and he shot her a dangerous glance. "Nothing a soak in a tub and a pair of tweezers couldn't fix. I could have done with some help, though. You look amazing. Your bruise has gone."

He was either kind or delusional. Kitty wasn't sure which. "We both know that's pure flattery on your part. I look a fright, but I'll take the compliment."

Daniel sucked in a theatrical breath. "Always so sharp, Ms Cameron. When will I get a glimpse of your softer edges?"

His eyes raked over her body. Kitty felt every single millisecond, her heart beating a little louder than before. She'd file the tingle his hungry gaze gave her for later under 'kissellaneous'.

"I'm afraid you'll have to take a rain check. The shower waits for no woman. I won't be long."

Kitty turned and walked into the house.

"Hurry back," Daniel called after her. "I'll have your drink waiting."

With a renewed spring in her step, Kitty headed to her bedroom and shed her clothes in a messy pile. Her bare skin burned hot in the warm air. Was she sure it was just the day's heat? Daniel always brought a smile to her lips, and his words made her blood pump just a little more than was healthy.

The sound of Julia's laughter in the garden filled her heart. How easy it was for him to make people happy. Daniel's life was so simple. He'd told her he dedicated himself to pleasure. Reliant on Amber to keep the pub and bistro running, he flitted in and out, spending his time on the golf course or getting up to who knew what. Kitty didn't dare guess. But fate was dangling a big, juicy carrot for her, and its name was Daniel Cunningham.

She stood under a cool jet of water and washed the smell of Small Oaks from her body. The memory of Josh's handsome face in the barn pricked at her brain. What had he thought when he'd seen her under the hose? And why was the thought of him watching her so pleasing?

Kitty's slick tan skin shone in the mirror as she exited the shower. Her previously pallid complexion was long gone, thanks to her hours in the sun. She twirled around, admiring her reflection. She'd never been so at home in her body. Daniel would probably give his eyeteeth to join her right now.

The corners of her mouth curled. The thoughts that popped into her head these days shocked her. Kitty hardly recognised herself. What the hell was Daniel Cunningham doing to her?

She brushed out her long, wet hair, put on some knickers, and shrugged into a simple cotton sundress that skimmed the top of her thighs. Examining her new freckles in the mirror, she added some bronzer to her cheeks, a light line of kohl under her lashes and a slick of mascara.

The woman who stared back was confident and beautiful. Satisfied, she added a final touch of lip gloss and a light spray of perfume, then padded downstairs barefoot to join Julia and Daniel.

24

DANIEL

WHEN KITTY CAME BACK out to the patio, Daniel's mouth gaped open. Her body gave off silent waves of energy. The golden glow of her skin pulled at his fingers, and they itched to touch the sumptuous hair that pooled around her shoulders like velvet. The thought of its length tangled around his fist sent a shiver right down to Daniel's cock.

"You're breathtaking," he said, his sexy drawl dripping with unspoken intent.

Kitty sat down, avoiding his gaze, and Daniel dragged his eyes over her. She smelled of flowers and lavender, and her thin dress hugged the curve of her breasts where they met her ribs. *Damn*, she'd improved. Life in the country certainly agreed with her.

He handed her a tall glass, filled to the brim with Pimms and lemonade, dressed with mint, strawberry, and cucumber slices. Kitty took a long sip.

"Oh, I needed that," she said, swallowing another icy mouthful. "I'd forgotten how refreshing Pimms is, and it's been a long, hot day. So, what did I miss?" she asked, licking the drink from her lips.

"I learned your mum is a romance writer," said Daniel. "Why didn't you mention that before?"

Kitty rolled her eyes, cursing Julia and her loose lips. "It's not the sort of thing I tell people when I introduce myself. To be honest, it's been the bane of my life. I've put up with a lot of teasing over the years."

"Fair enough," he said, "I won't hold it against you. I just find it intriguing. I mean, your 'birds and the bees' chat must have been sensational."

Daniel's dark eyes gleamed.

"And that is exactly why I keep it to myself," Kitty said, with a shake of her head.

"Kitty, don't be so squeamish," said Julia. "Daniel came round to lift my spirits. I didn't think you'd mind my telling him."

"It looks like you've had more than enough spirit for one day." Kitty giggled, eyeing the empty glass that sat in her hand.

"And on that note, I shall powder my nose," said Julia as she grabbed her stick and tottered off unsteadily into the house.

"Am I in trouble?" Daniel asked, his voice low.

He tried hard to maintain an expression of remorse but failed miserably. Women usually found it hard to stay annoyed with him for long. Kitty wouldn't be any different.

"Not this time, but consider this a warning," she said.

"Yes, Mistress Katherine," he said, one eyebrow cocked.

Sure, he was back on less shaky ground, he leaned in closer to Kitty. "Don't tell Julia, but I came to see *you*." He reached behind his chair and brought out an enormous bunch of plump peonies tied up in a dusky pink ribbon. "And to give you these."

Kitty's eyes shone. "How did you know they were my favourite?" she said, the heady aroma of the blooms filling the air between them.

"I have my sources. I'm glad you like them."

"They're stunning," said Kitty. "Thank you."

Daniel smiled. Thank goodness he'd taken the advice of the florist. He was one of their best customers, and it'd been a toss-up between the peonies and some red roses. He hoped his luck was a signifier of things to come.

The look on Kitty's face was enchanting. On a whim, Daniel took one of her wrists in his hand and stroked the skin at its inside with his thumb. Kitty's eyes widened as he lowered his voice.

"I could give you so much more than flowers if you'd let me."

A nervous giggle escaped Kitty's mouth, and her arm stiffened under his fingers. Her eyes flicked up to the open window, where the sounds of Julia pottering around in the kitchen reached them.

"I hope Julia has a vase big enough," Kitty said loudly for her aunt to overhear.

"Ah, so size matters, does it?" he countered.

"No! Yes, well, in vases, it might." Kitty's cheeks flushed. Daniel loved teasing her.

"Methinks the lady doth change the subject too quickly. Are you worried you won't have a vessel large enough to take my gift?"

Kitty's already pink cheeks darkened, and her gaze dropped. Had he gone too far?

"Daniel! Stop it! Julia will hear you," Kitty snickered.

Her giggles made him smile. He could listen to them all night.

"I can hear every single word, children," Julia said through the window. She was rinsing glasses and plates in the sink. "I'm more worried about running *out* of vases, what with all your admirers, Kitty."

Daniel's body stiffened, and he released her wrist.

"Enlighten me, Julia. Who else has been calling on fair

Katherine?" The smile he kept on his face belied the buzz of irritation in his chest. He turned his eyes on Kitty. "Do I have a rival?"

Kitty's eyes flittered around the garden, avoiding his. "Only the four-legged variety. I had a delivery of wildflowers from a dog at Small Oaks Farm. It was a thank you for babysitting."

Daniel's eyebrows lifted. "Babysitting at the farm? Another of your hidden talents. I hope you don't mind me saying, but I didn't think a life of domesticity would be your style. When I think of you, Katherine, I picture you standing astride a pile of broken men you've just slayed with your tongue. Metaphorically, of course."

Kitty shifted under his gaze, and she played with the hem of her dress. He had to ease up on her. He didn't want her to think he was jealous. That would put him at a disadvantage, and Daniel aimed to be in control of this seduction. He gave her a warm smile.

"Tell me who I'm up against. Don't say it's a pug. Even I can't compete with that."

Kitty's body relaxed, and she smiled.

"No, they were from something much larger."

"Joshua Fox?" As soon as the name left his mouth, he regretted his slip-up. Now she would know he was jealous.

"No. It was a giant mutt-sized admirer. With curly ears."

He wanted to offer Josh's name again but thought better of it. He didn't want to give her any reason to be cross with him. Unless Thea had switched teams, the flowers *were* from the vet. Daniel saw his outsized dog around the village occasionally. It was about the only female company Josh kept these days.

"Yes, they were from Josh's dog, Wendy!" Julia shouted through the window. "Such a friendly gesture from the family. Kitty has been spending quite a lot of time at the farm. She's been helping Thea Fox with her animals."

A sharp dagger plunged into Daniel's ego. Had they been

spending time together? Did Kitty actually have a thing for Josh? He cast his mind back to trivia night and the looks and smiles the two shared. He'd dismissed it as a potential concussion on her part, knowing Josh's monk-like tendencies. Was something going on between them? And if so, why hadn't Kitty said anything?

His brow furrowed, and he recalled Amber's question after the wine tasting. Why did he care so much? Daniel could shrug off a bit of competition, but somehow this was different. *She* was different.

He turned his laser-like gaze back to Kitty. It was time to go on the offensive.

"You're so beautiful in this light," he murmured. "The sun picks up all the colours in your hair."

Kitty's hand reached up and tucked one side of it behind her ear.

"You should wear it down more often. It's incredible," he said.

As Daniel spoke, he reached for the peonies on the table and picked a small bloom from the bunch.

"May I?" he asked, tucking the flower behind Kitty's ear, brushing the still-damp hair lying over her shoulders with the back of his hand. "Katherine, I think you're stealing my heart."

He trailed his fingers down her arm and, with satisfaction, noted the slight shiver that jumped through her body. The rapid rise and fall of her chest against the flimsy cotton of her dress.

Her reaction was a good sign. Now he'd pull back. Make her doubt his attraction to her. He was using every tactic in the Daniel Cunningham seduction manual. He didn't like to resort to it, but he couldn't bear the thought of anyone else having her.

"Can I take you to lunch tomorrow? I know a gorgeous place down on the river. How are your punting skills?"

Kitty's lips curled. "Untried and untested," she said. "I trip over my feet. I should never be in charge of a small boat and a large pole."

"Don't worry. I'd save you if you fell in... I think."

Kitty laughed. "I can't make it tomorrow. I'm sorry." She played with her hair, threading it around her long fingers. "I'm out for the day."

"Sounds exciting," said Daniel, an uncomfortable sensation churning in his gut. "Are you taking the goats on a field trip?"

"No, I'm spending the day with Josh. For work. Thea wanted me to see what Josh did."

The hairs on the back of Daniel's neck lifted. Why the hell would Thea Fox want Kitty to join her brother? She'd miss out on her help. It didn't ring true. Was she lying?

Daniel maintained a steady smile. He took one of her hands in his, stroking her knuckles with his thumb. Her body was as still as a statue under his touch.

"How lovely. I'm sure you'll learn a lot. I hear Josh is quite the miracle worker, second only to St Francis of Assisi." Kitty frowned. "I'm joking. I'm also a little jealous, so you'll have to make it up to me."

As Kitty nodded, the sun dipped around the side of the cottage, and the golden glow that lit her hair dimmed as if a spell had broken. Daniel looked at his watch.

"Damn, I have to go," he said. "Amber is off tonight, so I actually have to work."

"Thank you for the flowers," Kitty said as he let go of her hand. "They're beautiful."

"And so are you, Katherine. But please, don't have too much fun tomorrow."

25

KITTY

LONG AFTER DANIEL LEFT, Kitty sat on the patio, gazing into the fading light of the day. The early evening bird song lulled her into an almost hypnotic state. Even the silky brush of Herod, weaving through her legs and crying for food, couldn't shake her from her thoughts.

Kitty never expected to roll into Tottenbridge and find two men who made her heart beat so wildly. Two men she liked for such different reasons. While she'd willingly flirted with Daniel, she'd never factored in her preoccupation with Josh. It was true he'd spent most of the last week AWOL, but this morning, seeing him in the barn reminded her of all the reasons she spent far too much time thinking about him.

Kitty sighed. With Josh, she was all at sixes and sevens. Awkward and shy. He was handsome and kind and felt like home. But was he interested? She may have a raging crush on him, but he still had her in the friend zone. He'd told her his work and family life were all-consuming, and while it would be hypocritical to judge him for that, it didn't leave time for romance.

Josh wasn't a no strings attached kind of guy, though. That

didn't bother her, but she'd find it hard to leave for London if she slaked her thirst for him. Long distance never worked. A million romcoms couldn't be wrong.

On the other hand, Daniel was a wild card in all senses of the word. He was dangerous and sexy. He filled her with a confidence she'd never known, and it felt good. Every minute with him was exciting. Ronnie could be right. Maybe she should just get laid and live a little. Daniel was interested, alright. His motivation might be sketchy, but just like he'd told her, he'd be perfect for a quick, no-strings fling.

Daniel wouldn't interrupt her plans, and he'd always be nice to visit if the mood took her. Kitty's mouth curled up as she thought of what a quick fling with Daniel would look like. She was sure he'd know his way around the female body. How could it hurt? But what if Josh found out? What would he think?

Kitty reminded herself he might not even care.

Indecision rattled around in her brain, and she rubbed her temples. Her head thumped from the heat of the day, and her thoughts drifted to the animals in the paddocks. Time to put them to bed, then herself. She had an early start with Josh.

Tomorrow. She'd know more tomorrow.

26

KITTY

AFTER GETTING up at ridiculous o'clock to sort out Julia's animals, Kitty took a freshly brewed coffee to the old wooden bench in the front garden to wait for Josh. In the mugginess of the morning, glistening dew hung on every petal and leaf-like they were dressed in diamonds.

Another hot day was on the cards, and Kitty wore a sky-blue vest top, a pair of denim shorts, and her work boots. Butterflies skittered in her empty tummy, and she wasn't sure if her heart's thump was down to Josh or her strong coffee.

Perfectly on time, Josh pulled up outside the cottage in his old, mud-spattered Troop Carrier. *Be still my fastidious heart.* Punctuality was in Kitty's top five sexiest traits.

Josh opened the door, and before he could get out, an excited Wendy leapt over him and raced out to fling herself at Kitty's legs. She had a hard time stopping herself from falling into Julia's rose bushes.

Instead of the bushes, though, Kitty fell into Josh's sparkling eyes. She stood there, dumbstruck by his beauty, holding her coffee cup in two hands like Oliver Twist. Please, sir, could she have some more of him?

"Sorry," Josh smiled.

"You should learn to control your crazy mutt!" Kitty said as she crouched down to tickle Wendy's ears and accept her slobbering kisses.

"What can I say? She likes you."

If only *he* were so obvious.

"If you give me a slug of your coffee, I'll show you what Wendy brought you," Josh said.

He headed to the back of his truck and returned with a pair of pale pink and white polka-dot gum boots. Kitty's face instantly cracked into a grin.

"I can only apologise for Wendy's taste," Josh said. "She couldn't wrap them either. Obviously, she doesn't have thumbs."

Kitty's heart soared. The boots were adorable. Totally impractical but adorable. Was this how Josh saw her? Pink and dotty? The thought made her smile. Most people in her life would see her as grey and practical.

"I love them," she said.

"You hear that, Wendy? They're a hit." He tickled his dog's ears as she looked up at him, adoration in her eyes.

A frown knitted Kitty's brows together.

"I can't wear them, though. I don't want to ruin them. They're perfect."

"Sure you can. Boots are there to be trashed. Nothing's perfect. Wendy won't mind. She'd rather not watch you struggle each day in Phil's old ones. I would offer her services to clean them, but again, paws, not thumbs."

The amusement on his face had Kitty's frown unknotting. *Nothing needed to be perfect*. The notion was so Josh. She sat on the old bench again and undid her work boots, slipping them off to reveal socks covered in Mr Men and Little Misses. The corners of Josh's mouth twitched when he saw them.

Kitty stepped into the new boots and stood to model them.

His eyes skimmed down her legs, then drew up to meet hers. A flash of approval lay deep within them, and Kitty's heart skipped.

"Thank you," she said.

He shook his head. "Don't thank me, thank the crazy mutt. She makes up at least one-third of the Kitty Cameron fan club."

Kitty's breath pulled up for a millisecond. If Wendy was one of three, who the hell were the other members?

"Come on, Little Miss Long Legs. We'll make a country girl of you yet."

She followed Josh to the truck as he ordered Wendy to ride in the back. The dog sat sulkily, staring at Kitty, who'd buckled up in the front passenger seat. No sooner had they set off than Wendy clambered over the middle and sat straight in Kitty's lap, totally blocking her view.

"I think someone's jealous," Josh said as he pulled over to shift Wendy back into the middle seat between them. "There, you can keep us apart now. Happy?"

The day's first appointment in Josh's diary was a herd health check at a dairy farm.

"Are you sure it's okay for me to come along?" Kitty asked.

"They won't mind at all. I'm sure they'll welcome the distraction. You're far more

appealing than watching me with my arm up a cow's bum!"

"Is that meant to be a compliment?" asked Kitty, a giggle escaping her lips.

They drove steadily along the winding road, its edges fringed with cowslips and thick hedges heavy with ripe blackberries. Kitty pleaded with Josh to stop so she could pick some. He checked his watch and gave her five minutes. She hopped out of the truck and, with her bright new wellies, picked her way through the brambles to reach the fruit.

Without a container, Kitty pulled the bottom of her top out to form a makeshift basket, and after a few minutes of battling with thorns, Josh called her back. He'd found her a bag to carry the fruit and dutifully held it out while she tipped her harvest in. The blackberries were bruised and squashed into the fabric of her shirt, leaving one massive purple stain on its front and Kitty's hands.

"I thought you hated mess?" asked Josh.

Kitty held out her palms, examining them. "I do, don't I?" She shrugged her shoulders with a smile. "Maybe I'm becoming immune?"

"I'm very pleased for you, but I'm more concerned about how I'll convince my clients that you're not an axe murderer!"

Getting back into the truck, Josh's eyes crinkled at the corners, just the way she liked, and the muscles in his arms jumped as he ground the heavy gear stick. Kitty was grateful for Wendy sitting in between them. If she wasn't there, she'd have to sit on her hands. She couldn't trust herself not to reach out to trace a path along each and every one.

Back on the road again, Josh told Kitty about his assistant, Kate.

"She's like my second mother. She runs the show. My phone rings all day, and often I can't pick it up. Kate fields the calls and sends me where I need to go. I mostly hired her for her baking skills, though."

"Seriously?"

"Hell yeah. I haven't had to make myself lunch in years. I could probably judge that bake-off show by now. She'll be in phone contact all day, so get used to hearing the ping."

Kitty glanced down at Josh's washboard flat stomach. There was no evidence of a muffin top in sight. Perhaps she should enquire about local classes for goat wrangling or cow grappling. It seemed to work for him.

Eventually, they pulled up to a large metal gate. "Fitzroy Dairy" announced the bottle-green sign. Kitty jumped out and opened it. After Josh passed through, she clanked the mechanism across to secure it. *See!* She was even learning to close gates. They drove up to the farmhouse and pulled into the yard.

"Okay, everybody out," Josh said, turning off the engine.

Kitty hopped onto the muddy concrete, suddenly very aware of how silly she must look in her spotless, spotted boots. She wandered round to the back of the truck as Wendy sniffed every crevice and corner in the yard. The doors were open, and Josh pulled something out of a drawer.

"I'm expected to at least dress the part," he said, unfolding a pair of green overalls. "Though I draw the line at a flat cap and a pipe."

Kitty giggled. "I think you could carry off a flat cap."

Josh winced comically. "I'd rather not, thanks. But I'm tempted to make you wear one of these too," he said, holding up the overalls against her, his hands skirting the top of her bare shoulders. "At least you'd make them look good."

His cornflower blue eyes met hers, and Kitty bit her lip, willing his hands to slide down her arms, around her waist, and then down...*Holy crap*! She had to stop thinking lustful thoughts if she was going to get through the whole day.

"I have something that might help you," Josh said. He turned back to the truck and pulled out an old grey T-shirt.

"It's optional, of course, but you might freak the cows out dressed as you are."

Kitty frowned, then followed his gaze down to her top. The blackberry juice had dried, and she looked like she'd had a fight with a machete. She took the shirt and was about to ask where she could change when Josh peeled off his own T-shirt right in front of her.

Kitty's breath hitched. His golden chest and abs shone in the early morning sun, and the pink scar near his waistband drew her eyes down. Her mouth gaped open, and she froze. *Bloody hell!* His body was incredible. She didn't know they came like that. She quickly closed her mouth, realising she was probably staring like a halfwit! Thank God she wasn't dribbling.

Josh stepped into his overalls and pulled them up, his muscles rippling with every movement. She'd been right. Wrestling goats was good for more than just the soul. Nobody else could make a green jumpsuit look as hot as he did. Once he'd done up the buttons, Josh turned towards Kitty, who was still staring at him.

With a quick smile, she turned away, peeled off her vest top, and popped on his T-shirt as fast as physically possible. The shirt drowned her, so she knotted up the front. When she turned back around, his eyes rushed to the bare skin of her waist. A shiver of pleasure swept through Kitty as his gaze lingered on her stomach, but she couldn't read their expression.

A red-headed man wearing blue overalls wandered out of the farmhouse towards the truck.

"Morning, Josh. You come to see the girls?"

He noticed Kitty and offered a hand in greeting, an enormous smile on his face. "You must be Kitty. Josh said you were coming along to help. Nice to meet you."

She shook his offered hand.

"This is Keith," said Josh. "He owns the dairy. Let's get started before it gets too hot."

With Josh's impromptu strip show, things were already a little too hot, in her opinion.

Keith left to get things ready, and Josh turned to Kitty. "This might be dull. Tell me if you get too bored."

She nodded. This wasn't a date, and Josh needed to concentrate. She'd keep her ogling to a minimum.

He took his equipment out of the truck. Attaching a small screen to his forearm with Velcro, he put on a backpack.

"I didn't know you were auditioning for *Ghostbusters*," Kitty said.

Josh laughed. "It's an ultrasound machine. I'll show you how it works later. I'll warn you, though, it's not for the faint-hearted."

Once he'd organised his gear, they stepped inside the first of the big sheds. It was quieter than Kitty expected. The low hum of machinery blended with scraping hooves and the occasional soft bellow. The smell was overwhelming, however. A strange mixture of animal, mud, and disinfectant. Once she'd steadied her breath and conquered her gag reflex, Kitty watched Josh at work.

He described what he was doing with each cow, almost as if in meditation. Kitty drank in the intensity on his face, and the commanding tone of his velvet voice drew a blanket of calm over her. She'd willingly follow him into any battle at that moment. This Josh was far from the one she'd played Twister with, but this Josh was just as attractive. Maybe more so.

He moved further down the barn. Aware she wasn't doing anything remotely useful, Kitty was grateful to be joined by a ruddy-faced woman wearing a khaki T-shirt and a pair of leggings.

"They'll be at this for a while, luv. Fancy a cup of tea?" she asked, watching Josh as intently as Kitty. With a grateful nod, she followed the woman out of the shed and into the searing sunlight of the yard.

"I'm Becky, Keith's better half," she said.

Kitty introduced herself as they wandered into the cool interior of the stone farmhouse, sitting down at the cluttered kitchen table. Her fingers itched to clean the cloth that wore the remnants of what looked like toast and marmalade. Instead, she clenched her hands into fists.

Becky boiled the kettle and took four mugs from the cupboard.

"Nice boots," she said. "I can't imagine you've had those long."

Kitty winced. She must look so green. “No, not long,” she replied, her cheeks warming. She couldn’t admit they were roughly an hour old. She’d look like a newbie, for sure.

“So, are you a trainee vet or a vet assistant?” asked Becky as she added sugar to her and Keith’s mugs. Kitty shifted in her seat.

“Neither, I’m afraid.”

Becky smiled. “I did wonder. You were standing around like a spare part in the shed.” The woman’s bright laughter echoed off the orange floor tiles, and Kitty cringed.

“Is it that obvious? I’m a lawyer, hence the inappropriate footwear.”

“I think your boots are great! I was going to ask where you got them from.”

Kitty’s face relaxed into a smile. “I don’t know. They were a gift. I’m a groupie today. Josh wanted to show me what he did for work.”

A look of contemplation crossed Becky’s face as she joined Kitty at the table.

“A lawyer and a farm vet? Well, they say opposites attract. I suppose it’s best to know upfront if you’re suited to a life where any four-legged creature takes priority over you at a moment’s notice.” Kitty’s brow furrowed slightly. “I imagine you work very hard too, but it’s good to know what you are getting yourself into.”

Kitty should clarify that she and Josh weren’t a couple, but she wanted to know what Becky thought.

“See, that young man is very dedicated. He works long hours and rarely takes a holiday.” She took a sip of her tea and continued. “Many’s the time he’s come out here in the middle of the night. He’s always lovely, but I don’t need to tell you that. Such a gentle soul. His dad was the same. Not so easy on the eye, though.” Becky winked at Kitty. “How long have you been together?”

Heat rose up Kitty's chest. "I've known Josh for years, but we aren't together. We were friends as kids. I'm just helping his sister with her animal sanctuary. As adults, I really don't know him that well."

Becky huffed. "With him, what you see is what you get. It's rare these days." She picked up an ancient biscuit barrel from the shelf, removed the lid, and offered Kitty something from its depths. She shook her head.

"You may not be an item, but I saw how he looked at you. I spotted you both getting changed through the window and let's just say he enjoyed the view." Becky had a mischievous glimmer in her eye. "Usually, an undergrad or trainee are the only people he'd bring along on a visit. You might have yourself an admirer there." Heat flushed throughout the whole of Kitty's body now.

Clutching two mugs each, they headed back outside. After trying three sheds, they finally found Josh and Keith, the former with his entire arm inside a cow's bum. There was an image she'd never unsee. Kitty put her cargo down on an old bench, and Josh looked over. He must have seen the horrified look on her face.

"Not so glamourous, huh?" he asked.

"Erm, no, but I assume it's necessary and not just a pastime."

Josh laughed. "This is how you give a cow an ultrasound. Come over and have a look." He nodded towards the small screen he had strapped to his arm. Kitty's heart sped up at the thought of approaching the cow, but she moved towards Josh, using him as a shield. Like a human ultrasound, a vague white shape was visible in the dark grey void of the screen.

"So, it's not for ghost busting then," she said, almost to herself.

"It's easier to go in this way. The scanning probe can pass over the uterus. Back in my dad's day, it was all done by feeling. This tech makes me an amateur, really. See the legs there?"

Kitty nodded, the blurry picture shifting with each movement of the calf.

"You can just make out the ribcage. I'd say she's around 60 days along. The gestation period is about 280 days," he said, absorbed by the picture on the screen. All Kitty could think about was how a mini cow would make it all the way out, complete with hooves.

At Josh's direction, Kitty stepped back, and he extracted his arm and the scanning probe.

"Okay, that's the last one, Keith," he said.

Pleased to see that he'd encased his arm in a full-length plastic arm sleeve, Kitty gave him a wide berth as he washed up in a sink in the corner. The smell of disinfectant burned into her nostrils, making her lightheaded. This was the reality of his job and not the romanticised notion painted in the James Herriot books she'd read as a kid.

After he'd finished cleaning up, Josh headed over to Kitty.

"Well, that sight was a baptism by fire for you. There's nothing more confronting than seeing someone with their arm inside a cow."

She giggled. "You never know what weird stuff people are into."

"Sometimes, it's best not to ask. You know, you're the first non-veterinarian I've ever taken out for the day. I could get used to having you around."

Kitty's heart felt like it would burst out of her chest. "I bet you say that to all the girls."

Josh smiled at her, her head topped to one side. "Only those who swear blind that they hate mud. I don't buy it for a minute, Kitty Cameron. You're as at home here as in a boardroom."

The glow in his eyes sent Kitty's tummy butterflies flying around her whole body. The feeling was exquisite.

She followed Josh to the truck, where they said goodbye to Keith and Becky. Wendy was snoozing in the shade. The oppressive heat beat down on them as Josh opened both doors at the front. Grateful for the opportunity to get out of the sun, Kitty sat in the passenger seat, fanning herself ineffectually with her hand.

She watched Josh's reflection in the wing mirror as he walked to the back of the truck and stripped off the now crumpled green overalls. Kitty took a sharp intake of breath. He stood in the sun, jeans slung low around his waist, the lean proportions of his body perfectly balanced. Every angle was a delight, from his powerful arms to the scoring of the muscles on his abdomen, and a gentle tingle sprung between her legs.

Kitty's heart pounded. To spy on him was wicked, but she couldn't tear her eyes away. As Josh bundled up the overalls and stuffed them in the bag, the muscles in his back, shoulders and arms danced under his smooth skin. The sweat on his torso cast a subtle sparkle in the relentless sun like he'd been spray painted in glitter, and Kitty's mouth ran dry. If she touched his skin, would she leave fingerprints?

Wendy crept round to the back of the truck to join him, and he crouched down low to greet her, whispering into her silken ears and nuzzling her neck. What Kitty wouldn't give to be Wendy right now.

Josh gave his dog a last kiss on the top of her head and stood up. He reached into his back pocket and pulled out his phone, looking at the screen. Kitty hadn't heard any message come in. Perhaps he'd had it on silent. Anti-cow startle mode. A frown knitted Josh's brows, marring his beautiful face. His jaw was tight, and he placed his hand on his hip, looking heavenward.

This couldn't be good news.

27

JOSH

Josh was unimpressed. A message had come in from Kate about a lame horse. That was fine, but the horse in question belonged to his ex, and worse, her overbearing mother stabled her. Josh didn't know if he had the energy to deal with Patricia today, let alone for her to meet Kitty. She was hell-bent on him and Tabitha getting back together.

They would never get back together. Ever.

Josh looked at the truck, and Kitty's reflection in the wing mirror was the first thing he saw. Her dark eyes peeped out from half-closed lashes, threatening to strip off his skin with their intensity. Their gazes locked for a second, and Josh was suddenly very aware of being half-dressed. Fingers of sensation raked his chest as if invisible hands were running over him, and his breath sat in his throat.

Josh spun around, leaning against the hot metal of the car, steadying his quickened heartbeat. But the burn against his skin did nothing to take away the desire to have her. To own her.

Fuck. As the days went by, he was fighting a losing battle. Kitty was his first thought each morning and his last thought before falling asleep. The distance he'd put between them only added to his misery. That she'd leave soon only opened him up to the same feelings that had crippled him for the last few years.

Thoughts of Tabitha and now this visit to Patricia's made him uneasy. Would he ever be able to shake off her ghost?

His phone pinged again. It was Kate confirming the visit to Patricia's. With a sigh, Josh tipped his head back, looking into the vivid blue sky. He had to get his shit together. He was working, not on a date, not trying to seduce his friend.

With a quiet growl, Josh straightened up and grabbed a clean T-shirt from the drawer. After putting it on, he slammed the back doors and walked to the passenger side, grabbing them both a cold bottle of water from the car fridge.

He stood so close to Kitty that the sweet fragrance of her hair enveloped him. She sat in the passenger seat, gazing out into fields with her long legs stretched out of the door, and an urge to caress their silky skin consumed him. Instead, he grasped the bottles with tight fists and closed the fridge door.

Kitty looked up at him, shielding her eyes from the bright sun as he approached her.

"I imagine you could do with this?" Josh said, handing her the water. She took it, sitting up and bringing her legs into the car.

Her face remained passive. Had he just imagined her watching him in the mirror? Did she have any idea of the effect it had on him?

"Who was the message from?" Kitty asked.

Josh gulped down the entire water bottle, its chill tightening his throat.

"Kate. She had a call about a lame horse I need to check out. It's on the way back home."

He decided not to mention Patricia. Hopefully, she'd behave today.

28

KITTY

THE DRIVE back to Tottenbridge took longer than Kitty remembered. Perhaps it was the mood in the truck that made the journey seem longer. Josh was quiet, and getting conversation out of him was like pulling teeth. Kitty gave up halfway back, and they sat in silence. She shook her head. Why was this guy such a total head trip?

The truck pulled up just outside the village at a beautiful manor house that was covered in ivy. A lady with perfectly styled hair and too much makeup came out of the wide front door and glided down the steps, arms outstretched in greeting.

"Joshie darling, thank you so much for coming."

Kitty had heard Thea and Amelia call him by the name 'Joshie.' She'd assumed it was only family that used it. Did he and this woman know each other well? In a wave of perfume, the woman enveloped Josh in her arms, giving him a theatrical hug. His body stiffened, and his arms remained at his sides.

"It's Diva, darling," she said. "She's gone lame. It's been a few days, and I should have called you sooner."

The woman moved to lead Josh across the gravel, linking her arm through his. He hesitated and looked back at Kitty and

Wendy, still sitting in the truck. The woman noticed them for the first time.

"Oh, who's this?" she asked, a peevish look on her face.

Kitty scrambled out of the car and offered an outstretched hand in greeting. She was about to introduce herself when Josh jumped in.

"Patricia, this is Kitty. She's a colleague of Thea's who's come to help me today."

Kitty clamped her jaw tight enough to shatter her molars. Just a colleague of Thea's? She'd at least earned the title of *friend.*

Josh's eyes found hers, and there was a pleading look in them. He knew what he'd said would hurt her! What the hell was he playing at? Kitty stared ahead, smiling stiffly through the introduction.

After leaving Wendy with a large bowl of cold water, they followed Patricia to the stables at the back of the house. Kitty was ignored by their hostess, which suited her well, and she hung in the background as Patricia led the beautiful animal out of the stable and into the yard.

The horse was huge, with a long, winsome mane and a chestnut coat gleaming like shined copper. Kitty couldn't miss the rolling eyes and flared, snorting nostrils. Her wild beauty was mesmerising. The horse danced around the yard, the lameness in her front leg obvious even to her untrained eye.

Patricia moved forward and held the horse tight in her bridle, handing her to Josh. Diva soon relaxed under his examination, his calm singsong tones setting her at ease as his hands traced over every inch of her. After checking her lame leg up on his knee, he placed it down and turned to Patricia.

"She's got an abscess. I should be able to treat it easily enough, but it'll cause some pain. She'll be out of action for a week."

"Whatever you think best," Patricia said, suddenly

distracted. "Tabitha will want to know. She'll want to know that *you're* dealing with it.

Josh smiled, his lips shut together. It was a smile that didn't quite meet his eyes. "That's unnecessary. I'm certain Diva will make a full recovery."

Kitty narrowed her eyes. She picked up on the name 'Tabitha' and the muscle that flickered in Josh's jaw the moment he'd heard it. Curiouser and curiouser.

"No, I'd better call her. You!" she barked at Kitty. "Take the horse." Patricia held the leading rope out to her.

A rush of adrenalin coursed through her body, and her breathing turned rapid and raspy. She backed up against the stable wall, just staring at the giant horse, and a crazy urge to run gripped her. Still holding out the rope, Patricia scowled at her hesitance.

"Oh, for goodness' sake!" she snapped.

With a grimace, Josh took the rope from Patricia, and she stomped off, muttering. He turned to Kitty, his eyes running over her face.

"It's okay," he said, the honey of his voice soothing her. "She'll be calm if you are. She's only upset now because of Patricia. You saw how I settled her down."

"I... I can't," Kitty said, shaking her head. She'd come to terms with Jill the donkey and Simon, a more placid horse at Small Oaks, but this enormous beast terrified her.

"Yes, you can," Josh said, reaching out for her. As if drawn by a magnet, her hand lifted to him, and he took it, gently pulling her towards his body.

"It's okay. She'll trust you."

Josh moved Kitty in front of him and positioned her between his arms. She stood, cocooned in his warmth, trembling as Diva rolled her eyes and stamped her good feet in agitation. She winced and backed into Josh, her rigid body pushing against him. He stood his ground. He held her hand in his own and guided it towards Diva's shimmering neck.

"It's okay," he whispered. "She's going to love you. You're calm and in control, and she's going to sense that."

"I'm not calm or in control at all," she said through gritted teeth, pulling back her hand.

"Are you kidding? You're one of the most self-controlled people I've ever met," he said. You must have an inner calmness to handle the pressure of your job. Try to harness that."

Kitty swallowed hard, then took a deep breath, relaxing her body like she did before an important meeting. Once her breathing had stilled, Josh guided her hand up to Diva's neck again. He placed it there, leaving his own hand to cover hers. Diva's dense coat was velveteen under Kitty's touch, and the pressure of Josh's hand soothed her fear.

The horse seemed to settle under their combined pressure, and Josh continued to talk to Diva in a quiet voice. His breath at Kitty's ear was as light as a kiss. Gripping her lip in her teeth, she tried to match his breath, his chest rising and falling against her back.

Soon enough, her body relaxed, and Josh removed his hand from hers. The sudden loss of his warmth left her skin tingling like something was missing. He passed her the leading rope and stepped back from her.

"See, I knew you could do it. I'll be right back. Just keep doing what you are doing." Josh turned away and headed towards the truck.

Kitty stayed in the same position until he returned. She'd begun to stroke Diva's neck, and the horse was content. Josh put down the items he'd brought from the truck.

"See, she loves you," he said, pulling up close to Diva, his eyes on Kitty's face.

At that moment, Patricia came stalking out of the house, and Diva tensed under her hand.

"I couldn't get through to Tabitha. I had to leave a message."

Without a word, Josh took the rope and tied Diva up, setting to work, cleaning and trimming back her hoof to expose the abscess. Once located, he lanced it and allowed it to drain. He then applied a poultice and dressed the hoof. As soon as he'd finished, he stroked Diva and kissed the side of her neck.

"There, darling, that should help with the pain."

Kitty held her breath. She never thought she'd envy a horse.

29

JOSH

THE MIDDAY HEAT seared them as Patricia, full of thanks and praise for Josh, invited them in for a cold drink. Desperate to cool down, he accepted the offer, praying to the gods that she'd behave herself.

"We'll pack up, then come and join you," he called after Patricia as she disappeared inside her rambling home.

Josh took a compliant Diva and led her back to her stable. Once inside, Kitty gave her neck a last pat and whispered to her. He'd love to know what she said. Not to mention what had made her so afraid of horses. A soft smile settled on his lips as she turned to face him.

"I knew you could handle it," he said as they headed to the truck.

"Thanks. I could never have done it without your help."

He looked down at his feet. "It was the least I could do for a...."

"For a colleague of your sisters?" Kitty finished his sentence for him, a bitter edge in her voice.

His stomach lurched, and a burn of guilt gnawed at him

deep inside. "Ouch," he said, looking up to meet her eyes. "I deserve that, and I'm sorry."

Her face remained stony, and when she said nothing, he continued. "It's hard to explain, but there's a history with Patricia, and she can be bloody spiteful. I told her you were here because of Thea, to stop any of her nonsense."

"What could she have to say to me?" Kitty asked.

Hopefully, nothing.

30

KITTY

AFTER THEY'D CHECKED on Wendy and repacked the gear into the truck, Josh guided Kitty through the house's front door. They didn't say much to each other. She was still cross with him even if he did help her with Diva. She didn't press him to elaborate on the *history* he'd mentioned with Patricia. She'd try to get it out of him later.

They passed through an opulent hallway full of palms and plump armchairs and into a cavernous kitchen. Patricia motioned them to sit on an oversized couch next to a coffee table. Kitty sunk into its depths, but Josh excused himself to clean up. Without being given any directions, he disappeared into the hallway. Her eyebrows raised. He knew where he was going.

She sat in awkward silence as Patricia made herself busy with the drinks. Desperate for a distraction, she looked around the room. Several pictures of a gorgeous blonde woman smiled down from the walls. Her clear, blue eyes and angelic face were stunning, and her delicate features gave her the look of a fae. Patricia noticed Kitty looking at the photos.

"That's my Tabitha," she said with a triumphant smile. "Isn't she beautiful?"

"Yes, she is. Is she a model?" asked Kitty.

"I always thought she could have a career in front of the camera, but she chose a life behind it," said Patricia, warming to her subject.

"Oh?"

"Yes, she studied fashion and has built her own boutique label. She's quite a success in Europe,"

Patricia put a tray down on the table. It held three glasses and a pitcher of pale liquid. She took a seat opposite Kitty.

"How amazing," Kitty said, genuinely impressed.

"I was hoping she would settle for a quieter life in the country, but she wouldn't have it. Bright lights and adventure lured her away."

Kitty smiled as the ice cubes in the pitcher clinked together, increasing her thirst.

"When she and Josh parted ways, I kissed that dream goodbye." Patricia sighed, her mouth in a sulky pout.

Tight tendrils of heat crept up Kitty's neck. Josh and this glorious creature used to be an item? If that were true, what hope was there for her? She and the picture of perfection on the wall couldn't be more different.

"I'm always hopeful they'll reconsider, and she'll come back."

Kitty's stomach lurched. That sounded like a terrible idea to her.

"Where do you live?" Patricia asked, her eyes narrowing.

"I'm from Hertfordshire, but I've lived in London for a while now."

"I assume you aren't a veterinarian, my dear, judging from how you handled Diva and..." she paused, staring at Kitty's pink gumboots, "your attire."

Kitty shifted in her seat. "No," she admitted. "I'm a lawyer. I'm just in between jobs now, and...."

"Then our little village must be a change of scenery for you," Patricia said, interrupting her.

She gripped the arm of the wicker sofa. "Well, it's different. I used to visit during the holidays when I was a kid. I'd forgotten how much I loved wandering the fields and hearing the birds. We even picked some berries today."

Patricia's eyebrows lifted. "How, then, do you know Joshua and Thea?"

"I'm Jonathan Finch's cousin."

Patricia pursed her lips together. "So, you must be Julia's niece?"

Kitty nodded.

"Well, now," Patricia smirked. "I'd heard you'd arrived in our little paradise. Please give Julia my best wishes for a speedy recovery."

From the look on her face, she didn't care if Kitty delivered the message or not.

"Joshua said you've been helping Thea at the Sanctuary. I'm one of her biggest donors, you know." Patricia smiled at her, a smug look on her face. "Thea and Tabitha used to be the best of friends. I assume Jonty introduced you to Thea?"

"No, Josh introduced us," said Kitty.

Patricia's over-plucked eyebrows shot up. "Oh, so you already knew Joshua?"

Kitty was about to tell her about their childhood friendship, but a returning Josh interrupted her.

"Did I hear my name?" he said as he appeared through the doorway, fresh, handsome, and smelling like hand soap. He took a seat next to Kitty. Patricia's face lit up. The King had returned to his worshipping court.

"Oh darling, there you are. Your friend..."

"Kitty," he said.

Damn, she loved the way her name sounded on his lips.

"Yes, Kitty was just telling me about herself." Patricia poured out the drinks. "This is Tabitha's absolute favourite. Peach tea," she said as the liquid filled the glasses. "You remember, don't you, Joshie?"

Kitty threw him a surreptitious glance. He didn't move a muscle. Said nothing.

"I was also telling Kitty about Tabitha and her success," Patricia said, warming to her subject. She put the pitcher down and folded her hands in her lap. "She's worked so hard, but to what end? I'm still not convinced she's happy."

Patricia's eyes were pinned on Josh's face, but his expression remained deadpan. Regardless, she ploughed on.

"Tab has lived life in the fast lane long enough. I'm just hoping she realises it's not sustainable. What do you think, Joshie? You know her so very well."

Josh shifted on the cushions, his solid thigh brushing against Kitty's. It was almost more than she could bear not to return the pressure.

"When I've spoken to her, she seems happy," he said. "She has a great life,"

"Oh well, you'd know better than I," Patricia's voice dripped like treacle. "When did you last speak to her?"

"Last week," murmured Josh.

Kitty's hands clenched into fists at her side. Josh and his ex chatted recently, then. Was he still in love with her? Regret might account for his changeability.

"Yes, you keep in very close contact, don't you?" It was a statement, not a question, and she'd aimed it squarely at Kitty with a triumphant glare.

The tiny muscle twitched in Josh's cheek again, and his jaw was set, firm and steady. Kitty would love to know what was going on in that head.

The shrill tone of a phone ringing broke the silence, and

Josh shifted beside her. When Patricia jumped up to answer it, Josh gestured to Kitty that they make a run for it. Taking her hand, he practically dragged her into the yard to the distant excited screech of, "Tabitha darling!"

As soon as they were outside, Josh dropped her hand like a hot potato.

"I'm so sorry to put you through that," he said. "I didn't think. Patricia can be a nightmare." He looked at her, and she noticed the dark shadows under his eyes. "Please, let's get out of here," he murmured.

Kitty chewed her bottom lip. The conversation in Patricia's kitchen had been eye-opening and left so many questions unanswered. Who the hell was Tabitha? When did they split up, and why did Josh seem so upset with Patricia? Intending to find out, Kitty followed him back to the truck.

31

JOSH

WENDY, who'd been sleeping in the shade, greeted Josh with lazy tail thumps. The sun beat down, and he and Kitty were already hot and sweaty since leaving Patricia's. She leaned against the truck, her eyes on his face.

"I have questions," she said.

Josh gave her a wry smile and pulled his fingers through his hair. Damn Patricia and her obsession with him and Tabitha.

"I'm not surprised. That was an interesting hour. Jump in the truck and ask away. I got a text from Kate when I was in the bathroom. Our next stop is a bit of a drive."

Josh climbed into the truck and glanced to see Kitty slide into the passenger seat. She was settling Wendy down between them, her face flushed and shiny. Would that be how she'd look, underneath him, in bed? Josh sucked in a breath.

"One thing before we go," Kitty said. "Please promise me we're not dropping in on a menopausal goat. I don't think I could cope with the trauma."

"Don't worry. I get hazard pay for that sort of thing. I'll pay your medical bills."

Kitty smiled across at him. "You couldn't afford me."

They rolled out of the driveway and turned into the road, the car's air-con blasting them in icy waves. Kitty was the first to speak.

"So, what was all that about at Patricia's?"

Josh sighed and tapped a finger on the steering wheel.

"Do you want the long or short story?"

"How long is the drive?"

Josh laughed. "Okay then, buckle up." He'd try and keep his explanation light and vague. No over-sharing.

"Short story, Tabitha, Patricia's daughter, and I used to be together. We split a while back, and Patricia wishes we hadn't. She wants us back together as long as we're both single."

Kitty stared at him, her eyes slightly narrowed. Josh held his breath, waiting to see if his explanation would be enough.

"Well, that's very unsatisfying," Kitty said. "What's the long story?"

Josh's knuckles turn white on the wheel. *Fuck.* He really didn't want to go into detail, but then, he didn't want Kitty questioning his calling her a colleague. Not to mention all the passive-aggressive chat from Patricia about him and her daughter.

Josh took a breath. "We were getting married."

Kitty's eyebrows lifted, and the pitch of her voice lifted. "Oh, well, that's different." She waited a few seconds. "What happened? How long were you together?"

His earlier thought echoed around his head. *Keep it light and vague.*

"We were dating through high school. Tab was talented, beautiful, and fun. I adored her. She was all my *firsts*. We split up before university. We were heading on different paths. It devastated me, but you know, wild oats and all that. I mended, but I didn't forget her."

"You didn't speak at all? Didn't you run into each other during the holidays?"

"Not really. She travelled a lot, and I kept myself occupied. I'm not a monk, Kitty." Well, he wasn't back then.

"But you're both so good-looking. I can't believe either of you is single," Kitty murmured.

Josh's gut tightened, and his cheeks burned hot as he stared straight ahead at the road.

"Oh, shit, sorry," she said. "That kind of just came out. No filter."

Josh snickered. "It's okay. I'll take the compliment. When I took over from Dad, Tab was at her folks' place."

"Why was she back?"

"Well, that's where it gets interesting. She wanted to launch her own label but needed her dad's money to fund it. They're loaded, by the way."

"I noticed," Kitty muttered.

"He refused to bankroll her unless she cleaned her act up. She had a pretty wild lifestyle. When I came back, she must have seen me coming."

"What do you mean, saw you coming?" asked Kitty, turning in her seat to face him.

Josh looked out the window over the rolling fields of corn, smiled, and shook his head.

"We hung out a lot, and I fell straight back in love with her. She fell into more of a 'reliable old Josh will impress my dad to get the cash' kind of love."

"Oh. Wow."

Her voice was low, and a wave of nausea swept over Josh at the pity in it. She'd see him as weak and foolish. It was how he saw himself. He wanted to stop. Box his feelings and the story of him and Tabitha back up. But now he'd lifted the lid, he couldn't shut it again, and the words kept coming.

"Yeah. It worked too. With me as part of the package, she got her money. She planned this big launch party and a move to London. I could see her slipping away, so I panicked and proposed. I mean, it was naïve of me, but I was so in love with her. I really wanted it to work."

Josh grimaced. He was officially oversharing.

"She said yes?" Kitty asked.

"She did. All things considered, I wish she'd turned me down. Hindsight is a wonderful thing. She never loved me the way I loved her."

Kitty turned away to look out of her window. And her fingers stilled in Wendy's fur. "So, what happened?"

"I missed her launch party. I got called out to an emergency when nobody else was available. I sent her a message to let her know, but I didn't hear back."

"Was she angry?" Kitty asked.

Josh loosened his aching fingers from the steering wheel, stretching out their knuckles. "Not exactly angry. More vindictive or opportunistic. I guess with the cash in the bank, she felt at liberty to go home with someone else. I'm sure I don't need to fill in the details."

Kitty's head swung around to look at Josh, her brows knitted together.

"Because you missed one night?"

"It was more than that. I think the reality of being married to a workaholic had well and truly sunk in by then. I wasn't much fun to be with, and Tabitha wanted to have fun."

Josh breathed out. It was done. He'd told the story that he'd only confessed to two other people. His sister and Jonty. But opening up the wound hadn't hurt so much this time.

"She used you," Kitty said. "That's terrible. I'm so sorry, Josh."

"I was, too," he said. "I never found out who it was. Nobody seemed to know, and Tab certainly wouldn't tell me. Still won't. Anyway, we split. She skipped town and launched a successful fashion label. End of a very long story." Josh ended his words with a smile. An attempt to get Kitty to drop the subject. To see he was okay and move on.

"But you still talk?" she persisted.

"She's one of my oldest friends. Ultimately, I still love her in that way."

"And Patricia?"

Josh gave a wry smile. "Still heavily invested. She wanted hearts and roses and a comfortable life in the countryside for her daughter. She views any woman who comes within ten metres of me as a threat to her dream of a reunion. You happened to fall foul of that today."

"That's ridiculous," scoffed Kitty.

There was a deep furrow in her brow, and her hand was now knotted into Wendy's fur. Josh had hoped that giving her the whole story would clear the air. Lighten the atmosphere. Her face didn't look at all lightened.

"It is, and I didn't mean to tell you everything, but you did ask for the long story."

Kitty's frown lifted. "Don't worry, I'll send you a bill for my time." The second she'd spoken the words, her mouth dropped open, and she turned to face him, eyes wide. "I am so sorry. That was terrible of me. I have a habit of reverting to humour at the worst times.

Josh's chest lurched. *Great*. He'd dumped his sorry story on *her,* adding a big dollop of misery, and she was the one apologising. He took his hand off the steering wheel and moved it down to cover hers, giving it a gentle squeeze.

"It's fine. I know how ridiculous it all sounds."

Kitty's body froze, the tension in her fingers like steel against his skin. Silence ballooned between them, and Josh held his breath. What the fuck had he done that for? He'd squeezed her hand like a kindly uncle comforting a child. Now she really *would* think he was pathetic.

Kitty looked down at his hand lying on hers, and Josh

removed it, bunching it into a fist at his thigh. Kitty's shoulders dropped, and she looked out the bug-splattered windscreen. "On the bright side. At least you escaped Patricia's clutches. She'd be the mother-in-law from hell."

Josh chuckled, grateful for the light relief. "Oh, she's still trying."

He looked over at Kitty. She wasn't tugging at the door lock, trying to get out of the car. She didn't look panicked, and she wasn't quietly texting an SOS to Julia. Perhaps he'd gotten away with his clumsy attempt at touching her.

Apart from the game of Twister, when he'd tickled her, he hadn't been brave enough. He'd wanted to touch her, to feel her skin against his fingertips from the minute she'd smiled at him at the pub. And he'd thought about it, alone at night, a lot.

Josh slowed down as he came to the turning for the next appointment. With a grimace, he pulled into the gate and drove up the driveway.

32

JOSH

AFTER TREATING a sick alpaca and getting peed on for his troubles, Josh headed back to the truck. Kitty had elected to stay with Wendy under the shade of a large oak tree. She'd bailed after he told her alpacas spat. She joked she'd had enough excitement for one day. Still, Josh worried his confessions about Tabitha had put a downer on her mood, and he couldn't shake the sick feeling in his stomach.

The whole day was going wrong. They were supposed to be having fun. He wanted to show her what he did and why he loved it so much. Now he'd bored her with tales of his heartbreak.

"Hey there," he said, walking towards her.

Kitty and Wendy sat in a heap at the base of the tree. She was red-faced, and Wendy panted like a pair of broken bellows. Kitty raised her hand in greeting, then flopped it down in her lap again.

"How'd it go?" she asked.

"All good. Just a mild dermatosis."

"Ah yes, dermatosis, of course. All the best alpacas have it." Kitty smiled at him, and Josh's heart lifted a little.

"Are you ready to go?" he said. "You look melted at the edges."

"I am *so* ready. I think I've sweated my entire body weight today,"

A sheen of perspiration covered Kitty's face. His old grey T-shirt wasn't the coolest thing she could wear, not to mention the thick rubber boots. Josh, too, was struggling in the ridiculous heat. He wiped the moisture from his brow and headed to the truck to change out of his overalls. As he put on a new shirt, he had an idea. Something he could do to lighten their mood and cool them down. Somewhere special he could take Kitty to put a smile back on her face.

He returned to the front of the truck, taking out water and energy bars from the fridge and handing them to Kitty. She took the food but just stared at it.

"I'm still not hungry. It's too hot to eat," she said.

"I don't like to put my responsible adult hat on, but I don't want you passing out from low blood sugar. At least have a drink."

Kitty nodded and took the water, tipping it back. Josh eyed the shimmering skin on her long neck, imagining his lips moving over it, tasting her. *Damn.* He was the one who needed to cool off.

"Hang on," he said, taking his phone out of his pocket. Josh walked to the gate at the edge of the field. He made a quick call, watching Kitty the whole time. She'd climbed into the truck and waited for him to return, stroking Wendy's head and chatting to her.

After a couple of minutes on the phone, Josh walked back to the truck. He grinned as he opened the door and sat down. Gunning the engine, he turned to Kitty.

"Fancy a change of scenery?" he asked.

"Sure. Where to now? Can't we just stop off to give a

chihuahua an enema or something? I honestly don't know how you do this."

Josh laughed as they drove down the driveway and pulled onto the road. The windows were still wound down, and the hot, blustery breeze made the loose strands of Kitty's hair dance.

"I can turn on the air-con if you'd prefer?" he said. "I'm just trying to heat-torture you."

Kitty grinned. "Torture away. I like it."

Josh turned on the radio, and an old song came on. At first, he sang quietly but was soon belting the tune out the window at the top of his voice.

"You can actually sing!" Kitty giggled. "Is there anything you *can't* do?"

Josh gave her a cheeky wink and carried on, throwing in a couple of arm moves. Next, Wendy was up on her feet, making small yelping noises as if singing along with him. Kitty held her hands to her ears, refusing to join in.

"Is singing even allowed?" she shouted. "I thought you had to be always ready for action? How will you hear the phone?"

"I've turned it off," he said.

She looked at him, confusion in her eyes.

"I'm done. It's too hot to concentrate, and there may or may not be a corrupting influence on ride-along today." He side-eyed her with a smirk on his lips.

"Don't blame me!" she squealed, wrinkling up her nose. He loved it when she did that.

"Well, it's not Wendy, is it? She agrees with everything I say." He ruffled the top of his dog's head, and Kitty grinned at them. "Only because she relies on you for food."

They reached the outskirts of Tottenbridge after a few more songs and more 'singing' from Wendy. Josh pulled onto the side of the road in front of a small bridge. He turned off the engine and faced Kitty.

"What are you doing?" she asked.

"As I said, I'm done. I'm taking the afternoon off. Kate is diverting any calls through to someone else."

"Can you even do that?" Kitty asked, taking a last drink of her water.

It was a good question. In fact, he'd never taken an afternoon off before. The only time he'd ever missed a job, or taken time off, was when Phil died.

"I can," he said.

Josh walked around to open the door for Kitty. At first, she hesitated in the passenger seat before clambering onto the grass. Wendy bolted and disappeared into the cowslips without a second glance.

"Well, what are we doing here?" she asked.

"This is a secret spot of mine," he said, gesturing behind him, down the bank. "And now you know about it. I'll have to kill you." He giggled at her look of surprise, retrieving a four-pack of cold soda from the fridge. In the shade of the trees, the heat was already more tolerable.

"You hungry yet?" he asked.

Kitty shook her head.

"Well, I'm starving." He smiled, then grabbed a paper bag from the fridge along with the cans. He locked the car and followed Wendy into the bushes, beckoning Kitty to join him.

33

KITTY

After leaving the truck behind at the bridge, they headed downhill through the thick greenery. A gentle gurgle of water kissed her ears, and the bracken and grasses scratched and caressed her legs in equal measure.

"Watch your step," Josh said, reaching out for her hand.

She took it, enjoying the effortless way her palm slipped into his. When he'd touched her hand in the car, she hadn't noticed how smooth his skin was, considering what he did for a living. She'd been more shocked by his action. Now, thoughts of his soft hands on her, running all over her, invaded her brain and her mouth dried.

Moments later, they emerged from the greenery onto a sandy riverbank under the shade of a vast willow tree. Banks of blackberry bushes and wildflowers stood around them. Kitty stopped in her tracks.

"Holy crap! It's beautiful. I feel like I've been here before, though."

Josh smiled, his eyes glowing. "Isn't it? And yes, you have."

As if realising he was still holding her hand, he loosened his grip and let it go. Moving towards the water, they sat on the sand under the shade of the willow tree, its branches weaving lazily in the warm breeze. The boughs creaked as they swung, and the sun picked through the canopy to bathe their bodies in dappled light.

Settled on the bank, they both took off their boots, and Kitty wiggled her toes in delight, a sigh escaping her lips. Even the hot air was luxurious compared to the thick socks and rubber encasing her feet all day. Josh cracked open two cans of soda, and Kitty took one, drinking it in a series of long, greedy gulps.

No sooner had she finished it when a lump of searing pain hit her chest, doubling her over into her knees. Panic set in, and a cold sweat broke out on her back. She'd drunk the soda so fast, and now an enormous burp, brewing deep inside, threatened to explode.

What the hell could she do? She didn't want Josh to hear her burping like Barney from the Simpsons, but there was no way she could hold it in. If she did, the air might rush through her body and come out the other end. She'd never burped or farted in front of someone she'd fancied before. She'd never got close enough to anyone to let *that* final wall down.

Praying to the soda gods for mercy, Kitty sat back up, her cheeks puffing out like a hamster after a good meal.

"Are you okay?" asked Josh, looking concerned and scanning her face. "You look very red."

Kitty's eyes widened, and she pointed at the can, then clutched at her chest.

Josh's mouth dropped, and he looked at her, realisation glinting in his eyes. "Burp," he said, a smile twitching on his lips. "Before you explode. I don't want to be responsible for bits of you being splattered along the riverbank."

Kitty shook her head, desperate to stand up and run, but the pain was so intense she couldn't move. She daredn't answer him either, knowing that if she did, a terrifying force would rip out of her body, shattering any illusions that she was an attractive woman.

"Kitty! You look like you're about to die. You can't fight nature. I won't look." he said.

Kitty shook her head again, her breath and her resolve running out fast.

"Okay," Josh said, "I'll go and stand over there." He pointed to the edge of the bank. "That way, I won't hear you."

With a smirk, and a shake of his head, he stood to walk down to the water's edge, but he only got three steps away when Kitty's efforts to stifle the biggest burp in recorded history failed.

At the noise, both Josh and Kitty froze. She, with a look of horror on her face and he, with his back to her.

Oh god! What the hell had just happened? A blazing burn hit Kitty's face, and she covered her mouth with her hands. Josh still hadn't turned round, but looking on the bright side, he hadn't left either. Instead, he stood on the spot, his shoulders twitching. Hang on, they weren't twitching. They were bouncing. Bouncing with silent laughter.

After an excruciating few seconds, they stopped, and Josh let out a breath. "Pardon you," he said before bursting into a belly laugh and turning around to face her.

His smile was the same as the little kid in the pictures at Small Oaks. Cheeky and infectious. She hadn't realised quite how much she adored it. Kitty put her head into her hands.

"I'm so sorry. I've never done that before in front of a...."

Kitty caught herself before she said the word boyfriend. Josh *wasn't* her boyfriend, and after making such a joke of herself, he probably never would be. Her cheeks fired hot.

"Look, it's just that you brought me to this perfect place, and then I had to go and ruin it."

Josh's brows pulled together, and he rubbed the back of his neck. "Remember what Wendy said earlier? Nothing has to be perfect. Nobody needs to be perfect." One corner of his mouth twitched, and he stepped back towards her. "Look at it as payback for me spilling my guts in the car. One kind of hot air for another."

Kitty snickered. "But it's gross!"

"It's fine. It's perfectly acceptable behaviour in front of a ...."

"Colleague?" Kitty finished, one brow arched.

Josh winced, sitting back down next to her. "Exactly."

They settled back into a comfortable silence, the hum of the bees keeping time with the gurgle of the water. This magical place was just where she needed to be today. And she was sitting next to the best person to share it with, even if she had rendered herself unimaginable in the romance department. She wouldn't be able to do this when she was stuck behind a desk in a concrete tower.

Josh sat gazing at the opposite bank, and beads of perspiration formed on his upper lip. Kitty longed to kiss them away. She couldn't help it. Her promise to stay focussed on her career was slipping away by the second under the onslaught of his all-around gorgeousness.

Kitty raked her fingers through the sand of the bank, still wrapped in thoughts of soft, damp lips, when she noticed a movement out of the corner of her eye. She looked at Josh, who'd stood up, brushed himself off, and peeled the T-shirt from his body. *Not again!* His tanned, toned torso had Kitty's eyes on stalks, and her mouth dropped open.

What was he doing?

Her imagination went to all the wrong places as her thoughts tumbled over each other. Was he about to declare he was a rampant naturist, or was he about to jump on her? For all the expression on his face revealed, he could have been ordering a pizza.

A singe of heat crept over Kitty's face as Josh slowly unbuttoned his jeans, lava rushing to her cheeks. With his crotch at eye level, it was like watching her own private strip show. Her very own porno. Kitty's breath caught in her throat. Where was the pause button? Where was the emergency oxygen?

After a long, torturous wait, Josh slipped his jeans off and stood before her, a smile on his face. He wore small black trunks that moulded to every inch of him. Kitty swallowed. From where she sat, the inches he had looked impressive.

"I'm going for a swim," he said. "Join me?"

Wide-eyed, Kitty's brain went into overdrive, begging herself not to look at his package, say anything stupid, and to be cool for once in her life.

"Sorry?" she said, looking at him.

"A swim in the river. It's beautiful on a hot day."

Kitty froze.

"I...I don't have swimmers."

Josh shrugged. "You have undies on, though? Unless that's not your style, of course."

Josh grinned at her. Bloody hell. He must think she was some kind of deviant.

"Yes, I do, but..." her words trailed off.

"We're hidden here, so you can go full commando if you like."

He met her shocked look with a chuckle and headed down to the river, followed by an excited Wendy.

Kitty's eyes stayed glued to Josh's tight buttocks as they made their way down to the water's edge, the nails on each hand digging into her palms. How did they end up here? An hour ago, he was pouring his heart out, a few minutes ago, she was humiliating herself, and now he was half naked, tempting her into the water.

Kitty got to her feet, still mesmerised by the sight of Josh's butt cheeks, when a thought barrelled into her brain. *Crap*! What knickers had she put on this morning? With such an early start, she couldn't remember what she'd grabbed in the dark. Offering a silent prayer to St. Agnes, the patron saint of chastity and purity, she hoped at least that they matched her bra.

Josh stood in the shallows and threw a stick for Wendy, waiting for Kitty to join him. His broad back glistened with light perspiration, and its muscles jostled for supremacy under his skin as he moved. Kitty shivered.

She really had to get a grip. She was only taking a near-naked swim with an achingly sexy and unattainable friend. Kitty hadn't read the instruction manual for these types of situations, but as long as she looked and didn't touch, things would be fine.

Taking a deep breath and a leap of false confidence, Kitty stripped off Josh's T-shirt and her shorts, glancing down to check what undies she was wearing. Relief flooded her as she noted they matched. They were utilitarian and plain black, but at least they matched.

The giggle that escaped her lips caused Josh to turn around. When their eyes locked, his lit up, and a flash of embarrassment swept through her. What if he thought she was too gangly? He'd already used the word once. Did he prefer bigger boobs? Why hadn't she checked if her bikini line was fuzz-free?

Wendy barked in the shallows, urging Josh to throw the stick again. But as if the moment locked him in time, he stood there, a smile settling on his lips. Kitty was on the verge of turning around and running all the way back to Rose Cottage, even if it meant sprinting up High Street in her bra and knickers. Steeling herself, though, she took a deep breath and untied her hair.

Okay, so far, so good. Her clothes had been removed with little fuss. Now to enter the water. Kitty set off down the bank, trying to muster all the poise and grace of a classic movie star. Instead, she trod on something sharp. A full-throated "Fuck!"

left her mouth, and the offending stone sent her tripping and hopping right into Josh's chest.

She caught him off balance and almost bowled him over into the water. His muscular arms and legs kept them both upright, and he set Kitty back on her feet, laughter in his eyes. Their bodies were so close that she swore she could feel the molecules dance under her skin, attempting to join with his. It would be so easy to reach out and touch him. To run her lips across his glowing....

"So sorry. I'm so clumsy," was all Kitty could say as their lips drew level.

The corners of his mouth twitched. "Been hanging out with many sailors lately?" he said quietly, his soft breath brushing her cheek.

"Shit! I'm sorry for my language," she said, wincing at the irony of her statement.

"I've heard worse," he said. "Shall we do it?"

Kitty's eyes widened.

"Do it?"

"Take a swim," Josh said.

"Oh, yes. Take a swim. Sure, you go first."

Kitty breathed out the minute he turned away. What the hell did she think he meant, for goodness' sake? And why had she suddenly turned into a gibbering wreck unable to form proper sentences?

Taking a few more steps into the river, Josh dived straight into its cool depths. The sight of his body slicing through the crystal water was glorious, every muscle on his hard, chiselled flesh defined in the sharp sunlight. He came up out of the darkness and pushed his wet hair back. He looked like a Greek god. Kitty licked her lips.

"I thought you were joining me?" he shouted.

"Sorry. I got side-tracked." *Very side-tracked.*

Kitty walked into the river, wading in until the gurgling

water covered her thighs. She held her breath before executing a tidy dive into the dark green water. Grateful for not belly-flopping, the river's cool tendrils wrapped around her hot skin. She stayed under as long as possible, working out the perfect angle to exit the water. If she judged it right, she'd come up with her long hair fanned out behind her. If not, she'd look more like Cousin It.

Much to Kitty's relief, her exit from the depths went according to plan, and with her hair in place, she trod water alongside Josh.

"This is amazing. Thank you for bringing me here."

A stunning grin lit up his face, and Kitty's heart fluttered.

"We can go back down memory lane if you like," Josh said. "Swim down under the bridge where it's shallow. We used to fish off the bank there. Do you remember?"

A furrow hit Kitty's brow. "I'd forgotten. But coming here brings it all back. You taught me how to spear worms on hooks," she giggled.

"Is that all you remember from my fishing lessons? Worm spearing?"

"It was memorable. And to think, you ended up being a vet."

Josh's eyes crinkled at the corners.

As they trod water together, the only sounds were the droning of the insects, the lapping of the river against their bodies, and their laboured breathing. Josh stared at Kitty, his eyes roaming her face, and she longed to ask him what he was thinking. Sucked in by the same spell, she took in the light freckles on his nose and cheeks, the droplets of water that clung to his skin, and the gentle furrow of his brow. He was like an angelic, mythical creature sent to tempt her, and she was falling for him hook, line, and sinker.

In the current, the swirling water drew them closer together, like bobbing corks in a whirlpool. Nothing Kitty did could stop it. Would she even try if she had the chance? Their bodies were almost touching now. She ached for Josh to reach out and touch her skin, to do anything. Eyes glued to each other's, they drifted ever closer, and Josh's lips parted as if he was about to speak.

A sniffing and scrabbling noise behind Josh attracted Kitty's attention. Wendy stood on the high bank, staring down at them with what looked like a giant grin. Was that even possible? Her front paws were tapping with excitement on the grass, and her back legs were bent, gearing up for movement. She was going to jump!

Josh had his back to the dog and, oblivious to what was happening behind him, reached out a hand to Kitty's face. Her eyes widened, not sure what to focus on; Josh's outstretched hand or Wendy, who looked like she was about to launch into the air.

Josh spoke. "Kitty, I..."

With enough time to act, Kitty shut her eyes, grabbed Josh's hand, and braced for impact. A shrill bark sounded out before Wendy took a flying leap, landing in the water between them. The force of her body pushed them underwater, and they all came up, a shocked, spluttering mess. Josh wiped the water out of his eyes and scowled after Wendy, who was paddling to the bank.

"Bloody dog!" he laughed. "You can't stand not being the centre of attention for five minutes!" He rolled his eyes as Wendy retreated to the side.

"Never work with animals or children," Kitty spluttered, pushing her hair out of her face. Now she *did* look like Cousin It.

Kitty's heart hammered, and she took shuddering breaths, having swallowed half the river. She wasn't sure what surprised her the most; Wendy's theatrics or that Josh had tried to say something to her before they crashed underwater. Had she imagined it? Maybe she had a leaf stuck to her face or a bit of weed. Perhaps that was the reason he'd reached out.

He'd done it before, with the paint at Thea's, but his time it was different. *Something* was different now. Sure she hadn't imagined it, Kitty searched Josh's face, willing him to start over again. Press rewind and go back to the moment he'd held her eyes and her heart in his hand. Instead, he avoided looking at her.

"Josh, what was it you wanted to say?" Kitty asked in desperation, reaching out for his shoulder as he swam away.

He didn't turn.

"It was nothing," he said, his voice tight in his throat.

Kitty's heart sank to the bottom. Really? Nothing? It hadn't felt like nothing. His eyes had burned into hers. His breath was fast and hard. But as she looked at him, Josh pulled away towards the bank, his powerful arms slicing through the water, each stroke taking him further away from her. Kitty was left cursing Neptune, Poseidon, or whoever was the God of the rivers at the fact that her hopes were scuppered.

After a slow swim back, Kitty's feet found solid ground. Half out of the water, Josh leaned over and offered her his hand with a strange look on his face. She took it, feeling his palm curl around hers, each finger and thumb leaving a print on her skin. Kitty followed him back up and out of the water, his body gleaming like gold in the sunlight with rivulets of water dripping between his shoulder blades. Just being with him was torture.

After returning to dry land, Kitty and Josh flopped onto the bank, the sand coating their backs.

"You hungry yet?" he asked as he stretched his arms over his head.

Kitty nodded, not trusting what would come out of her mouth if she opened it.

Josh undid the paper bag he'd brought from the truck and

took out two iced cupcakes decorated with ladybirds. He handed one to Kitty, and she examined it, turning it around in the air.

"Well, I *am* impressed," she said. "You're a wasted talent in the veterinary world. Did you ice them yourself?"

"Compliments of Kate."

Kitty saw a chance to reconnect with him after their disastrous swim. A chance to make him laugh. "*Sure* they are." she giggled. "You can't fool me. If you can deliver a calf, you can handle a piping bag."

Josh laughed, screwed his bun case into a ball, and threw it at Kitty. She ducked it, and it landed on the sand behind her.

"That's littering. It's a punishable offence in some parts of the world," she said, taking a huge bite from her cupcake.

"So is getting icing on your nose," Josh said as he gestured at Kitty's face. She reached her hand up to check, but there was nothing there. Josh snickered, a glow in his eyes.

Despite the disappointment of "Wendygate," this was what she loved about him. He was fun to hang out with, and he made her laugh. And okay, he was extremely easy on the eyes, but the remnants of doubt still lingered.

He'd been sketchy and absent the last couple of weeks, and she didn't know where she stood with him. It was like hanging out with a best friend, not the sexiest single vet for miles around. Thoughts of Josh had pushed everything else out of her brain today. It wasn't a good sign when she was trying to land the job of her life.

They ate the cupcakes, washing them down with the remnants of soda. Josh fed half of his to a slobbering Wendy, then turned to Kitty, who'd flipped over onto her stomach. She lay with her knees bent, swinging her feet in the air behind her.

"I've told you all about my woeful love life," he said. "Anything you want to share about yours? Put us on an even footing. I'm sure nothing can be as bad as my sorry tale."

Kitty's blood ran cold. *Great.* If it wasn't enough to burp in front of him, then be half-drowned whilst imagining he was going to make a pass at her, now it was time for the ultimate humiliation. Her non-existent love life.

"I haven't had a relationship for five years," she said, getting it over and done with as soon as possible.

Kitty scanned Josh's face for some reaction, but he just lay back on the sand.

"I'm surprised," he said. It was as if she'd announced the next day was Wednesday, not admitted to being a freak of nature.

"It really hasn't been a priority. My career doesn't leave much room for romance and all things fluffy," she said, feeling the need to explain.

The corners of Josh's mouth turned up.

"I mean, I have *had* sex," she blurted, screaming at her brain to stop her mouth from moving. "I'm not suggesting I'm easy, but I've had sex. With people I've met. At conferences." Nope, her brain wasn't obeying at all.

"I'm glad to hear you'd at least met the people you had sex with." Josh snickered. "I think it's essential unless you just skipped the formalities because of your work schedule.

"I'm so embarrassed," Kitty said, burying her burning face in her arms.

"Don't be. I'm only teasing you. I understand a job getting in the way of the fluffy stuff."

Neither of them spoke, and as Kitty's heart thumped in the heat, the song of the skylark hovering high overhead punctuated the still air. Josh looked at his watch.

"I have to get back," he said.

"What time is it?"

"It's just after five."

"Really? I need to sort out Julia's brats."

Josh's brow wrinkled.

"The goats," Kitty said. "If I don't have their dinner on the table by six pm, I'll face an organised rebellion."

Josh let out a belly laugh, its resonance making Kitty's stomach curl up in delight.

"Then I shall return Cinders to her cellar. Try not to leave a gumboot behind on the sand."

Josh stood up, and his impressive physique again dominated Kitty's view. She eyed the angular planes of his chest in the willow's shadow. When he reached down to help her, she stood awkwardly against him, the heat from his body pulsing against her bare skin.

"You okay?" he said.

Kitty took a deep breath, smothering the urge to touch his soft lips. To throw caution to the wind. Kiss him and see what he'd do. What was the use, though? She'd had a lovely day with him, but they'd been nearly naked together for the last hour, even touched, and he hadn't flinched. Hadn't let her hope for anything more than a friendship.

Instead, Kitty reflexively crossed her arms over her chest and began babbling about giving Julia's cat his flea treatment. She quickly gathered her discarded clothes and dressed as if she was escaping a one-night stand the morning after. Josh put his clothes on as well, but at a leisurely pace. How could he be so calm?

The sun lowered behind the willow tree, and they gathered their rubbish and trudged back to the truck. All Kitty wanted to do was get home and process the day with an enormous glass of self-pity.

34

JOSH

JOSH AND KITTY drove the short distance to Julia's. Wendy had showered them in a fall of sand when she'd vaulted into the middle seat. She was now crashed out, with her head on Josh's lap and her entire back half draped across Kitty, who played with her curly tail. The clammy heat clung to Josh's body. He'd left the windows down again but wasn't in the mood for singing. After they pulled up at Rose Cottage, Josh killed the engine. Both he and Kitty sat, frozen in their own thoughts.

He didn't want the day to end like this. He didn't want it to end at all. Regret tugged at his heart when he remembered the river. He wasn't sure if Wendy had hindered or helped him with her flying leap. He'd been about to tell Kitty how he felt. How much he liked her. Perhaps Wendy'd saved him from making a complete fool of himself, not to mention future heartache when Kitty left the village.

Josh sighed. Who was he trying to fool? He'd lost his nerve.

"Come in for a cup of tea?" Kitty said, snapping him out of his reverie. "I know Julia would love to see you."

Josh closed his eyes. The last thing he wanted was a hot cup of tea, but he'd gladly scald his throat if it meant more time with Kitty.

Since they'd left the riverbank, he'd been playing out different scenarios in his head. What if he spoke to Jonty and told him how he felt about Kitty? He could honestly tell him he wasn't just lusting after his cousin, and he would do everything he could to make sure she stuck to her plans. Even if it meant saying goodbye at the end of her stay. But was he prepared to say goodbye?

What if he told Kitty how much he wanted her? They could try to make the distance work if she felt the same way. It would mean a lot of travel for her. He couldn't take weekends off. There would be a lot of her kicking her heels at his cottage. But she could work if he was out on a call. He had decent enough Wi-Fi. Perhaps he could partner with another practice or maybe find a locum to take his weekend callouts.

"Josh?" Kitty's voice broke into his racing thoughts. "Are you coming?"

She was standing on the path, peering back in through the door. Wendy had stretched her long body across Kitty's seat and looked in no danger of moving. Josh nodded and got out, leaving the windows down to give her some air.

He followed Kitty up the path, resisting the urge to reach out and take her hand. His eyes stayed fixed on her now dusty gumboots and the long, lean calves they covered. A wave of nausea overwhelmed him, and he swallowed it down. If he didn't say something now, he could lose the opportunity forever.

If things went wrong, he'd just avoid her for the next six weeks. He'd become pretty good at that already. All he had to do was summon up the courage to speak.

Heat raged through his body. They'd made it to the door now, and Josh saw the window of opportunity closing. His heart was beating like a jackhammer as he opened his mouth to speak. Kitty opened the door, but before Josh could reach her, the sound of voices and laughter drifted from the house.

Kitty looked back at him, a comical, puzzled look on her face, one eyebrow raised to the sky. Josh shrugged his shoulders and followed her inside, cursing his terrible timing.

As they walked through the cottage, Josh spied one of Julia's cats high atop a cabinet, peering down at them like a waiting assassin sent to slay him before he even had time to grab the treasure.

The further they travelled towards the back of the house, the louder the voices grew. A man was talking, his words punctuated by peals of a woman's laughter. As they emerged through the kitchen and out onto the patio, Josh spotted Julia. She was sitting at the table, clutching her stomach and had tears running down her cheeks. Opposite her sat Daniel Cunningham. Josh's eyes widened, and his teeth locked together. Why was Tottenbridge's answer to Casanova here?

Daniel held a book in one hand and a glass of something clear and icy in the other. Both his and Julia's heads snapped around when they saw Kitty and Josh at the door.

"Kitty! You're back!" Julia squealed in delight.

She clapped her hands together and gestured for them both to sit down. Josh shook his head, and the look Daniel threw at him raised his hackles. It was a look of pure smugness.

"Come and join us," Daniel said, looking at Kitty with a serpent's smile.

Kitty hovered at the edge of the table with wide eyes. The shadow of the house hollowed out her cheekbones, and she looked like a Victorian street urchin in his knotted T-shirt.

"Hello, Julia." Josh bent down to give her a kiss on the cheek. "Daniel," Josh said as he nodded, unsmiling.

Kitty greeted Julia with a kiss, then walked towards Daniel. He'd put his glass and the book down and rose to greet her.

"Hello, Katherine," Daniel said, his husky tone deep. His

eyes swept over Kitty with a hunger that had Josh's gut churning. "Life out in the fields seems to suit you."

Daniel opened his arms, giving Kitty a soft kiss on the cheek, his eyes finding Josh's. She moved away from him, but he held onto her hand, sitting back down to make room for her on the bench.

"Come and sit down, darlings," Julia said. "Daniel has been the most wonderful company this afternoon, Kitty. We weren't sure what time you were returning, so he helped me sort the animals out and brought us a lovely quiche and salad for dinner."

"Not to mention plying you with gin," Josh said, eyeing the half-empty bottle on the table. He'd found his voice but hadn't liked its bitterness.

Daniel's eyes tore away from Kitty and glared at him.

"For medicinal purposes. As a pick-me-up," Julia said, her clear laugh ringing out again. "We've had a wonderful afternoon."

"You didn't mention our literary misadventures," Daniel said, gesturing to a pile of scattered paperbacks on the table. "One has to take care of both the body and mind. I've found these lofty tomes quite instructive." His eyes flashed, and he turned his wolfish smile to Kitty.

"You're reading my mum's books?" she squealed with a look of absolute horror on her face.

"Yes, and they're marvellous! You interrupted us just as Lord Anthony De Wain was confessing undying lust for a Miss Cressida Fanshaw in the formal gardens. Things were getting quite heated." Daniel's mocking tone dripped with innuendo, and Josh glared at him with open hostility.

Julia unleashed another girlish cackle and clapped her hands together. Just how much gin had she had?

"Will you join us for a chapter, Joshua? You never know what you might learn, old boy." Daniel grinned.

Josh gave an unsubtle eye roll and shook his head. He'd had enough of Daniel already.

"As much as I'd love to, I'm going. I was just dropping Kitty off."

"Are you sure you won't stay?" she asked.

Her eyes were wide and pleading, and Josh's heart sank. He would have loved to join her and Julia. But with Daniel Cunningham in the mix, he couldn't guarantee he'd hold his temper. They'd never got on, and Josh hated how he'd left a trail of broken hearts in his wake since moving to the village. If he stayed, the afternoon wouldn't end well.

"No thanks. I better get to the farm." He backed away towards the kitchen, and Kitty stared after him, her brows drawn together. She jumped up from the bench.

"I'll see you out."

"Hurry back," Daniel called after her, his sing-song tone making Josh's stomach curdle.

35

KITTY

AFTER A HURRIED WALK through the house, Kitty and Josh reached the front door and stepped outside onto the step. Boughs of honeysuckle swathed the doorway, and she breathed in its heady scent. The last of the afternoon sunlight cast a golden glow onto their skin. Kitty looked at Josh, marvelling at his beauty, even wearing the world's biggest frown. Her fingers itched to smooth the furrow at his brow away, to ask what was bothering him.

If, as she suspected, Daniel's presence irritated him, it could be a good sign. Kitty wasn't averse to encouraging just a little jealousy for the greater good. Perhaps it was just the nudge he needed.

Awkwardness filled Kitty's body, like a teenager waiting for a goodbye kiss after a first date. Clearing his throat, Josh turned to Kitty, the frown still present.

"Do you see Daniel very much?" he asked, kicking at a stone on the path. His voice was quiet, hesitant.

Kitty's heart fluttered in her ribcage. His question was as loaded as they came. He *was* jealous. All he needed was a gentle shove in the right direction, and she might be in with a chance.

"A little, I suppose," she said, a small smile on her lips. "He comes over sometimes, and then, of course, I go to the pub. We have a lot of fun."

Josh's searching blue eyes met hers, and as a million unnamed emotions flashed across his face, the bottom of Kitty's stomach took a slow-motion freefall. What was she doing? Why didn't she just deny even knowing Daniel? Trying to make Josh jealous was a crazy risk to take.

He nodded and let out a breath. "Thank you for today," he said, the warmth coming back into his face. "I'll see you soon," he said.

Kitty smiled at him. It was the last thing she felt like doing, but she was desperate to cling to the conversation and keep him there.

"I had so much fun. And thank you for your help with Diva. I may even be ready for that riding lesson soon."

He laughed. "I know, I know. I promise we'll do it."

"You're a hard man to pin down, Joshua Fox," Kitty said, looking at him from under her lashes, willing him to respond to her.

It had been ages since she'd tried to flirt with anyone, and it didn't seem to have the desired effect. He wasn't taking her into his arms and carrying her off into the sunset. His hands were in his pockets, and he was still kicking at that bloody stone on the path. Kitty didn't want him to leave. She wanted to go with him and hang out with Thea and Amelia. She needed him to know it.

Thoughts of taking Josh's face in both hands and kissing his mouth—kissing his mouth hard—filled her mind, and Kitty felt a swell of confidence in her chest. Under the promise of his lips, her breath quickened, and her body flushed with heat.

She was going to do it. She'd tell him how much she wanted

him. Blood screamed in her ears, and her heart beat hard enough to break out of her chest. But as Kitty opened her mouth to speak, without warning, Josh took her in his arms in a big hug.

His embrace was unexpected, but after her initial surprise, she welcomed the feel of his warm, hard body pressed against hers. His closeness and smell set her senses on fire, and she longed for more. She wanted his hands to move, to explore her body. Craved the mouth he'd buried in her hair to find her skin, kiss her hot neck, and bite into her.

The hug seemed to last forever, but Josh's hands didn't move. His mouth never found her neck, and he held her at arm's length when he pulled away.

"I'm sorry. That was rude and presumptuous of me," he said, looking at Kitty.

She wanted to scream that no, it was fine. In fact, it wasn't anywhere near enough.

"I just want you to know how much I value your friendship," he said. "And how much your help with Thea means to me."

Kitty's heart plummeted as the realisation kicked in. He valued her *friendship*. He was grateful for her helping Thea. There was no "Kitty, you're smart and sexy, great with goats, and I want to jump your bones." Nothing.

"I loved today," Josh said, his usual beautiful, soft smile appearing.

Kitty nibbled at the side of her lip. "I'm happy to offer my services any time," she said, her mouth feeling disconnected from her brain.

Josh gently squeezed her arms and looked into her eyes. "You'd better get back. I wouldn't trust Julia with an open bottle of gin and the company of Daniel Cunningham." He smiled and turned to leave.

Everything in Kitty's body screamed at her to stop him. To

tell him no. To keep him with her. If she could erase the last five minutes and re-record the movie, she wouldn't hesitate. Rub out her stupid attempt to make him jealous. But as Josh disappeared into the dusk, her legs wouldn't move, and her voice wouldn't come. He was in the truck now, about to turn the key and drive away.

When he started the engine, Kitty's body sprung to life. "Josh!" she called after him, but the engine was too loud, and he didn't hear her. Kitty's heart twisted in her chest, and she fought the urge to vomit. Standing motionless on the step, she watched him drive off towards the farm.

36

KITTY

When Kitty arrived back on the patio, the sinking sun was creating a magnificent light show over the fields. She slumped on the cushions of the bench, deflated and exhausted.

"Joshua cut and run?" Daniel said, tracing the patterns of his cut crystal glass with long fingers.

"He had to get back. His sister needed him."

Daniel snickered. "Of course, he's a busy man. You looked very cosy when you came in."

"Oh, Kitty and Joshua are excellent friends," Julia said, swaying in her seat.

"Is that right?" Daniel poured Kitty a glass of gin, adding a splash of tonic and a mountain of ice. "I didn't know you were close."

"We're not *that* close. We just get on." The edge in Kitty's voice was as subtle as a sledgehammer.

"You seem tired, Katherine. How about I start dinner, and you can unwind out here with Julia? From the colour in your cheeks, I'd say you'd been outside and on your feet all day."

If only he knew.

The yawning emptiness in her stomach returned when she thought of her day with Josh.

"No, you two chat," said Julia. "I'll manage. I need to re-sharpen my culinary skills. I can't rely on Kitty forever."

"You have me as long as you need me, Julia," Kitty said, absentmindedly brushing away the condensation on the outside of her glass. Kitty took a sip of her drink, the icy cool sending a shiver through her body.

"Does that apply to everyone?" Daniel asked once Julia weaved towards the kitchen and was out of earshot.

Kitty's eyes flashed up to his. The smile that greeted her was so different to the one Josh had given her. His eyes shone, full of desire, and a little smile formed on her lips. Though she hated to admit it, Kitty needed to feel wanted, and Daniel knew how to kiss her bruised ego better. Was she really that shallow?

She'd sat on the step after Josh had left, trying to work through the maelstrom of thoughts in her head. The day was so confusing. Josh was so confusing. Was she deluding herself, wasting her time on someone who didn't feel the same way?

And here was Daniel looking at her like he was starved, and she was the last pastry in the bakery. Overtly interested, charming Daniel. He made it all seem so simple.

Kitty took her glass and tipped it up, draining the contents. The sour tang of the gin hit the back of her throat like razor blades. Daniel picked up the book he'd been reading to Julia and opened it up with grand ceremony.

"Daniel, do you have to? My mum's stuff is pretty grim, and I'm so tired."

"I think you'd find it soothing if you just tried it *my* way," he said, looking as if he'd devour her given half the chance.

Kitty giggled. Something done Daniel's way would be anything but soothing. "I spent my childhood being tortured by this stuff. Can you imagine the hell I copped at school?"

Not giving in, Daniel stood up and walked behind her,

massaging her neck and shoulders with gentle fingers. Kitty melted under his expert touch. He'd done this a few million times before, no doubt. He bent down and whispered into her ear.

"Why don't you lie in the hammock, and I'll read to you."

Kitty looked up. Daniel was standing over her in the fading light, wearing a smile that would crumble anyone's best intentions. His seduction skills were top-notch, and he left her little question about what he wanted. The contrast with Josh was jarring.

Admitting defeat, she nodded. "Fine, but just don't expect me to laugh."

A grin of triumph spread across Daniel's face, and he topped up Kitty's gin and tonic.

"You must be exhausted," he said as he guided her over towards Julia's hammock. As she clutched her glass, he knelt and took off her boots, one by one. Kitty held onto his shoulder and stood on each leg while he pulled her socks off. The whole ritual of his actions was intensely intimate, and his soft fingers on her calves sent a rash of goosebumps up her legs.

"That feels amazing, thank you," she whispered.

"My pleasure." Daniel smiled as he moved her to the edge of the hammock.

"Just lie down, and I'll take care of all your needs."

Kitty sucked in a breath but was too tired to find a witty comeback. "I need a shower," she said.

"You're perfect just the way you are."

Kitty wanted to tell him that Josh said nothing had to be perfect, but as his insistent hands and low voice guided her down into the soft hug of the fabric, she couldn't summon the energy. The gin had hit her now, and Kitty's head swam.

"I smell like cow poo!" she protested, her gaze dropping.

"Not from where I'm standing," he said as he stared down at her, his eyes smouldering with longing.

Once Kitty was settled, Daniel set the hammock on a gentle rock, walked back to pick up the book, and joined her, laying on the adjoining sun lounger.

"Are you lying comfortably?"

"You know I am," Kitty murmured, struggling to find the energy to talk.

"Then I'll begin."

In the dwindling light, Kitty could see the twinkle in Daniel's eye as he read her a steamy scene from one of her mum's books. He made every single word count, rolling them around on his tongue, his cadence matching the pulse thumping in her ears.

Kitty's body, full of excitement and unrequited lust from her afternoon, was crying out for release. Her mind flashed back to the riverbank. The way Josh undressed in front of her, every moment an exquisite torture. A dull ache settled in her core as she recalled his taught, golden skin and the way the water snaked across it.

But Daniel was here, and Josh wasn't. All it would take would be one touch, one hand to stray to his thigh, and all her frustration could disappear. Daniel's body, his mouth, could mend the confusion and hurt. He'd be a willing band-aid.

But it wouldn't be right. She'd be using him, hurting herself, and it would put her past the point of no return with Josh. Why she still hung onto the hope that he wanted her, Kitty didn't know, but if she gave in to temptation, she'd never forgive herself.

Kitty glanced at Daniel, his aquiline profile catching the shadows as the sun set over the horizon. His long dark lashes fluttered as he read the words in the book, and Kitty shut her eyes to block out his beautiful, tempting face. The sexy lilt of his voice and the hot and busy day merged to create a perfect storm, and it wasn't long before she drifted off into a fitful sleep.

Kitty woke with a start. Disorientated, she glanced down to see Herod nesting on her legs, his paws kneading imaginary dough on her lap. She was still lying in the hammock, feeling sweaty and needing a good stretch.

Julia must have gone to bed and left some hurricane lanterns burning, their light casting a soft glow. A patchwork blanket covered her, and someone had laid a sprig of lavender on the cushion next to her head, its fresh smell hanging in the air.

Kitty tried to get up, but something hard pressed into her side. She reached under the blanket, and her hand touched something solid and angular. Retrieving the offending object, Kitty's hand drew out the book Daniel had been reading from.

The picture on the front showed a busty, dark-haired lady with oversized lips and far too much bronzer for Regency England. A rugged blond hero was bending her backwards over a rosebush. His oversized muscles seemed to be in the fight of their lives under his torn shirt. The castle in the background looked more Disney than highlands, and Kitty rolled her eyes at her mother's taste.

As she held the book, a piece of paper poked out between the pages. She extracted it and read its flowery script.

"My beautiful Katherine," Daniel whispered into her ear. Despite the anguish in his voice, she didn't stir from her heavy slumber. He gently traced along her fragile collarbone with his strong, thick, masculine fingers. Despite his touch, she gave him nothing. He gazed upon her innocent face. Long, dark lashes brushed freckled cheeks, and her perfect bosoms heaved steadily against her clothes. How he longed to reach down and release them from their confines. He was burning with lust for this woman. Cruel, cruel Katherine. How much longer would she keep him waiting? Under his ardent gaze, Katherine shifted in her sleep. Could he take her now? Would she end

his torture and confess her own hunger? Her soft, luscious lips parted in sleep, and when Daniel reached down to kiss them, she whispered, 'Josh.'

Sleep well, my beautiful, cruel Katherine. Until we meet again.

Kitty's breath caught.

Holy crap! What did she do?

37

JOSH

JOSH'S PHONE BUZZED, rudely waking him. He'd fallen asleep a few hours ago with the help of a bottle of red wine. The thumping ache in his head reminded him of the drawbacks of drowning your sorrows alone.

Thin morning light crept into the room, and the shrill dawn chorus beginning outside seared into his brain. Josh tried to move his legs but couldn't. He looked down at the white sheet twisted around his body. As if escaping from a straitjacket, he kicked himself free, avoiding Wendy, who snored at the end of the bed. He rubbed his eyes and picked up his phone to see a brief text from Thea.

Thea: Coffee? I'm outside.

Josh frowned. What the hell was she doing up so early? He climbed out of bed and went to the open window. Thea was standing outside his front door with a sleeping Amelia in her arms. The little girl clutched a threadbare stuffed rabbit and sucked on her thumb, oblivious to her dawn adventure. His sister grinned and shrugged her shoulders.

"Hang on a minute," Josh said.

He ran his fingers through his hair, and on hearing him up

and about, Wendy lumbered to her feet and stretched, wagging her tail in greeting. Dressed only in light grey boxers, he walked from his bedroom to the living area and unlocked the front door. Thea stepped into the room, lay Amelia on the couch, and covered her with a blanket. The little girl stirred, sighed, and drifted back off to sleep.

"You didn't come over last night," Thea said, her eyes scanning Josh's face. "And I know you weren't working because your lights were on. I thought you might have company, but then I thought, no, Josh never has company." A smile danced on her lips as one of her blonde eyebrows raised.

Without answering, Josh turned away and removed two mugs and a coffee pot from the cupboard. Wendy came wandering out of the bedroom. She nuzzled Thea's hand, then jumped up on the couch to curl up with Ammy.

"Joshie, is something wrong?" Thea said.

"No," he replied, "but I have to pee." He disappeared into the bathroom. "Turn the pot on," he shouted over his shoulder.

Josh took care of business, then set about brushing his teeth. He caught his reflection in the mirror and examined his face. The bags under his eyes reflected his night. He'd struggled to sleep in the muggy heat, his senses dulled by too much wine.

Sweaty and frustrated, he'd tossed and turned, replaying the day repeatedly in his head. Every conversation was inked into his memory. Still, he'd tortured himself with thoughts of what could happen between Kitty and Daniel at Julia's. The fact he'd come so close to telling her how he felt terrified him.

Josh walked back into the kitchen. Thea had opened all the windows, and the cacophony of the morning birds filled the room. She was busy brewing coffee on the stove, and he sat at the kitchen table. He dragged his fingers through his messy hair, examining the empty wine bottle in front of him.

"Did you have company?" Thea asked.

Josh sighed heavily. "Nope. Just too much to drink and plenty to think about."

"Why? What's going on?"

"Not here," he said, nodding towards a stirring Amelia. "Let's go outside."

Josh carried two mugs of steaming black coffee into the garden and sat beside Thea on the bench. The vapour trails from their cups curled and wound upwards through the cool morning air.

"Okay, spill the beans, little bro," said Thea.

Josh recounted the entire day. He told her about the new gum boots, the time at the dairy, their disastrous visit to Patricia's, and Kitty's courage in dealing with Diva.

"Then I took a few hours off, and we swam at the river."

Thea scoffed. "You took time off? You *never* take time off. Spontaneity strikes my all too serious brother, it seems. What caused that?"

Josh rolled his eyes, a tiny smile on his lips.

"And swimming in the river, no less. Don't tell me you went skinny dipping?" Thea giggled and took a sip of her coffee.

"No, no skinny dipping. I'll leave that sort of thing to you, dear sister. We wore undies."

Her eyes glittered with mischief. "Interesting. But this doesn't sound bad. Why the sad face and empty wine bottle?"

"I told her about Tabitha," Josh said.

"*All* about Tabitha? Meaning you left nothing out?"

"Not much. I kind of skimmed over all the worst bits."

"Oh, dear. Oh well, at least she'll know why you're...."

"So emotionally retarded?" Josh interrupted.

Thea cringed. "I wouldn't say that. I was going for 'unavailable.' The rest of the female population of this village can't work it out. Again, though, what's the problem? It sounds like a great day."

"Well, when we got back to Julia's, I planned to tell her I

wanted to be less 'unavailable.' Let her know I like her."

"Holy shit Joshie!" Thea's face shone, her eyes sprung wide, and her lips curled in a smile. "Are you kidding? Way to go, little brother! I had no idea. What did she say?"

"I didn't get that far. Kitty had a visitor waiting for her when we got back."

"Who?" asked Thea, hanging on his words.

"Daniel Cunningham," Josh said, unable to keep the sneer off his lips.

"Oh gosh," said Thea. The grimace on her face marred the sunny smile she'd worn. "What on earth was *he* doing there?"

"What do you think, Thea? Turns out they've seen quite a lot of each other."

"Are you sure? She hasn't mentioned him to me. We don't share every minute detail of our lives, but would Kitty be into someone like him?"

"Well, he can be very charming."

Thea huffed a breath. "That's one word for it. A few of my friends would describe him as insatiable. He makes Don Giovanni look like a boy scout."

Josh sighed and sipped his coffee.

"It surprised me, but she didn't deny it. I guess you don't know somebody until you scratch the surface. Yesterday was more of a deep gouge, though."

"Hence the drinking for one?"

Josh nodded, his head thumping anew.

"I'm going to assume that you like Kitty a little more than you're letting on and that she doesn't have a clue about Daniel Cunningham. When are you going to tell her?"

"I'm not," Josh said, blowing on his coffee, the pollen-laden smell of the morning competing with the thick aroma of his drink.

"But you have to. She should know what he's like."

He shrugged. "It would make me look petty. Anyway, it'd be

weird. She's got no idea how I feel."

"Are you sure?"

Josh rubbed the back of his aching neck. Thea was there for every minute of the misery Tabitha had wrought on him. Looking into her earnest face dredged up the unpleasant feelings he'd buried well.

"She's a grown woman," he said. "She can make up her own mind. If he's the sort of man she wants, that's her choice. I'm not getting involved."

"Josh, don't cut off your nose to spite your face."

He shook his head. Burying it in the sand seemed very appealing.

"He won't be able to hurt her. She's not interested in love."

"What do you mean?"

"Kitty's only here until she can get back to her career. This was only ever a stopgap. She's told me as much."

Thea straightened on the bench. "So let me get this right. You and she have talked about love and relationships?"

"A little," Josh said. "Enough to know that anything between us wouldn't go anywhere."

Her face sprung to life. "Kitty likes you?"

"I didn't say that."

"But what if she did?" asked Thea.

Josh rolled his eyes.

"Josh, look in the mirror, will you? There's not a single woman within thirty miles who wouldn't be happy to be with you if you would just talk to them!" Josh pouted his lips and put down his coffee cup. "So, let's examine this. You like Kitty. Kitty *may* like you. And now you're worried because Daniel Cunningham is, what, at her house?"

"What point are you trying to make, Thea?" Josh said, irritation creeping into his voice.

"My point is you don't know why he was there. They may just be friends, like you and she are friends. Kitty doesn't seem the type to throw herself at anyone or to be taken in by false charm. I think you'd know if she was into him."

Josh shook his head and stared into the dawn mist as it sat low in the fields.

"I can't take the chance."

His eyes narrowed. The thought of Kitty becoming another notch on Daniel Cunningham's bedpost bothered him. She was worth so much more.

"Why don't you just ask her what's going on between them? Slip it into the conversation. Then you can tell her how *you* feel about her," said Thea.

Josh looked down at his mug, rubbing at an imaginary mark in silence.

"Oh, Joshie! You're over thirty years old, and you still can't talk about your feelings with someone you actually have feelings for?"

Josh put his face in his hands, elbows resting on the table. Here he was again. It was the same old story. The thought of getting hurt crippled him. Paralysed him.

"It's not that easy. What if she looks at me like I'm bonkers? She might not be interested."

"Then at least you'd know, and you could stop this self-torture."

Josh screwed up his face.

"What's the point Thea? Kitty will leave my life in a few short weeks and get on with her own. What's the point of even telling her how I feel?"

Thea pursed her lips together. "Because heaven forbid, she might like you too. You could have a great time while she's still here. It's called 'fun' Josh. Take it from me. It's important to take advantage of all the fun available while you can. You'll have to put your heart on the line one day or end up a lonely old man."

Thea gently prodded her brother in the ribs.

"Just talk to Kitty."

38

KITTY

THE WEEK PASSED in a blur for Kitty. She'd been to London twice, overnight, and gone through a rigorous set of interviews, meeting her potential new bosses and some teams she'd work with. She was happy to return to the city but couldn't help comparing it to the country.

Surrounded by the perpetual hum of traffic, Kitty missed the bird song. She even listened out for the rooster's screeching dawn alarm each morning. Not sure what the rules were for keeping roosters in London, Kitty recorded his crow as an alarm tone on her phone. That way, she could have the best of both worlds.

Staring out of taxi windows, to and from meetings, Kitty admired the order and symmetry of the city's buildings. They were laid out like dominoes, and their uniformity was pleasing. But still, her mind drifted to the rolling hills and fresh air of the little village she'd started to think of as home.

Now back and lying in her small bed at Julia's, Kitty's mind worked overtime. The role she was interviewing for was incredible. Everything she'd always wanted. And the thought excited her during the long days in the city. Still, she had trouble summoning the same enthusiasm when she was back in Tottenbridge.

To make matters worse, Kitty hadn't heard from Josh in six long days. Not that she was counting, of course. She'd sent him an airy text the morning after their day together. He'd sent a disappointingly brief reply, but she assumed he was busy and hadn't paid it too much attention.

She'd sent him two more texts from London but had no response. Daniel's presence at her house and Kitty's over-exaggeration of their closeness were the only reasons she could find. Giant burp notwithstanding, Kitty hadn't said or done anything to offend him.

Even texting Thea had been pointless. She'd been annoyingly vague when Kitty had contacted her from her hotel to check if he was okay. As a result, she spent her nights lying awake, reliving the day she and Josh had spent together and its strange ending.

In contrast, Daniel peppered her with supportive and suggestive texts all week. He made her laugh and mad equally, but at least he was there. He'd even forgiven her for her slip of the tongue in the hammock. She'd blamed it on tiredness. He'd blamed it on rabies.

Proudly wearing her polka-dot gumboots, Kitty walked into Small Oaks farm that morning, a woman on a mission. It'd been a week since she'd been there, and today she'd decided to find Josh and ask him why he was ignoring her.

She entered the yard via the gate next to Josh's cottage, but there was no sign of him or his truck. Even his vegetable garden looked withered and scorched, a bit like her heart. Kitty wandered to the farmhouse, feeling at home in the old yard. Things weren't as tidy as she'd left them, but she let it fly.

The door to the office was wide open. Kitty was about to complain about the bags of guinea pig pellets lying abandoned on the step, but the sight of Thea sitting with her head in her hands stopped her in her tracks. Thea's shoulders heaved, and small, strangled sobs escaped from her mouth. Kitty's immediate thought was for Josh. Was he okay? Had something happened to him? Bile rushed into her throat as she approached.

"Thea, are you okay?" she asked. "What's wrong? Is it Josh?"

Thea looked up at Kitty, tears streaming down her face. She shook her head, pushing away the moisture with the back of her hand.

"No, he's fine. He's taken Ammy out with him today."

Kitty exhaled, relief washing over her. "What is it then?" she asked, massaging Thea's tense shoulders. Seeing her this upset was awful. Kitty adored her kind, crazy boss.

Thea calmed, and as her tears dwindled to an occasional sniff, Kitty pulled up a chair and sat beside her.

"What's going on?"

After taking some steadying breaths, Thea tried her best to smile.

"Sorry for being so dramatic. I've had bad news about this place. The bank is questioning our viability."

Kitty was confused. Thea owned the property, and Kitty assumed the sanctuary ticked over on donations and grants without too much trouble. There were always plenty of food deliveries.

Gathering her up and out of the office, Kitty made Thea a hot cup of tea and sat her down at the kitchen table. Each cup ring on its surface was like an old friend to her now.

"What's the bank worried about?"

Thea sighed. "We've been limping along for ages on fundraisers, and a smattering of regular donations, but the administrational side of things is a real mess. We're running out of money, and I'm scared I'll lose the whole place."

"But isn't this your family home?" Kitty asked. "Don't you own it? That must give you some comfort?"

Thea sighed and bit her lip.

"I had to take out a loan, quite a big one. Phil had little to leave us, and my family owns the farm, yes, but they don't know about the mess I'm in. Josh has been bailing me out for months, but I can't keep asking him to do it. It's not fair." Thea let out a shuddering breath, the kind that followed a good cry. "I wanted to make things a success for Phil. The sanctuary was always his dream, and when he died, it was one of the few things I had left. I feel like I've let him down, letting things get as bad as they have."

"Does Josh know how bad things are?" said Kitty, screwing up her face.

"I haven't told him everything. I don't like to bother him. He's so busy."

"But he's your brother. He'd want to know."

Thea nodded and scratched at a paint stain on the table. Kitty noticed the washing up stacked in the sink and the toys scattered around under the table.

"I need to think of ways to bring more money in," said Thea. "I need to make upgrades. The old barn is falling apart around the pigs."

"When did you last look at your processes?" Kitty asked, ever practical. "Do you have a business plan lodged at the bank?"

Thea blinked at her.

"Okay, I think it's safe to say that you don't, but you need one, Thea. You need to know how you're tracking and where you're heading."

She slumped in her chair. "I'm terrible at that stuff. I'm great knee-deep in manure but hopeless on the business side of things."

"When is Josh back?" Kitty asked, partially digging for information, partially on the hunt for a solution.

"He'll be back before Ammy's bedtime. He's taken her to the dairy farm."

The corners of Kitty's mouth curled up as she remembered Josh with his arm inside the cow. She said she'd never unsee that image. A momentary flash of worry crossed her brow.

"He's okay, isn't he? He hasn't replied to any of my texts."

Thea's face blanched.

"He's fine, just under the pump. Today was his first 'run of the mill' day all week. He knows you've been away and busy. I've kept him updated."

The placid smile on her lips seemed forced, and jitters attacked Kitty's hands as she wondered what was happening behind it.

"How did London go?" Thea asked, changing the subject.

Kitty told Thea about her time away. The job she described sounded amazing, so why wasn't the prospect as enticing as before? What she didn't describe was the terrible loneliness she'd felt when she was on her own, back at her hotel.

Daniel had been amazing. He'd checked on her often and even sent a fantastic bunch of peonies to her hotel. His flirty texts had been the only thing that kept her sane. But she'd rather have heard from Thea's brother.

Instead of dwelling on Josh, or the lack of him, a need to assist Thea grabbed Kitty. To help her write out a business development plan and save the sanctuary. It would be a way to kill two birds with one stone. She'd be helping Thea keep Small Oaks going, plus keep herself occupied until she left to go back to London.

That she may run into Josh now and then was a bonus.

After a morning of clearing and cleaning out enclosures and re-organising the food stores that'd become messy, Kitty spent an hour and a half with Thea questioning her on the minutest details about the sanctuary. They talked about her hopes and dreams to grow the place and all the limitations and potential opportunities. Satisfied she had enough information, Kitty promised she'd go away and come up with something Thea could show to the bank.

39

KITTY

THAT EVENING, Kitty had a dinner date with Daniel. They were going to a small French restaurant in the next village. He'd described the food as orgasmic. Under his persistent texting, she'd agreed to the date, and as she applied dark eyeliner to already smoky shadowed eyes, her thoughts, as always, drifted to Josh.

He hadn't contacted her. She'd given up analysing the minutiae of their last conversation. Now she was just plain cross with him. Her thoughts and stomach churning, Kitty almost stabbed herself in the eye with her kohl pencil when her phone pinged on the side of the sink.

She checked the notification, expecting it to be Daniel asking her not to wear knickers or something equally silly, but the name that flashed up on the screen had Kitty's heart skitter. With shaking hands, she opened the message.

Josh: I delivered a foal today. Thought of you.

That was all he had to say? Kitty's temper flared. He hadn't contacted her for a week after their wonderful day together, and then, when she finally *did* hear from him, this was all he had to say. Kitty replied with:

Kitty: ???

It took only seconds for him to respond.

Josh: Legs x

Did his words mean he liked her legs, or did he mean her knees were knobbly? Hoping he meant they were long and coltish, Kitty couldn't contain her smile as she stroked the screen of her phone. Maybe things would be okay. Maybe he *had* just been busy. She'd track him down tomorrow.

A horn beeped outside, signalling that Daniel had arrived, and sweeping another layer of gloss over her lips, Kitty checked out her bottom in the dress she wore. It was a black satin sheath, high-necked at the front but cut tantalisingly low at the back.

She popped her hand down on the side, balancing while she added black stilettos to her outfit. Something hard poked into her skin, and she glanced down to see her broken glasses. They'd remained on the side in the bathroom since trivia night. Kitty couldn't throw them out. It was as if they signified a part of her life, a stability to which she wanted to hang on. With a widening grin, she picked them up, threw them into the bin and walked out to meet her date.

After what felt more like a ride in a rocket than a car, Daniel drove them into the restaurant carpark and turned off the engine.

He liked to go fast in more ways than one.

Daniel activated the roof to retract over them, and Kitty ran her fingers through her hair to remove the tangles created by the wind. She wrote a mental note to herself to bring a sleek 1950s headscarf or even a beanie when travelling with Daniel Cunningham.

He walked around the car and opened the door for her,

taking her hand and helping her out of the low seat. His eyes glinted with delight as they wandered over her in the moonlight. A wave of satisfaction washed over Kitty. At least *somebody* appreciated her.

Kitty's heels crunched across the gravel, then into inside the beautiful restaurant. The Maître D', obviously knowing Daniel, fell over himself to accommodate them. He showed them to a secluded table at the back of the room. The lighting was low and sensual, and each table held a delicate vase of irises and a long thick candle. Kitty's gaze landed on it immediately, and noticing, Daniel cocked an eyebrow.

"It's a bit on the small side, wouldn't you say?"

Kitty's eyes grew wide. *Damn*, he was starting the smut offensive early. She'd hoped they'd make it to dessert before the innuendo started. But then again, she was on a date with Daniel Cunningham. Why was she surprised?

They began the evening with champagne and canapes. Kitty was ravenous, having forgotten to eat earlier. Daniel, as attentive as usual, made a great show of appreciation for her dress. As they'd entered the restaurant, he'd traced a hand down her back, between her shoulder blades, sending an electric shiver through her body. Nobody had touched her with such sensuality for years.

Kitty found it hard to believe this sexy, confident man was on a date with her. She still couldn't entirely lose the picture she had of herself: *Clumsy Kitty* with the heavy glasses, the obsession with order, and a hatred of mud. The girl least likely to be propositioned at the office Christmas party.

Daniel ordered for them both, something that Kitty would never typically allow. She was far too much of a control freak. When the food arrived, though, it was, as he promised, orgasmic. However, the portions were small, and Kitty made sure not to load up on too much champagne.

After four delicate courses, they ended their meal with a

decadent dessert wine. Daniel gazed into Kitty's eyes as he poured their drinks and picked up her hand, massaging its palm with his thumb. Perhaps it was the champagne, but Kitty found the continuous, circular motion arousing, and a hot ache grew between her legs. If nothing else, Daniel had magical fingers.

"You look beautiful this evening. So sexy," Daniel purred, brushing a strand of her long hair behind her ear.

Kitty looked into his clear, dark eyes and died a little inside, wishing she was sharing this evening with Josh instead. She wasn't sure this restaurant would be his style, though. He'd be more at home with a pizza and a bottle of wine in front of the TV. Her lips curled at the thought.

"What?" asked Daniel, searching her face.

"You don't brush up too badly yourself," she said. Although he knew that already, he seemed content with her answer.

Kitty removed her hand from Daniel's and laid her hands to rest on the white tablecloth. She had to give this night a chance without her attention wandering off to thoughts of Josh. She owed it to Daniel. He'd been there for her when it mattered. He understood her and supported her drive to get the new role. More importantly, Daniel made her feel wanted.

"I've been thinking," he said softly. "When you return to London, you'll need someone to massage your feet at the end of a long, hard day."

Where was he going with this? He'd put emphasis on the words 'long' and 'hard', so it was bound to be a destination below the belt.

"I mean, you wear very, very high heels in the office, don't you? I'm just offering my services."

Kitty recalled the way he'd removed her gumboots at Julia's. The slow care and attention he'd given to each foot. She'd never experienced anything like it before, but she hadn't minded it, either. Quite the opposite.

"I'm sure Amber could hold the fort if the need arose," he said. "I could be there in a couple of hours. It could become a regular thing."

It took Kitty a few moments to realise he was discussing the future. The future when she was back in London, smashing out long days in the office, and he was miles away in Tottenbridge. She hadn't ever factored Daniel into her post-goat-wrangling life, and his suggestion jolted her. Did he think they had some sort of future together? She was sure it wouldn't ever be marriage and children, but his serious expression set off butterflies in her tummy.

"I only wear heels to intimidate little men in meetings," Kitty said, attempting to steer him off the subject. "At my age, I need to think about arthritis and bunions. High heels aren't conducive to healthy feet."

He picked up her hand again and ran his thumb along the back of her knuckles.

"With your legs, even a pair of Crocs would look sexy. Particularly teamed with the right underwear."

Kitty's cheeks simmered under his stare. He really knew how to speak to her baser sensibilities.

"I have something very special to ask you this evening," Daniel said, an enticing glint in his eyes. "Now you've lived in the village for a few weeks. I think you're ready."

"Ready for what? The next Women's Club event?"

"Alas, no. Even I can't pull those strings, but I think you're ready for the splendour of the Tottenbridge Annual Cricket Match and Ball." Kitty giggled, and Daniel gave her a disapproving look. "I've weighed the pros and cons up carefully, and I think, with the perfect chaperone, you'd survive the experience intact." His eyebrows lifted, and the dirtiest of smirks grew on his lips.

"And I suppose you'd be the perfect chaperon?" Kitty asked.

"Well, if you hold my bat at morning tea and don't upset my stumps, I think we'd rub along nicely together."

Kitty dissolved into peals of laughter. She could always rely on Daniel's dirty humour to cheer her up.

"Don't mock. I'm deadly serious. Every year, Tottenbridge's finest young bucks turn out to trounce the elderly gentlemen in a game of cricket. It really is quite a spectacle for the ladies." His eyes twinkled in the candlelight. "Naturally, as star batsman for the Young Guns, I have a reputation to uphold. And you, young lady, will do nicely."

Kitty beamed at him. He was really winding this whole invitation up. "Is it really such a big deal?"

"It's the jewel of the social calendar for miles around. The actual match is just a formality. What really matters is the opportunity to get very drunk and unnecessary with yours truly at the ball afterwards. And come to think of it, the Women's Club does host it. It could be your last opportunity to dazzle them. Lifetime membership beckons!"

Kitty tipped an eyebrow to the sky. "Did you say you'll be playing for the elderly gentlemen's team?"

"Steady," Daniel said. "They prefer to be called The Veterans. Far more dignified. To be honest, it's probably one of my last years on the Bucks team, so I plan to go down in a blaze of glory with the most beautiful woman in Tottenbridge on my arm."

As Daniel spoke, he continued to draw his thumb across Kitty's knuckles, and each sensual, seductive stroke made her toes curl. Being out with Daniel was like dating the big bad wolf.

Kitty ordered coffee, and declining a cup himself, he leaned in towards her.

"I think it's time for me to whisk you back to my place and ravage you," he said, his smile dripping with desire.

Kitty sucked in her lips. "No ravaging tonight," she said. "I have my last interview at ten thirty in the morning, and I need to be on the ball."

Daniel pouted like a spoiled child. "I won't say I'm not disappointed, but at least it's a reasonable excuse. How about a glass of wine instead? I promise I'll have you back home by the time the clock strikes midnight."

"No. I need time to prep, and I can't go into the Zoom meeting looking like I've had one too many the night before."

Daniel cocked his head to the side. "I could think of things I'd rather be doing than prepping you, but if anyone could wing an interview, you could. Go on, live a little."

She was well prepared, and the interview felt like more of a formality than anything. Kitty looked into Daniel's eyes, their fire promising far more than friendship and a quick glass of wine. Why shouldn't she have a bit of fun? She'd only have one glass and then walk home. If she was in bed by twelve-thirty, she'd be fine.

"Okay then. But if I don't get this job, you'll have to hire me in the pub until I find another."

Daniel smiled. "You'd look fantastic pulling a pint, but you'd be far too distracting for me. Come on, let's go."

Daniel stood and guided Kitty's chair away. His warm breath was at her ear as she stood up, and he inhaled deeply. "You smell incredible," he whispered. "It's all I can do to stop myself from devouring you right here in front of everyone."

Words caught in her throat, and as his breath tickled her skin, her nipples hardened against the silk of her dress. Worried someone would notice, she glanced around her, left and right, unsure which way to turn. A smiling Daniel caught her hand and drew her in closer.

"You can't escape me, Kitty. I will have you." His soft lips brushed her cheek. The shivers that erupted across her skin and the tingle that sprung at her core would have sent one of her mother's heroines to the nearest nunnery. But Kitty stood still, enjoying the sensations. It'd been so long since a man had desired her like this. *Damnit,* she was lonely. Why shouldn't she enjoy Daniel's attention?

After settling the bill, they stood chatting with the manager. As they spoke about wine and brandy, Daniel reached out his arm and, trailing it around the bare skin of Kitty's back, rested his warm palm on the silk just above her buttock. Once again, he circled his thumb slowly against her skin, and the delicious ache in her core returned.

Kitty's breath quickened. She turned to look at him, and Daniel gazed back, his lips slightly curved. Nobody had made her feel like this in a long time, not even Josh. Daniel's touch was bringing her back to life.

When they left the restaurant, stepping into the hot air of the summer evening, Kitty turned to him

"Thank you for a lovely evening," she said.

"It's not over yet. I have a beautiful bottle of red with our names on it."

Kitty's lips opened to remind him she had to be up early, but he shook his head and fished out the car keys from his pocket.

"Have no fear," he said. "You'll leave my place within the next hour and a half with your dignity intact, along with my erection, unfortunately. You'll be the death of me, Katherine. Promise to put me out of my misery soon."

Rolling her eyes, Kitty suppressed a grin. She moved to the passenger side of the car and waited to get in. Daniel hadn't pressed the button to release the lock. Instead, he strolled to her side, his handsome face in shadow. Kitty held her breath as he drew nearer.

"I've spent the entire evening battling to keep my hands off you. That dress..." He smiled, his eyes full of fire. "In that dress, I'd be your slave." He grinned, taking her hand in his and kissing the inside of her wrist. "Would it be okay if I kissed you?"

He was so close to her now that she could feel his body heat through the silk she wore. She bit her lip and closed her eyes. What if she let him kiss her, opened her mouth to him, and who knows what else? It could be amazing, but something unspoken ached in her gut and held her back. *Josh.* She hadn't had a chance to speak to him about the way he'd left Rose Cottage. To confirm, even for herself, that he wasn't interested. Regret was a terrible thing to carry, and Kitty had no intention of adding it to her baggage.

She couldn't even spend one evening with Daniel without thinking of Josh, wishing she was with him instead. Dishonesty wasn't fair to either of them. She opened her eyes.

"Daniel, I..."

Kitty watched as his face fell and the hunger left his eyes. He stepped away from her.

"Still not quite on the same page?" he murmured. "What's stopping you?" he asked, rubbing his forehead. His face was a picture of rejection, and as he backed away from her, Kitty moved to follow him, reaching out for his hand.

"I honestly don't know," she lied.

Daniel looked at her, his dark brow furrowed. He looked like a child whose candy was taken away, and a burn filled Kitty's gut. She wasn't being fair. She wasn't giving him a chance.

"Can I still come for that drink?" she heard herself say.

Daniel eyed her through narrowed lids.

"Please don't play with me, Katherine."

He bent down and kissed the top of one lightly freckled shoulder, unlocked the car and opened the door for Kitty. Stunned, she slid into the seat, not sure what would happen when she entered Daniel's lair.

40

KITTY

By the time they arrived at Daniel's flat, Kitty already had misgivings about agreeing to join him. Could she trust herself to have a drink, then cut and run when Daniel whispered sexy suggestions in her ear?

His door was part of the facade of the antique shop on High Street. Bright red and ornately carved, it stuck out like a sore thumb in the quaint village of Tottenbridge. He fumbled with the key in the lock.

"I'm more pissed than I thought. Probably shouldn't have driven."

He opened the door and led Kitty up a steep set of stairs.

"Why don't you live at the pub?" she asked.

"And have Amber keeping tabs on my every move? She lives there. It would be like living with my mother. I'd never be able to breathe. Besides, it's embarrassing for somebody our age to still be living at home."

Did he just make a dig at Josh?

At the top of the stairs, Daniel opened a second door, and they stepped into his flat. His sitting room was larger than she'd expected. Muted colours filled the walls, accented with cream.

Two standard lamps provided the light, and a large leather couch dominated the room, along with a pile of cushions on the floor next to a coffee table. Kitty wandered over to a cabinet, its shelves brimming with books.

"I didn't know you enjoyed reading?"

"Don't you remember? I loved reading your mum's stuff."

Kitty's brow creased.

"I'm just kidding," he said. "I don't read much. It just makes me look smarter."

"You are smart."

"But not as smart as you, my beautiful Katherine." He took her hand. "Your brains turn me on. However, there seem to be some gaps in your education. Let me get that wine, and I can provide you with a lesson."

He disappeared into the kitchen, and Kitty found the bathroom. It was smart with a beautiful, standalone roll-top bath with clawed feet. She appreciated the simplicity of the room and the lack of clutter. She'd tidy her own bathroom at Rose Cottage in the morning.

In the morning? Did she hope to expect to spend the night? The thought terrified her, but here she stood in his apartment, against her better judgement and not exactly nipping Daniel's advances in the bud. Bile rose in her throat as she looked at her flushed face in the mirror, not recognising herself. She swallowed it down and washed her hands.

When Kitty returned to the lounge room, Daniel sat on the floor against the large cushions, rolling a joint. The bottle of wine lay open and poured on the coffee table. Kitty kicked off her shoes and joined him, a tight smile on her lips. He lit up the joint, took a deep drag, and offered it to her. She hesitated.

"It's okay," he said. "It'll help you relax."

Why the hell not? Kitty hadn't smoked since university and then only once. She didn't like the lack of control. It had certainly loosened her up that night, though. It was the night she'd lost her virginity, seduced at a party by one of the smartest and sexiest guys on her course.

She'd later found out that it was a dare to see who could score with the plain, quiet girl. She'd wiped the sniggers off their faces at graduation, though, when she'd taken top honours and landed the best job.

Kitty eyed the joint, then took it from Daniel. Just one drag. She'd still be fine for the interview. The smoke hit the back of her throat, and Kitty's eyes watered. She resisted the urge to cough her lungs up and held the smoke down for a while before finally blowing it out. Her head spun, and she lay back on the cushions.

"Steady on," Daniel purred, a provocative smile on his lips. She took another drag and passed it back to him. As he drew on the joint, its tip glowed a bright ruby colour, and she examined his face in the haze of smoke that escaped.

It differed from Josh's in every way. Daniel's dark, slicked-back hair never seemed out of place. Strong eyebrows framed intense eyes that were fringed by thick, ebony-coloured lashes, and shadowy stubble clung to his hollow cheeks and defined chin. His angular features provided him with jaw-dropping beauty. He wasn't Josh, but damn, he was hot. Daniel placed the joint in the ashtray and rested his head on his hand.

"You know, I've wanted you since the first minute I saw you," he breathed. "If I'm full on sometimes, I'm sorry. It's just needing you this much is torture." Daniel's hand reached towards Kitty, and his fingers gently brushed her hair. Each stroke sent her deeper into his hypnotic eyes, and the pull of his lips, so close to hers, was magnetic. "You look incredible right now. You don't know the effect you have on me," he whispered.

He stopped stroking her hair and gently picked up one of her hands, his voice low and husky. "I want to please you, to show you how much I want you." Daniel brought Kitty's hand to his mouth and kissed the inside of her wrist, just like he had earlier. Hot lips against her pulse, his stubble engraving her skin. When she didn't pull away, he intertwined his fingers with hers.

Kitty stared into Daniel's eyes, exhausted. She only wanted to see and feel Josh, and her body burned with desire for his touch. Kitty closed her eyes and pictured his face, her mouth curling into a contented smile. Without him here, her imagination would have to do.

Daniel kissed her neck, soft lips mixed with the drag of his stubbled skin. Kitty's nipples hardened against the silk of her dress as his kisses crept down to her shoulder. With her eyes shut tight, she pretended it was Josh. She could see him, smell him, and believe it was *his* body next to hers. Fingers nudged her dress aside as warm lips glanced against her collarbone.

Letting out a small moan, Kitty turned her head towards her lover and found his mouth, kissing him hard, tongues searching each other. Giving in to her pent-up need was the only thing she could think about.

She was doing the wrong thing with Daniel. Using him. But she didn't care. She'd just keep telling herself it was Josh.

Daniel moved on top of her. His breath came fast, and his hardness pressed against Kitty's thigh. She moved her hand under his shirt, across his hard midriff, and curled her fingers around his back, pulling him closer.

His fingertips were at her breast, brushing her hard nipple through the fabric of her dress. With a sigh, Kitty dug her fingers into his skin, dragging them across his back. Blood pounded in her ears, and her heart thundered as she pressed her full lips against his, their tongues dancing together.

Daniel's hand moved to her knee as it inched up the silk of her dress, bit by bit. Higher and higher, it travelled, caressing the inside of her thigh, teasing strokes expertly placed. When his fingers reached her aching core, Kitty took a sharp intake of breath,

"Oh, Josh," she moaned.

Her words stung the air, like an assassin's knife, straight at Daniel's groin. He rolled back from her as if he had been scolded, his eyes burning with horror.

"Oh, for fuck's sake!" he roared.

Kitty looked up at him with stunned, wide eyes, not believing what she'd done. What she'd said. She scrambled up the cushions to rest on her elbows, her breath coming in quick gasps. Daniel threw himself back against the bottom of the couch like a sulky toddler. He took a slug of his wine, appraising her through narrowed eyes.

"Daniel! I'm so sorry! I don't know what I was thinking."

"I'd rather *not* know what you were thinking," he spat.

"Oh, crap. What a mess," said Kitty, her head in her hands.

Daniel narrowed his eyes. "Dr Fox got under your skin?"

"Something like that," she mumbled. Kitty sighed. It felt so nice to admit it to someone, even if that someone was the man she'd just humiliated.

"I can't say I'm surprised," Daniel said, pouting. "I mean, he only needs a red cape and a hammer, and he'd have a successful career in Hollywood. Plenty of women have made fools of themselves over him. I only hope you have more luck."

Kitty grimaced. "It's not like that, Daniel."

"Oh, so there are feelings?" he asked.

"I'm not sure," she said.

"Well, I only hope you have a strong constitution. He's a tough nut to crack, according to Amber. She didn't get him past first base."

Kitty scowled, but Daniel continued.

"That's two times you've let his name slip in inappropriate circumstances. It's brutally clear that it's *him* you want, not me." Daniel reached over and drained his glass of wine.

Kitty drew her knees up to her chest, wrapping her arms around them.

"I don't know what to say. You're amazing. You're everything a woman could want...."

"Except the woman *I* want. This isn't helping me feel better, Kitty."

She bit her lip. "I think it's best if I just go home."

"I'll drop you," Daniel said, getting up from the cushions.

"I can walk."

"No chance. We can't have you crushing any more hearts in the moonlight."

Kitty thought back to their walk through the village on trivia night. He'd been there for her from the moment she'd arrived, even if his motives had been murky.

"Can we still be friends?" Kitty said. "I know I don't have the right to ask, but you make me smile."

Daniel sneered. "If the role of tragic clown is all I'm being offered, I'll take a rain check. Come on."

Daniel stood and turned to leave, and Kitty got to her feet to follow him. By the time they reached the street, she'd sobered up. By the time they made it to Rose Cottage, Kitty was full of panic about her job interview. The last thing she needed was what happened this evening distracting her. What had she been thinking? Kitty undid her seatbelt as they sat in the car outside Julia's.

"Crap. What if I stuff up the interview? I should never have come back to yours. Again, I'm so sorry."

Daniel sighed, his chiselled cheekbones shadowed in the streetlight. You're still not making me feel any better. You'll be fine. In fact, you'll kill it. Now, go, get some beauty sleep," he said, not meeting her eyes.

Kitty climbed out of the car and closed the door. Just as she turned to head up the path to Julia's, the window of the car wound down. Kitty turned back to see Daniel leaning over the centre console.

"I just thought of something," he said. "A bit of a tip for your interview."

"Yes?" said Kitty.

"Just try to get everyone's names right, and you'll have nothing to worry about."

With that, he gave her a rueful wink and drove away.

41

DANIEL

THE NEXT MORNING, Daniel sat at the bar, nursing a very strong coffee while Amber crashed around him, moving boxes of glasses out of the storeroom. The Five Bob was running the bar at the cricket ball, and Amber had the bit between her teeth. Was she trying to make as much noise as possible?

He'd spent most of his night ruminating about Kitty's slip of the tongue and her outright rejection of him. She'd bruised his ego more in the last week than anyone had in the last ten years.

"Amber!" he shouted. "Please. I'm trying to languish in self-pity over here."

Amber strolled into the bar and stood with one hand on her hip. Daniel took in her ample curves and how her unruly curls attempted to escape from her ponytail. She stood in a pool of light that made it through the window. It lit up the scattering of freckles on her nose, and his irritation melted under her steady gaze.

"Like that, is it? I didn't like to ask, but you rarely make it in before midday, and that coffee looks strong enough to stand up a spoon in."

Daniel sighed. "You have no idea."

The corners of Amber's mouth twitched, and her eyes danced with amusement.

"Oh, dear. Don't tell me you crashed and burned with Rapunzel of Rose Cottage again?"

"That's one way to describe it. Honestly, I don't know what I'm doing wrong."

Daniel looked down at his cold coffee and then checked his watch. It was eleven in the morning. Well, the bars were open somewhere in the world.

"Fancy a drink?" he said.

Amber tipped her head to one side.

"Not for me, but I'll keep you company."

She walked around to the other side of the darkened bar and, extracting Daniel's usual bottle of brandy, added a generous amount to a freshly polished glass. Pushing it towards him, she leaned one elbow on the surface between them.

"So, what happened, Tiger?"

"I crashed and burned, as you so decorously put it. I wined and dined her and said all the right things. I swear, at one point, she was going to melt into a puddle, but when the moment came—when we were really into it—she forgot my name and said someone else's.

Amber's face screwed up into a grimace. "Ouch! Dare I ask who's?"

"Joshua bloody Fox. The monk of Tottenbridge."

Amber sucked the air in between her teeth. "That makes sense. He's way more her style. No offence, Daniel, but she's always struck me as too wholesome for you."

"What do you mean? I'm everybody's style, you know that. One only has to try a small sip to want an enormous glass of this." He drew his arms down over his body, and Amber erupted into giggles.

"Apart from her," she said.

Daniel huffed, his body slumping into the bar stool.

"Apart from Kitty."

Amber's eyes sparkled. "I mean, how could she resist?"

"Precisely. In all seriousness, though, I'm at a loss for what to do. None of my usual tactics has worked. I've never tried so hard."

"Maybe that's a clue for you. But why do you care so much? I've never seen you fretting so hard over a woman before. Usually, it's onwards and upwards and into the knickers of the next."

Daniel gave Amber a withering look.

"Maybe I've turned over a new leaf. Hung up my raffish ways."

"I seriously doubt that, darling. She's got under your skin, that's all. It's like a cold. You'll get over it."

"I don't want to get over it." Daniel took another sip of his drink.

"Well, I can't stand you mooning around here anymore. If you're going to come to work early, at least make yourself useful and order some wine. I'm going to check the champagne delivery."

Amber reached out and gave him a friendly clap on the shoulder.

"You'll be fine."

She walked away towards the bistro room, and Daniel drained his glass. If he was going to be okay, why did he feel so terrible? Usually, if someone was such hard work, he'd lose interest, but nobody had ever challenged him the way Katherine Cameron did. There was something different about her.

He'd thought it was because she was unattainable, but now he wondered. Was it more? Could he have feelings for her? All he knew was he couldn't stop thinking about the time they'd spent together, and the thought of her with Joshua Fox made his blood boil. He needed to convince her to give him another chance, but how?

Kitty still wanted to be friends. Okay, he could be a good friend. That seemed to have worked for the vet.

Daniel reached into his pocket and brought out his phone, sending a text to Kitty.

Daniel: I'm sorry for being a selfish prick last night. I'd love to stay friends. But I have a favour to ask. Still come to the ball with me? I need you to make me look good. D x

He hit the send button and thought of her face. The memory of her body lying under his. Last night, in her dress, she looked devastatingly gorgeous, and she'd wanted his touch in the restaurant. But then...the insult she'd delivered. What was a man to do?

Daniel's phone buzzed on the bar, and Kitty's name flashed on the screen. The speed of her reply was a good sign. She must be about to start her final interview. That he was in her thoughts in the middle of a momentous occasion pleased him.

Kitty: Sure. I'll still go with you. I'm sorry, too. x

A smile grew on Daniel's lips as he put his phone on the bar. He was officially back in the game, and he'd drawn the score level.

42

KITTY

THE DAY of the cricket match began in a dewy haze. Kitty woke as the sun inched towards the orange horizon. She crept downstairs, careful not to wake Julia and the cats, and made a strong coffee. The thick brown liquid dripped into the cup, and her body tingled with trepidation.

Last night, she'd received the news she'd been waiting for. Wilbur Reed offered her the job at a far higher salary than she'd imagined. The firm wanted her to start orientation in the next couple of weeks.

It was time to leave Tottenbridge.

She'd called her sister to tell her the news. Ronnie was ecstatic for her, planning where to go apartment hunting and shopping trips to update her corporate wardrobe.

"You're getting just what you wanted! All that hard work has paid off. And think, no mud under your fingernails!"

Her sister beamed at her on the screen and asked her a million questions. Kitty just wanted to talk about the sanctuary and Josh. She hadn't, of course, but even amid her ultimate triumph, he was all she thought of.

She'd seen him only fleetingly in the last few days, and his texts had been short and sketchy. Kitty sighed and pulled her hair in a rope over one shoulder. After the events at Daniel's, she'd hoped something would happen. That fate was going to smile and deliver her a happy ending. However, Josh was a fly in the ointment, and she longed for the days when they'd chatted easily and laughed until their faces ached.

Thea said he was playing in the match today, so a tiny firefly of hope buzzed in her chest. At least she'd get to spend the day looking at him.

Kitty hadn't bothered to get dressed. Who else would be up this early to notice? She gripped the cup of fresh coffee and stepped out into the garden, wearing a pair of tiny black knickers, her pink wellies and Josh's T-shirt, still tied up at her waist. She slept in his T-shirt every night.

As she wandered down the path, running her fingers through the fragrant lavender, Kitty came to the wildflowers near the stone wall. She stood, taking in the glorious dawn as the dewy grass kissed her knees. She'd miss everything about Tottenbridge. Last night, excitement filled her, but now her energy flatlined.

A sudden warmth hit her skin, and Kitty turned to see the sun emerge over the rolling fields. She breathed out and submitted to its warming, golden glow. Drawing on its energy, she could feel herself powering up in its rays.

43

JOSH

JOSH WAS UP EARLY. He'd spent a wasted evening at the pub attending a Young Guns warm-up event hosted by Daniel. After they finished the tactical discussions and decided on the batting order, Daniel took charge, taking bets on the outcome and urging everyone to drink all the alcohol in the pub.

Heavy drinking wasn't the best tactic before a match, but even Josh had joined in. Daniel was on form but looked at the door each time it opened. He wasn't the only one. Every time Josh heard its familiar swish, he hoped to see Kitty. She never came.

Daniel was unnervingly friendly, disarming him with his legendary charm. He'd obliged him last night but wasn't sure he could maintain the pretence. When he looked at Daniel, he only saw green.

Although he presented a calm demeanour to the world, Josh was in absolute torment. His attempt to distract himself with work had failed, and he'd spent most evenings moping around at Thea's. He'd asked her not to say anything to Kitty. He preferred to ride out the time until she left Tottenbridge, keeping a low profile. Self-preservation. Thea had agreed but imposed a rule of her own. If she couldn't talk to Kitty about Josh, it was only fair it should work the other way around.

Josh spent yet another sleepless night thinking about her. He now found himself out before dawn, running off his frustration. An overwhelming need to be near her guided his feet, and he ran toward Rose Cottage, unsure what to do once he got there.

The sun had come up, and as he approached the house, a lone figure stood in the garden. *Kitty*. Her long, long hair, crumpled from sleep, hung down at her waist, skirting the hem of his old T-shirt. He'd forgotten, and now she wore it, still knotted just above her tummy button. The sun's early rays hit her flat, brown stomach and skimmed down her endless legs. She reminded him of a sunflower, standing still and tall, eyes closed in the blinding, golden light.

Josh's breath caught, and he broke his stride, slowing down. She looked so peaceful. He felt like an intruder. He had time to leave and turn back, but a boisterous Wendy had other ideas. She bowled straight through a gap in the gate, barking at the top of her lungs. Kitty startled and staggered backwards to prepare for an incoming dog-shaped missile. She steadied herself just in time and caught a hurtling Wendy in both arms.

"Slow down!" she shouted.

Kitty laughed as Wendy covered her legs with a shower of excited licks and wriggles. Josh took out his ear pods and ambled to the garden wall. It was a solid stone barrier between them. He leaned on the gate, trying to look as casual as possible. Feeling anything but.

Kitty saw him and glowed a beautiful pink as she walked towards him, pulling down on her T-shirt. Her beauty took his breath away. Why the hell had he stayed away?

"Hello, stranger. How've you been?" she asked.

Wretched for not seeing you didn't sound very casual, so

instead, he kept things vague. "I've been good. A little busy, though."

"I see," she said, her brow creasing.

If she was going to give him a piece of her mind for his behaviour, he deserved it. Avoiding her had been rude and arrogant. A hot burn rose in his chest, and he swallowed down hard. He'd never dare to tell her why.

Just then, Wendy spotted a rabbit and tore down the paddock to chase it, her shrill barks echoing off oak trees that ran along the garden. Grateful for the distraction, Josh smiled.

"We missed you at the pub last night. You didn't feel like coming?"

Kitty bit her bottom lip. That was her tell. A little clue that she was thinking hard. He had spent an unhealthy amount of time figuring out little things like that.

"I felt a bit off. I couldn't drag myself off the sofa," she said.

It was probably a lie.

"Well, you missed the beer pong tournament to end all beer pong tournaments. Don't blame me when your form drops off."

The corners of her mouth lifted. "Ha! Sounds like it was a good night to miss. But beer pong? Really?"

"Blame your friend, Daniel," Josh said.

Kitty's face clouded, and her lips pursed together. *Great.* In just one throwaway comment, he'd opened a chasm between them.

"What time are you heading to the match?" Kitty asked, her face pinched.

"The game starts at ten. You?"

Josh cringed inside. Could their conversation be any more stilted? Kitty shook out her hair, then wrapped her arms around her waist. The smell of spring flowers reached Josh's nose, and he battled the urge to reach out and tangle his fingers in the long, dark strands. He ached to touch her.

"By the looks of the kitchen, Julia is feeding the entire village. We're moving quiches and cakes down a few hours in advance," said Kitty, a mischievous smile lighting up her face. He'd missed that smile.

"Need any help?" he asked, hoping she'd take up his offer. Even if she ignored him, she'd be near. Their awkward conversation irritated him. All he wanted to do was jump over the wall, take her in his arms, and kiss the life out of her.

"I think Jonty's helping. Thanks, though."

"Sure. Just try not to exhaust our best bowler, okay?"

Kitty's lips curled.

"I can't believe you all take this cricket game so seriously. It's weird!"

Josh smiled too. No weirder than avoiding the woman you want because you don't want to lose her. That was just crazy.

"Hey, I better get back to my pre-match warm-up," Josh said.

Kitty's eyes swept over his body, and he felt a stirring in his groin as they lingered on his chest before levelling up to meet his. *Damn*, he should have worn a top.

"Well, don't you exhaust yourself either," she said. "Daniel tells me you're the team's secret batting weapon."

Josh smiled, then glanced towards the house to see a sleepy-looking Julia emerging, complete with a head full of curlers and a cat under her arm.

"It looks like you're about to be given your marching orders," Josh said, nodding towards her.

"Oh lord, she'll have a rolling pin in my hand before I know it. 'Sausage rolls do not roll themselves, young lady'."

Kitty delivered the last line with a cracking impersonation of her aunt. Josh couldn't help but laugh and watched in pleasure as her smile grew. It was just the quirky type of humour he'd missed from Kitty.

Josh's heart hurt. Ached. He had to leave before it cracked on the hard mud at their feet.

"I better go," he said, extracting a returned Wendy from behind the gate. "I'll see you at the match."

Josh turned to walk away, feeling like the soles of his shoes were coated in glue. He put his ear pods back in, but before his music started, he heard Kitty's voice behind him.

"Josh," she murmured.

When he turned around, Kitty's face was full of worry, her shoulders tense. The hairs on his neck stood up.

"I got the job. I leave in three weeks."

In that instant, Kitty's words pulled Josh's world out from under him. His breath caught in his chest, and his heart pounded in his ears.

He'd known it would happen. That Kitty would leave, but the reality hit him like a demolition ball. A dread filled his body, and his hands gathered into fists at his sides. His brain screamed at him to say something and beg her to stay, but all he could do was nod.

"I... I'm so happy for you, Kitty. We'll all miss you," he said, forcing a smile.

Her dark eyes bore into his like she was reaching into his soul. Josh's stomach lurched. He was making this worse. He had to get away before he said something even more stupid, so he turned and ran.

He ran hard. His feet pounded the smooth tarmac of the road, and his arms pumped at his sides. His legs were heavy, but he kept running, oblivious to everything around him. Once he reached his cottage, he bolted inside and paced in the kitchen in frustration.

No matter how hard or fast he'd run, he couldn't outrun his feelings. Kitty was going, and he only had a few weeks left with her.

Josh battled to steady his breath, but nausea overtook him,

and he ran to the bathroom, vomiting in the toilet. Once the retching stopped, he slid down the wall and sat on the floor, knees to his chest, head in his hands. Regret filled his every fibre. What the hell had he done?

Josh let out a low growl. Now that the reality of a Tottenbridge without Kitty had hit, a burning need for action seized him. He had to tell her how he felt. Even if she turned him down flat, even if she was with Daniel. He had to put himself out of this misery. He couldn't live with himself if he said nothing and let her walk away forever.

44

JOSH

JOSH SQUINTED INTO THE SUN. His sunglasses were still on the top of his cap. His stint in the outfield was quiet, thanks to Jonty's bowling skills. The other team was being picked off one by one, leaving him free to think about Kitty.

Since seeing her this morning, he'd settled on a plan of action. He'd find her at lunch or after the match, and—assuming she'd talk to him—he'd tell her how much he wanted her. And if she didn't feel the same way, he'd go back to the farm and lick his wounds. It all sounded so simple. The problem was growing the balls to do it.

Another wicket fell, and yet another batsman walked onto the field to face Jonty. One of Josh's teammates called his name and pointed for him to move to a spot nearer the action. Although disappointed to be leaving the shade of the trees, he was sick of the self-pity party he was having on his own. Lowering his sunglasses onto his eyes, Josh walked towards the pitch and took his position, covering the batsman's left.

He glanced around and couldn't help but smile at the quintessential scene of rural England before him. Like Wimbledon's centre court on a rare hot day, the grass this close to the pitch was verdant green. A patchwork of picnic rugs and pastel colours at the fringes mingled with pink, sweaty skin, and sun umbrellas.

He loved his life in this little village.

Jonty was ready to begin, and Josh, needing to be far more alert this close in, bent over, ready to catch.

"Hello, old sport. Fancy seeing you here."

His head turned to find a grinning Daniel Cunningham standing a few meters away.

Awesome.

Josh wasn't interested in chatting with Daniel. He wanted to get the match done and dusted and then find Kitty.

"Looks like we're going to be working together for a bit," Daniel said. "How does it feel to be brought in from the cold? I thought you were asleep back there."

The sarcasm in his voice set Josh's teeth on edge. He shrugged.

"Perhaps you needed the help. One good thing about being on the outer fringes is you can tell who's on their game."

Daniel raised one eyebrow. "I'm always on my game. It seems to be others who drop the ball."

The grin on his face made Josh's blood boil. He was referring to Kitty, no doubt. His brow knitted together. Don't bite. It was just what he wanted. He looked at Daniel and shook his head.

"Let's get through the next few innings without talking."

"That's the spirit. Eyes on the prize, Joshua."

Jonty delivered a blistering ball which was hit far to the boundary. In the game's lull, a murmur of voices flowed through the spectators.

"Now that's a prize worth keeping your eye on," said Daniel.

Josh looked at him and followed his eyes into the crowd. Like she had a spotlight shining on her, Kitty arrived. He held his breath as she picked her way through the picnic blankets and ice buckets, her long legs glowing in the sun. She looked incredible. The white sundress she wore skimmed her thighs, and her bronzed shoulders wore her thick, dark hair like a cloak.

She carried a cooling bag in her hand, and on her feet, she wore flip-flops. From where he stood, open-mouthed, he could almost hear the clack-clack of their rubber against her feet. At that moment, all his focus was on her, his brain tracking every tiny movement of her body.

Kitty spread out her rug on the grass, sat alongside Julia and opened a bottle of something bubbly, the pop of the cork reaching his ears. She scanned the field, and the moment her eyes found him, a smile lit her face. Josh's mouth ran dry. She'd looked for *him*. Not Daniel, but him. Kitty put up her hand and gave him a tentative wave. Blushing behind his sunglasses and with a ridiculous grin on his face, Josh waved back.

Out of nowhere, a hard red sphere flew towards him. Distraction delayed his reaction, and although he got his fingertips to the ball, it sailed past him, accompanied by a cacophony of groans.

"Hey! Wake up, Josh!" yelled Jonty, a furious look on his face.

It should have been an easy catch, but it rolled to the boundary for a score of four. *Damn!* Josh held up an arm to Jonty in apology.

"Dropped the ball, eh?"

Josh's head spun around to see Daniel and his mocking grin.

"You got a problem?" said Josh.

"Not at all. I just thought that if you kept your eyes on the game, you wouldn't miss any obvious opportunities. Fumbling the ball isn't the best look."

"Go fumble your own balls, Cunningham," Josh muttered.

"I'd rather have someone else do it for me," he replied.

Daniel winked at Josh. Heat filled his body, and he bit down on angry words. It would take a superhuman effort to get through the rest of the match without throttling the smug prick.

Another cry of "Josh" rang out. This time, sharpened by irritation, his hand flew up to catch the incoming ball, dismissing the batsman. To loud cheers, his nearby teammates came up to clap him on the back and offer congratulations. All but Daniel. He took off his gloves and stood, one leg bent across the other, examining his nails.

They spent the rest of the half in stony silence. Josh kept his eyes on Kitty in between points. He loved how her face softened as she talked to Julia, and the sight of her legs as she crossed and recrossed them was the ultimate distraction.

The minutes ticked away on the enormous clock hanging on the pavilion. Josh felt every single second. He was counting down the minutes until he could speak to her. Soon enough, Jonty took the last wicket, and the game stopped for lunch.

45

KITTY

"HELLO GORGEOUS," the now familiar greeting, in its warm, low drawl, hit Kitty's ears through the hum of the crowd. She lay on the rug, not wanting to be part of the throng that moved towards the pavilion for lunch. After half a bottle of prosecco, she didn't trust her legs to get her there in one piece. Instead, she practised her defence in court, should she unwittingly trip and fall into someone's picnic: *The boredom of cricket drove me to drink, your honour.*

Kitty giggled at her joke—never a good sign—and peeled open her eyes to see Daniel. He kneeled on the rug in front of her, arms folded, his cricket shirtsleeves rolled to his elbows to reveal sinewy olive skin. *Nice.* His face wore a rakish look, and he had grass stains on his thighs.

"You're dirty," she said.

"You know better than to say things like that to me. It's only asking for trouble, and it's hardly in keeping with our new status as friends, is it?"

Kitty pushed herself up to her elbows.

"You know what I mean. Is it over?" Daniel's eyebrow raised. "The game, I mean. It's taking a lot longer than I thought."

"Most women wouldn't complain about that," he smirked.

"It's just not cricket!" she said in a plummy English accent and dissolved into fits of giggles.

"How much have you had to drink?"

"Too much, I think. The sun makes me thirsty."

Daniel rolled his eyes and offered her a hand, pulling her to her feet. She steadied against him, and the world spun. The spicy smell of his cologne mingled with the scent of fresh grass clippings, and she swallowed down the sour acid of wine.

"Let's get you some food. I think we need to find Julia. She can keep an eye on you for me."

"And I thought *you* were my chaperone?" she asked. Daniel's eyes met hers.

"Give me the opportunity, and I'd chaperone you nonstop."

"Daniel...."

"I know, just friends. Message received loud and soul-crushingly clear."

After making slow progress across the grass, they found Julia holding court at the buffet, force-feeding anyone who dared to linger too near her sausage rolls. The tables groaned under a payload of vol-au-vent and cheese straws. Kitty's head swum with all the noise and colour in the room, the ancient ceiling fans doing little to move the sultry air.

"Can you prop Kitty upright for a bit?" Daniel said, pushing her towards a startled Julia. "I need to powder my nose."

"But she was fine half an hour ago!" squeaked Julia.

"I'm fine now!" Kitty argued.

Daniel shook his head, smiling.

"Just give her some food. I'll be back."

Daniel disappeared into the crowd.

"What was that about?" asked Julia.

"Some men like to pull out before things get too messy." Kitty giggled with a snort.

"Food," said Julia sternly.

She took Kitty to the edge of the room, sat her down on a wooden chair and fetched her a crisp roll, a large mound of butter, some plump, ripe strawberries, and a large glass of sparkling water.

"Thanks, Julia. I'll be okay. It's hot out there, and I had an early start. I'll slow down, I promise."

"Stay here. I'll track down a bottle of water to take back outside," she said, heading into the milling crowd.

Kitty sat in the noise and commotion of pink-faced ladies and portly gentlemen eating pork pies and coronation chicken, picking at the roll on her plate. Her head cleared in the pavilion's coolness, and in the crowd's jostling, she was aware of a tinkling laughter somewhere to her left.

She glanced around and spotted Patricia Gore standing in a group of older ladies. She was hanging on to Josh's arm and his every word. As he spoke, though, his eyes were on Kitty, not Patricia, and her stomach fluttered when she saw them crinkle at the corners.

Kitty turned away, but in her peripheral vision, she could see Josh moving towards her. A knight in cricket whites, coming to rescue the damsel in distress. Her heart sped up as he approached, all the questions he'd left her with this morning melting away. All that mattered was being near him.

"Hello again," Josh said with a beautiful smile. "You survived the pastry delivery unscathed?"

Kitty put her plate down on the wooden floor and stood to meet him.

"I did. I even had time to make myself look respectable."

Josh's eyes took her in, deep and intense.

"You look beautiful," he said, watching her from under his lashes. "But I think I preferred this morning's outfit."

Kitty's cheeks heated as she remembered her little knickers and T-shirt combo. Was he flirting with her? He'd said things like that before, but this was different. The energy between them was different.

Jostled by a passing player, Kitty fell into Josh. He met her body with his, and his arm snaked around her waist. His fingers caressed her skin through the thin cotton of her dress.

"I've got you," he said, his voice low. His breath tickled her ear, and every nerve ending in her body awoke.

"I think I've had too much to drink," she said, turning towards him.

"Whatever you've had too much of, it suits you."

Kitty's eyes widened. He *was* flirting with her! The glow in his azure eyes was unmistakable. She'd have killed for that look over and over. Now she had it. She froze, her heart drumming in her ribcage.

They were so close. Kitty couldn't tear her eyes from Josh's lips. He hadn't let her go, maintaining a delicious steady pressure against her, drawing her into his body.

"How are you enjoying the match?" he said, the corners of his mouth lifting.

"She's enjoying it so much. She's polished off half a bottle of bubbles already," came Daniel's voice. The pressure from Josh's arm released, and they both spun around as if he'd caught them stealing cookies from his jar.

Daniel stood, one hand on his hips and a glass of icy lemonade in the other. How long had he been there? He gave Kitty a broad smile, handing her the drink.

"I believe this is what the lady ordered," he said.

Kitty took the drink while Daniel and Josh nodded curtly at each other. She glanced at Daniel and couldn't help but notice a lipstick mark on his collar.

"You've a little something on your shirt," she said with a smirk, pointing to the offending smudge. Daniel followed her finger to look down at his neck.

"Oh dear, a hazard of the job," he said, with not the slightest guilt. "Some of these older groupies are very demanding. One of them chased me across the pavilion, asking me to sample her cream horns."

Kitty smiled, knowing it was more likely to be a brush with someone far younger. She didn't care about whose cream horns tempted Daniel.

Josh stepped forward, about to speak, but a loud clanging rang in the room. It was time for the match to resume. *Saved by the bell.*

"We'd better head back out," Daniel said as he gave Kitty a quick kiss on the cheek and headed towards the bar. "Are you coming, Joshua?" he said over his shoulder.

The fury on Josh's face surprised her, but when his eyes returned to hers, the murderous look slipped away.

"I'll see you soon," he said as he headed towards the changing rooms.

46

KITTY

"How much longer?" asked Kitty, comatose with boredom at this point. Julia laughed, looking at her watch.

"At least another hour, I'd say."

"Kill me now," Kitty replied, pouring the rest of her prosecco into her plastic cup. Thank goodness she'd brought her headphones. She could at least listen to an audiobook. Reading her mum's novels at Julia's had ignited a new hobby. Right now, she was in the middle of a steamy mafia romance that would make even her mother blush.

The sun beat down hard on her skin, draining her energy. Things perked up, though, when Jonty's batting stint ended after an excruciatingly long forty-seven runs. Josh now joined Daniel as the batting pair in play. Kitty watched him stride onto the pitch, his cricket whites clinging to his powerful body and a green cap pulled low down over his blond hair. Shirt sleeves rolled up, Josh flexed and unflexed his fingers in preparation. Every muscle jumped under his skin.

Cricket suddenly got interesting.

Still none the wiser as to the rules of the game, Kitty watched from behind her shades. They could have been performing a ballet for all she cared. The athletic efforts of both Josh and Daniel were a treat to behold.

Josh was sporty, and each time he smacked the ball away from the stumps and fired up his fast twitch muscles to run, Kitty was mesmerised. His solid and sinewy arms gripped the bat hard, and his powerful legs rocketed him along. Try as she might, she couldn't erase the memory of him standing in the river in wet underwear. What she wouldn't give to relive that afternoon.

Daniel was a gritty player, full of passion and bravado. His arrogant glares at the bowler and fielders were very sexy, and he swaggered around the pitch like a rock star. Kitty didn't know what he looked like in his underwear, but with that much self-confidence, he'd be far from disappointing.

They were egging each other on, needling and supporting each other in equal measures. The display captivated Kitty. After clocking up a respectable eighty-four runs between them, the bowler changed. Within two deliveries, he got Daniel out.

He stopped to give Josh a back slap and left the pitch to the rowdy applause of the spectators. Greeted by the rapturous congratulations of his teammates, Daniel headed to the bar with a group of local youngsters. The last Kitty saw of him was his back as he disappeared into the crowd, whispering something in the ear of a giggling blonde.

Kitty turned her attention back to Josh, who was now joined in bat by a dark-haired lad who was built like a God and very popular, judging from the cheers sent up from a cohort of noisy youngsters. Shouts of "C'mon Jesse" and "Light 'em up!" accompanied applause. He, like Josh, like Daniel, was devastatingly good-looking. Who knew such a small village could have so many attractive young men in it?

The man blew a kiss to a long-haired woman in the crowd, and she blushed and blew one back in return. The glow in their faces had Kitty's insides roiling. If only Josh would look at *her* like that.

The Young Guns were only twenty-two runs off the veterans total now, and the crowd sensed victory. Six runs off, Josh took advantage of a poorly delivered slow bowl and ripped it across the field for four points. Kitty sat up on her knees, amazed to be excited by the outcome. Perhaps watching Josh had everything to do with that.

After a few bowls with no score, Josh approached his teammate, put his arm around his shoulder and whispered words of encouragement or a quick joke in his ear. Kitty's heart swelled at his kindness. He retook the crease and scored an extra run.

It was now his teammate's turn to face the music, and at one run down, the pressure was on. His fan club was chanting his name, much to the amusement of Josh, who joined in. The young man proved up to the task and became the hero of the hour when he cracked the ball over the boundary for six points to the cheers of the delighted spectators.

Josh ran over and, after giving him a big hug, lifted him up on his shoulder. *Holy crap*, Josh was strong. The rest of the team took to the pitch in triumph, and after good-natured handshakes, they walked off together towards the changing rooms. Kitty couldn't see Daniel among them, but she saw the blistering look Josh threw at her as he walked away.

47

JOSH

JOSH LEFT the changing rooms after a lightning-quick shower and some celebratory swigs of champagne. Thoughts of Daniel and Kitty flooded his head while under the hot water. He couldn't bear to see her with someone like him. The last time Josh saw Daniel, he was at the bar, swapping numbers with another woman. His arrogance was astounding.

Josh headed into the brutal heat and saw Kitty walking towards him, gloriously dishevelled. She had a light smudging of black eyeliner under her eyes and was trying to secure a bundle of hair with a pen. His lips curled.

He loved her.

Nothing else explained the crazy feelings in his body, the obsessive analysing of every conversation and the desperate craving to touch her.

Kitty had given up on her hair and let it hang around her shoulders. Kissed pink by the sun, her cheeks glowed, and she held her flip-flops in one hand, red-painted toes threading through the grass. When her eyes landed on Josh, her face lit up with a beaming smile. It was the grin that had captured his heart all those years ago. The one that transformed her entire face and rendered him a hopeless wreck. Was he ready to lose her smile again?

"Josh!" She reached out and gave him a wobbly hug. "That was awesome."

"Yeah?" At almost the same height, she fitted into his arms perfectly.

"I thought I'd hate cricket, and I did, but you made it bearable."

He grinned. "I noticed you were asleep most of the second inning."

"Not true. I was resting my eyes in between points. And now I've lost everybody," she said, glancing around them in the crowd.

"Well, you found *me*."

Kitty's smile turned into a frown, and she stared at Josh, the colour draining from her face. A faraway look settled in her eyes as if she couldn't quite see him, and her hand reached to cling to his chest. He put a protective arm around her and drew her in.

"Josh, I feel sick," she said.

Kitty brought a hand up to her mouth. With her eyes full of panic, Josh led her away from the crowd, finding a quiet spot behind a large oak tree at the edge of the field. By the time they got there, she'd gained her composure, and colour had crept back into her cheeks. Still, Kitty melted against him, and Josh's body moved to cradle hers. Having her so close was everything he wanted.

"I'm so sorry," Kitty said, burrowing into his chest.

"It's okay. I think you've been on borrowed time since early afternoon," Josh said, breathing in the scent of her hair.

"No, it's not okay. I shouldn't have drunk so much, and it's so hot."

"We all need to cut loose sometimes." Bloody hell, he could have done with it today.

Kitty pushed away from him.

"It's more than that. Josh, I..."

"What is it, Kitty?" he asked, dreading her reply but desperate to make her feel better. Was this the moment she'd tell him she was in love with Daniel Cunningham?

Kitty leaned back against the trunk of the gnarled tree. Her body swayed, and her eyelids were heavy, tendrils of long hair framing her face. At that moment, she was so beautiful, so abandoned, that it took all Josh's restraint not to lean in and steal a kiss from her soft mouth.

"It's been a big day," she said. "I just wanted you to know I meant to tell you properly. About the job. It's just I haven't heard much from you."

Josh's stomach lurched. He'd acted like such a fool. As they stood on the grass in silence, staring at each other, bright sunlight streamed down through the branches, casting their faces in a dappled, golden glow. As if in slow motion, Kitty lifted her hand and reached out to trace her fingers along Josh's cheekbone, her dark eyes full of warmth.

"You look like an angel," she said. "I think you're so beautiful, and I'd really like to kiss you."

Time and breath stopped for Josh. He stared at Kitty's full mouth, wanting nothing more than to cover it with his own. Their bodies were so close he could almost feel her heart beating, pulsing through the heavy air. He shut his eyes but could still smell her sweet perfume and hear her gentle breath. Everything he'd wanted to say had flown out of his brain, melted away by the ferocity of his desire.

His mind filled with the memory of her lying on the sand at the river, the sun kissing her skin, and her chest's slow rise and fall. If he'd been braver that day, things might be different.

The reality of how badly he wanted her ached in his chest. He needed to feel her skin under his hands and all of him inside her. Taste her sweetness and hear her sigh his name.

Josh opened his eyes, but Kitty's were half closed, fringed by heavy lids, her pupils large and unfocused. With a sigh, he smiled ruefully. He couldn't trust anything she was saying or doing right now. After the amount she'd drunk, she may not even remember they'd spoken, let alone her last words to him.

"Come here," he breathed, holding his arms out towards her. She fell into his embrace, and he wrapped around her, pulling her close.

"We need to talk." His mouth was millimetres from her ear, and he paused, taking a full breath. "I can't let you go."

"Please don't," Kitty said.

Josh buried his face in her hair. Being this close to her was intoxicating. His head swam, and his chest was so full of joy that he thought it would burst. It was the only time he'd allowed himself to believe she might want him too. That they could make a future together work.

The first time Josh's phone vibrated in his pocket, he ignored it. He'd check the text in a minute. He dropped a kiss on the top of Kitty's head, and she looked at him, eyes full of need. Drunk or not, he had to kiss her.

As he leaned in to capture her lips, his phone buzzed again, but it didn't stop this time. Only Thea or Kate would call, but they knew he was off duty. Josh tutted and shook his head.

"Take it," Kitty murmured.

With a frown, Josh took the phone out of his back pocket and answered. It was Kate. A local stud farm had an emergency with a valuable racehorse. No other vets could attend, and if the horse didn't get treatment, it could die. Josh ended the call and closed his eyes, his brows squeezed together tight. He had to go, but he didn't want to leave Kitty alone with Daniel Cunningham circling like a shark.

"I'm so sorry. There's an emergency, and it could end up being nasty."

"Oh." Kitty's face fell.

"I know. It's terrible timing, but it's my job."

Kitty gave him a half smile.

"Please go. It's what you need to do."

What he needed to do was get her home to bed. Not his bed, but her own. She should sleep off the prosecco. He wanted her wide awake when they spoke. When he'd finally tell her how much she meant to him.

Josh took a breath, his eyes on Kitty. "Please, don't leave with Daniel. Wait for me at the party." Josh had no right to ask, but the thought of them leaving together filled him with dread.

Kitty nodded, and as Josh placed a gentle kiss on her forehead, she exhaled.

He spotted Julia wandering towards them from the corner of his eye. She must have seen them duck behind the tree.

"Julia!" he called. "Can you see Kitty gets home for a sleep? She's tired."

"I hope she's okay," said Julia. "I tried to keep an eye on her, but she likes to do her own thing."

Josh smiled. He wouldn't want it any other way.

48

KITTY

KITTY WOKE in the amber light of late afternoon and checked the clock on the side table. How long had she been asleep? She sat up against the plump pillows and thought back over the day. A lot of it was a hazy blur, but her body buzzed with excitement as she remembered the best bit of all. Sure she hadn't dreamed them up, Josh's words turned around and around in her head. Words he'd said as he held her close.

"I can't let you go."

Thank goodness for prosecco! She'd never have had the courage to touch him if she was sober.

Kitty sat on the edge of her bed, looking at her closed laptop lying abandoned on the floor. She gave it a small kick. The sheen of the thing she'd craved, the shiny new job offer, had dulled.

Kitty sighed. The thought of leaving Julia and the village twisted in her gut. She'd grown to love her life amongst the chaos of the animals and relentless rolling fields. There was peace here, and a purpose. No relentless pursuit of goals, no drive to prove herself in the cocoon of Julia's quiet house.

And then there was Josh. The corners of her mouth curled, and she stretched luxuriously before heading to the shower.

Fifteen minutes later, there was a knock at her door. It was Julia. The room was in chaos, clothes strewn everywhere. Kitty was in a tizzy, picking what to wear. As her eyes scanned the room, dresses were draped on every available piece of furniture.

She hardly recognised herself. The mayhem around her was a far cry from the woman who arrived in this house a month ago. *That* Kitty always kept her room perfectly ready for a kit inspection. *That* Kitty craved order and calm. *This* Kitty grunted in exasperation as she threw items out of a drawer, looking for the perfect pair of knickers.

"We have a visitor, Kitty," Julia said outside the door.

Josh! Had he gotten away early and come to see her before the party?

"I'll be down in ten," she said, holding up the successfully located knickers with a grin of triumph.

After applying some makeup, Kitty chose a silk dress of dark jade, slipping it on over her head. The fabric caressed her skin as it slid over her body, and her thoughts drifted to Josh's lips. The dress clung to her long, willowy frame, its thin spaghetti straps raking over her collarbones and the neckline plunging between her small breasts.

She wouldn't have had the courage to wear the dress before, but her lips spread into a smile as she admired herself in the mirror. Kitty popped her phone in her bag, picked up the matching green heels she'd bought with the dress, and headed downstairs in a spritz of cherry blossom.

Low voices drifted from the garden, and her heart skipped a beat. She followed the sound of laughter and swept onto the patio, ready to see Josh. The face that greeted her wasn't his but Daniel's. He looked like the hungry, big bad wolf as his eyes moved up and down her body, and Kitty's heart sank.

"Christ, Katherine. You look incredible," he said, standing up and drawing closer to give her a lingering kiss on the cheek.

Doused in spicy cologne, he wore a simple but beautifully tailored black suit and white shirt. He looked and smelled expensive.

Kitty plastered a smile on her face when she saw him, telling herself to go through the motions until she saw Josh. She'd agreed to go to the ball with Daniel, so she had to see it through. Julia disappeared to get changed. Kitty and Daniel sat on the patio, the bees still buzzing in the honeysuckle around them. He settled his dark, dangerous eyes on her.

"Where did you disappear to after the match? Last time I saw you, you were slipping into the trees."

Kitty's body crackled with heat. Had he seen her and Josh? Based on recent slips of the tongue, she hoped not.

"I was dizzy. I'd had too much to drink." Kitty's smile was laced with deceit. "Julia took me to get some fresh air."

One of Daniel's eyebrows raised. "Well, I have to say, Julia looks great in jeans and a T-shirt."

Kitty's face scorched hot. He *had* seen them, and he knew she'd lied.

"And are you feeling better now?" he asked, unscrewing the top off the bottle of single malt he'd already opened.

"Thankfully, yes."

He tipped up the bottle and poured some of the amber liquid into a glass.

"It was probably the sun more than anything. I wanted your opinion on this, but I understand if you'd rather not. I bought it with you in mind, though. It's a thing of beauty. Smooth and dark."

The last thing she wanted was to drink hard spirits with Daniel Cunningham. Her track record in that area wasn't the best. "No, I won't, thank you. You go ahead, though."

Julia joined them for a drink, looking like a bird of paradise in a feather-trimmed kimono, golden curls pinned up on her head. Daniel made a fuss of her, making a great show of "taking them to the ball." He had Julia in stitches as he escorted them to their *carriage*. Kitty smiled at her aunt's delight. For all his faults, he certainly knew how to be prince charming.

Daniel left the top of his car down, and they quickly covered the short journey to Patricia's house. She was hosting the party, and this time Kitty remembered to hold her hair back as they whizzed along the lanes, the warm breeze lashing at their skin.

They pulled up to the beautiful stone facade of the manor house, and Daniel parked right at the front of the gravel driveway, much to Patricia's annoyance. She walked towards them, tutting and muttering about flowerbeds and tyre tracks, but Daniel soon soothed her irritation, insisting on escorting her and Julia into the party.

The festivities were in full swing. The garden was decorated with hundreds of fairy lights and lanterns, keeping with the midsummer night's dream theme.

A bar, run by Amber, was set up near the ornamental fishpond. Whoever thought glasses, booze, and fishponds were a good mix was crazy. Kitty had already wobbled in her heels on the paving. Judging by the look of some of the other partygoers, it was only a matter of time before somebody fell in.

Julia and Kitty waited in the dusk for Daniel to get drinks. Garden statues of stone nestled in the hedges, and a smile touched Kitty's lips. Someone had drawn a moustache and glasses on a statue of Eros, and a reproduction Venus de Milo sported a cocktail umbrella at her groin. Kitty giggled. Take that, Patricia.

Julia spotted one of her friends across the garden. With a wave and a kiss, she drifted into the throng of the crowd. Julia and her friend jostled and swayed to the music, a riot of colour. Kitty was left alone, wishing she had access to a Sharpie and a blank statue, but Daniel soon returned, holding two glasses in his hands.

"Thank you," Kitty said as he passed her a flute of champagne. "I can't believe how much effort people have gone to."

"But none can hold a candle to you, fair Katherine." He touched his glass to hers and looked deep into her eyes. "You're doing wonders for my reputation. There's not a man, and perhaps a few women here, who wouldn't swap places with me tonight."

A warm glow touched Kitty's cheeks. Even if Daniel wasn't the man for her, he never failed to make her feel desirable. She'd miss his compliments and naughty jokes.

49

DANIEL

AS THE EVENING wore on and the light faded, the party ramped up. Daniel had never had so much fun with a woman before. Usually content to conquer and then move on to the next, spending time with Kitty was different. She was smart and witty, and tonight she had a glow about her he'd not seen before.

Daniel had been far more attentive than he normally was with any woman. He'd made himself scarce when she chatted with her cousin, proudly introduced her to the rest of the Young Guns team and stifled several yawns during an awkward conversation with Patricia Gore.

There was no sign of Josh yet, but Kitty checked her phone every few minutes. When he'd asked her where Josh was, she'd breezily mentioned an emergency call out. So, she was waiting for him to arrive? It irritated him to think that her mind was on someone else while he was trailing her around the party like a puppy dog.

Daniel had spotted them after the cricket match, tucking themselves behind a tree. Unnoticed, he'd seen enough to convince him that he was dead in the water where Kitty was concerned. Seeing them in each other's arms was a punch to his gut. Desperation grew within him. He wanted her so much. He needed to get her mind off Josh's whereabouts, to give himself one last opportunity to win her.

The DJ hammered out pop hits from the 90s to a grateful crowd of dancers. Others would see a happy crowd of people having fun. But Daniel saw an opportunity to separate Kitty from her phone as he watched some of the more flamboyant movers. He seized a passing Julia and suggested that Kitty take her to dance. Julia, full of gin, grabbed a reluctant Kitty's hand and led her to join the others already gyrating raucously on the dance floor.

"I'll keep your bag safe," Daniel said, relieving her of her clutch and waving her off wide-eyed behind a disappearing Julia.

Daniel turned away as soon as Kitty was out of view and opened the small bag to find her phone. There on the home screen was a message from Josh. He couldn't have timed his interference better if he'd tried.

Josh: Just got back in the truck. Heading for the shower first, then straight to you. J x

The corners of Daniel's mouth curled down when he read it. *Fuck.* Golden boy was on his way. He estimated he had about forty-five minutes to change Kitty's mind. To convince her he was the right choice. To save himself from his first-ever heart-break. He quickly stashed her bag, including her phone, behind a massive urn filled with hydrangeas. *Out of sight, out of mind.*

50

KITTY

FUELLED BY GIN AND CHAMPAGNE, Julia kept Kitty busy on the dance floor. Any form of public dancing would typically be her worst nightmare. Still, tonight she was happy to see Julia having fun and was so excited at the prospect of seeing Josh that she didn't care.

As her body fizzed with excitement, she bumped and ground with the best of them, hair flying wildly around her. The garden spun almost as much as she did, and the heat of the evening dulled her senses.

Daniel was never far away from her side. Like a protective older brother, he leaned against the wall next to the dance floor, a smile playing on his lips.

People assumed they were an item all night. She hadn't *exactly* shut the idea down. He showed her off like a peacock, and she'd given in to the ego massage.

Josh was still nowhere to be seen. It'd been hours since the end of the cricket match. Was he even coming? He could have got a message to her somehow. She'd been checking her phone all evening, and nothing.

At that moment, it occurred to her that she hadn't seen her phone or bag for a while. Daniel had put it somewhere safe.

The DJ put on a sexy, slow track, and from the side of the dancefloor, Daniel her the full high beam of his smile. He straightened up as she walked towards him.

"Hello gorgeous," he said. It was his standard greeting, but the look on his face was anything but standard. Taking one of her hands, he drew Kitty in closer.

"Would you dance with me? One last hurrah before the clock strikes midnight?"

The look in his eyes flashed a warning, but he'd been so good all evening. There'd been no going back on their 'friends' deal. She'd rather dance with Josh, but he wasn't there. Her brow furrowed. Why the hell not?

Kitty nodded. Daniel squeezed her hand and pulled her across the dimly lit dance floor to a quiet corner. Fairy lights twinkled around them, and the muggy cloy of the evening air clung to her skin. Many partygoers gravitated into Patricia's house, and the dance floor was quiet. Now, as they swayed to the music, Daniel's snaked his hands around her waist, the silk of her dress easing their path. Kitty's eyes flitted around the garden as his hands rested above her buttocks.

"Who do you keep looking for?" he asked.

"Nobody," she said, smiling at him, firming her grip on his shoulders.

"Good," he said in a quiet, low tone. "I want you all to myself for this song. I have to give you up soon." He took a breath. "You know, something funny happened earlier." Daniel's eyes shone.

"Don't tell me you actually succumbed to the cream horns?"

His lips curled. "Not today, though I was sorely tempted. I was talking to Amber. Telling her all about our new status as friends. And do you know what she said?"

Kitty's pulse quickened.

"Do I want to know?"

He flicked his eyebrows. "She said I was in love with you." Kitty's eyes widened, her shoulders tensed, a slow burn creeping up from her chest. What the hell was Daniel talking about?

"But that's silly. What gave her that idea?"

"She said she's never seen me so into anyone before. That I've never really cared about anyone like I care about you. And she's right." Daniel's eyes glittered dangerously, like a cobra hypnotising his prey. His angular face, serious and hungry, drew closer to hers.

"*I'd* never let you down. You mean too much to me," he said.

"What are you talking about?"

Daniel leaned forward to whisper in her ear.

"*I'm* the one who's actually here, Katherine."

Kitty swallowed hard as they moved together to the music. As the woody, musky smell of his cologne filled her head, the ghost of Josh's words hung over her. "*Wait for me at the party.*"

Kitty opened her mouth to speak.

"Daniel..."

"He's not coming."

Kitty's stomach lurched. Did Daniel know something she didn't?

"He's selfish. He'll always put his work before you. You're worth more than that. And I want to show you what you're worth to *me*."

Daniel's palms spread across her lower back and gently pulled her into him. Her mind swirled with his words.

"Who's not coming?" she asked.

"Your precious vet. I saw you together today, and it broke my heart."

Kitty flushed hot.

"He won't worship you like I would."

Kitty's jaw set tight. Daniel was wrong. "You don't know what you're talking about," she said.

"Well, where is he then?"

Daniel's hands tightened, and he pulled her towards his body.

"I love you, Kitty."

No sooner were the words out than his lips were on hers. His kiss stunned her. First, she froze. Then, when his mouth didn't leave hers, Kitty put all her energy into her arms, gripping his shoulders and pushing him away. At first, he tried to hold himself against her, but when she managed to separate their mouths, she lifted a hand and slapped him around the face.

"What the hell are you doing, Daniel?" she yelled.

Daniel staggered back onto the dance floor, and his hand flew to his cheek. His eyes were wide, and his chest heaved as he regained his footing. As Kitty glared at him, he put his hands up in front of his chest, palms towards her.

"Shit! Oh, fuck. I'm so sorry. Katherine, please. I'm so sorry. I don't know what came over me."

Daniel's face was pale and drawn. Kitty almost felt sorry for him. Almost. There was no excuse for what he'd just done, and she stood, hands on her hips, ready to let him know.

"How dare you! So much for being friends. I trusted you."

Daniel's shoulders slumped in defeat. He looked at Kitty, devastation on his face.

"I don't know what to say. I love you. I can't believe I did that. Kitty, please, that's not who I am."

She sucked in her lips. "I don't know who you are, Daniel, but I'd rather not hang around to find out."

His eyes darted around the garden as people noticed the commotion.

"You stay. I'll go. Please, believe me, I truly am sorry. I'll understand if you never want to speak to me again."

Kitty's frown eased, and she shook her head.

"Just go."

Daniel nodded and turned on his heel, heading towards the front of the house and his car.

51

KITTY

As Daniel fled the garden, Kitty spotted Jonty hovering on the edge of the dancefloor, a confused look on his face.

"What was that all about? Who lit a rocket up Cunningham's arse?"

Kitty shook her head, not wanting to get involved in a post-mortem of the evening's events.

"At least tell me what was up with Josh," he said.

Kitty's stomach dropped, and bile rose in her throat. *Josh?* Where was he?

"Jonty, where;s Josh?" Kitty asked in a tight voice.

Her cousin shrugged his shoulders.

"I have no idea. He was here a second ago. Then he took off, looking like he'd seen a ghost. Nearly knocked the beer out of my hand."

Kitty's heart hammered in her chest as the music pumped up, and revellers again took to the dance floor. Had Josh seen Daniel kiss her? Had Josh seen Kitty push Daniel away? Slap him? Surely if he had, he'd be the first to defend her. But instead, he'd taken off without a word.

"Which way did he go?" she asked, her breath tight in her chest.

"I don't know. The last time I saw him, he was heading out of the front door."

Kitty nodded and moved off the dance floor. As she stepped onto the paving, something squelched under her feet and looking down, her heart sank. Laying trampled on the ground was a bunch of wildflowers tied up in a piece of brown string. She recognised the same flowers Wendy had delivered her so long ago. Josh had been here. He must have seen Daniel's kiss.

Racing through the house as fast as her stilettoed feet would carry her, Kitty headed straight out of the front door, scattering several canoodling couples hanging around the front steps. She noted with satisfaction that Daniel's car had gone. Providing even more satisfaction, Patricia's gravel now sported two deep gouges where his tyres had been. There was no sign of Josh, so Kitty headed towards the lane, stopping only when she reached the gate.

Running out onto the smooth tarmac of the road, Kitty checked left and right, desperate for some sight of Josh or at least his truck brake lights. There was nothing, though. She squinted into the darkness in the direction of the village. The tall trees and their spreading canopies hugged the road like an archway.

She saw movement at the end of the tunnel of trees. It had to be Josh. The figure was tall, and its golden hair glowed in the light of the moon. Tearing the shoes from her feet, Kitty threw them down on the grass verge, tucked the sides of her dress into her tiny G-string, and took off down the road.

Muttering curses to the heavens, the stones tore into her feet as she covered the ground soundlessly. For once, she was grateful for her long legs. When she reached him, she shouted, her voice lost in her heaving breath.

"Josh! Wait. Where are you going? Slow down."

Josh stopped, still as a statue, the back of his shirt illuminated in the moonlight. His large shoulders tapered down to his waist, and Kitty bit on her lower lip. She'd only seen Josh in jeans or shorts and couldn't help but notice how impressive he looked, polished and dressed smartly.

"What is it, Kitty?" he asked.

Josh's silky voice had a sharp edge to it. He made no move to turn around, so she stood in front of him. The look of fury on his face filled her with dread.

"Where are you going?" she asked.

Josh exhaled loudly, a sneer on his lips.

"I saw everything, Kitty. You couldn't wait one evening for me?"

"I'm sorry?"

"I know you were drunk this afternoon, but I didn't think you would go and kiss Daniel. Not after what I said to you. Not after I told you what happened with Tabitha. How she couldn't wait one night for me either."

Kitty looked at his face. In the pale light, he was achingly gorgeous but oh so angry. He *had* seen Daniel's kiss.

"It's not what it looked like. He kissed *me*."

Josh huffed. "From where I stood, it didn't look like he was the only one doing the kissing."

Kitty's mouth gaped. "I'd never do that. I waited all evening for you. You didn't even send me a message."

"I did. I texted to let you know I was on my way."

"I don't even know where my phone is. I gave it to, to..." Kitty's voice trailed off. "Daniel." Kitty sighed.

Daniel had taken her phone and put it somewhere safe. She would've never seen Josh's text.

"It doesn't matter. It doesn't change anything. How can I trust you? I can't be on a relationship rollercoaster where I don't know where I stand. Not again."

Kitty's brows knotted, and fury bubbled up from deep

inside her. The anger she didn't know she held surged up through her body, and she screwed both hands into tight fists.

"Are you serious? You're insisting on certainty from *me*? Josh, you've done nothing but mess me about. One minute we're fine. Then I don't hear from you for days at a time, weeks even. I don't care how hurt you've been in the past. You can't treat people like that! It's not fair."

His face remained a mask as if he hadn't heard her. This cruel, closed-off Josh wasn't the one she'd fallen in love with. Kitty's stomach curled up at the irony as the thought struck her. She'd lost her heart to an unattainable idea, not the reality that stood before her. A hot breeze ruffled through her hair, and she held it to the side of her neck, coiling it into a tight bunch.

"If you can't trust me, that's your problem. But you need to grow up, Josh. I refuse to be with somebody who runs away or buries his head in the sand at the first sign of trouble. It's exhausting, and I don't have the time."

A stunned look settled on Josh's face. "What was I meant to think?"

"I don't know, but if you can't trust me, then there's no point in us even having this conversation."

Josh's hand left his side and hovered at his thigh. He clenched and unclenched his fingers over and over as if wondering whether to reach out to her.

"Can we talk about this?" he said. "I don't even know what to think or feel right now."

Kitty let out a breath, letting go of her hair. "No, we can't. I really care about you, but right now, I'm done."

As soon as the words left her mouth, Kitty regretted them. There was no going back. With one final look at his startled face, she turned back towards Patricia's house and walked away. Kitty listened for steps behind her, waited for a hand to touch her arm and bid her to wait, but it never came. In one day, she'd loved him, and now, she'd lost him.

52

KITTY

KITTY PICKED up her phone from the side when it buzzed. She'd found it last night, stowed safely in her bag, stuffed behind an urn in the garden. It was hard to believe Daniel had hidden it from her, but it was the only logical explanation. Kitty already had a message from him begging for forgiveness.

Daniel: I suppose love will make you do silly things.

She was tempted to text back that he'd never have put her in such a position if he did love her, but she resisted. The less contact, the better.

Kitty also found the text from Josh telling her he was on his way. Would last night have gone differently if she'd seen it? She'd spent most of the morning discussing that with Julia. It felt good to finally tell somebody else what'd been going on for the last few weeks. How the tug of war between her heart and her brain had consumed her thoughts.

Her phone chirped again. Half expecting it to be a second text from Daniel, Kitty was surprised to see it was from Thea.

Thea: Are you free to chat?

Kitty pulled herself up to a sitting position. She'd been lying on her bed, reliving last night over and over in her head.

She'd battled the urge to call Josh, despite her bitter disappointment in his words. Nausea brewed in the base of her stomach. Thea's message had to be about her brother. Kitty took a breath and dialled her number.

"Hello?" said Thea, her soft voice reminding Kitty of Josh.

"Hi, it's Kitty. Is everything okay?"

There was a short silence on the other end of the call.

"I was hoping to ask you the same thing. This is a bit awkward, but did something happen last night? Between you and Josh, I mean."

Kitty bit her bottom lip. How much should she say to Thea?

"I only saw him briefly. Is he alright?"

"Well, he was out at the crack of dawn riding the hell out of Madonna, and now he's holed up in his place, as miserable as sin. He's refusing to tell me what's wrong. If you call that alright, then I guess he is."

"I don't know how I can help," Kitty said, knowing that wasn't strictly true.

Thea sighed. "Kitty, Josh has talked to me about you. I know how much he likes you."

Kitty's heart skipped several beats, and a glimmer of hope ignited in her. He'd told Thea he liked her. But then she remembered his words from the night before and his lack of trust in her.

"If something's wrong, you'd tell me, wouldn't you?" said Thea, an urgent edge in her voice.

Kitty paused, choosing her words carefully.

"We had a bit of a disagreement. We're still friends, but he needs to sort a few things out. For himself."

A bit of a disagreement? He'd split her heart in two.

Kitty waited for Thea to respond. She could almost hear her brain cells churning over the phone. "But I want you to know that it won't affect my helping at the farm. I'm totally committed to you and the sanctuary."

Thea's exhalation rattled down the phone. "That means a lot, thank you. I promise not to bring Josh up again."

There was so much Kitty wanted to say. She wanted to pour her heart out to Thea and get her take on what she should do.

"It's okay. I'm an adult. It's not as if we won't bump into each other in the next couple of weeks. I'll see you in the morning, boss."

Kitty hung up the call, and a crushing weight hit her chest. She only had two more weeks in Tottenbridge. Two more weeks of feeling free. Two more weeks of being surrounded by wonderful people and two more weeks of seeing Josh's face. She didn't even have a photo of him, and stealing one from the farmhouse was all kinds of wrong.

The likelihood of her returning to Tottenbridge soon after she moved to London was slim to none. Her new job would require focus and commitment. She'd have to travel, meet the right people, and get up to speed. Kitty frowned. She wasn't remotely excited by the prospect. This was all she'd wanted, all she'd worked for. And now, she felt like a prisoner being led to the executioner.

53

KITTY

THE FOLLOWING DAY, just as she'd promised Thea, Kitty made it to work at the sanctuary. After thirty-six hours, her anger with Josh had fizzled out to a disappointed sadness. Already she missed the excitement of walking into the yard, wondering if she'd see him. The way his smile across the yard made her toes curl and the look of intensity on his face when he talked about his job. She couldn't excuse his accusations, but she didn't want to leave their friendship on such a wrong note.

After mucking out the pigs and then going over some final figures for Thea's business plan, Kitty needed some fresh air. She poured herself a glass of water and wandered outside. Ammy was playing in the sun, digging large holes in the herb garden against the stables. She'd left little piles of dirt on the cobblestones.

Kitty walked over to chat with the little girl. They'd become close, and Ammy had taken to calling her *Pretty* instead of Kitty.

"Hello there. What are you up to?" Kitty asked.

"I'm busy." The little girl waved her plastic spade around her, pointing to the little mounds of soil on the cobblestones.

"Well, I can see that. But what are you doing?" Kitty sat down and crossed her legs, the knobbly ground digging into her bottom.

"I'm making mud pies for Joshie."

Kitty's heart skipped a beat. Would she ever be able to hear his name again without having a coronary? "Why does he need mud pies?"

"Because you made him sad." Ammy looked up into Kitty's eyes. "Mud pies might cheer him up. Do you want to help?"

Kitty was floored by the little girl's words. She had to find out what Ammy knew, but grilling a four-year-old about her uncle's emotional state probably wasn't ethical. Electing for a gentler approach, Kitty grabbed a green garden trowel and helped Amelia add to her piles of dirt.

"Who said I made your uncle sad?" she asked.

"He did. I heard him and Mum talking last night. They were in the kitchen, and I crept down the stairs. They didn't see me." An impish grin stretched across her face. "I'm good at hiding."

"I'll bet you are. So, they didn't see you at all?"

"No. But I heard Joshie say he was devilstated, and then he hugged Wendy. She can't make him mud pies, though. Joshie says she doesn't have thumbs."

Kitty had to smile. He'd made the same joke with her. Josh was devilstated? Ammy must mean devastated. Was he really devastated? It wasn't a word the little girl would make up.

"And then Mummy said you were going away. Is that true?"

Kitty gazed down at Ammy, her blue eyes innocent and trusting. Her gut twisted at the thought of telling her she was leaving, but she shouldn't lie. It wasn't fair.

"It is. I have to go back to London. I need to earn money."

"But wouldn't you rather stay here? Jeffrey is going to miss you, and I'll miss you. You're good at playing Barbies."

Kitty smiled, her heart bursting with affection, but at the same time, tears threatened to come. She was so confused.

"I'll miss you too," she said.

Ammy stared back at Kitty before nodding her head. "If you're leaving, then we'll have to dig harder. We'll need to make much bigger pies because my uncle will be double devilstated."

54

KITTY

Over the following week, Kitty worked like a slave at the sanctuary to ensure things ran like clockwork after she left. She lost weight, and the dark circles under her eyes told a tale of sleepless nights and rumination.

Today was the most challenging day so far, though. It was the first time she'd seen Josh since the party.

He was fixing something underneath his truck, and Kitty hadn't seen him when she wandered up from the pond. As she drew level to the vehicle, a delighted Wendy shot round the corner, greeting her by pawing the metal buckets Kitty carried out of her hands. They clanked rudely against the cobbles, and she giggled, fending off the licks Wendy covered her with.

As she grappled the giant dog back to the ground, a movement behind the truck drew her eye, and Josh stood up, wiping his hands on an old rag. Her mouth ran dry, and her heart thumped in her chest. Incredible didn't begin to describe how he looked. He wore faded jeans slung low around his hips, and his T-shirt, abandoned in the heat, was tucked into his waistband.

Kitty had seen his body before, but it never failed to amaze her. His skin was as golden as she remembered, and every muscle was imprinted in her memory.

Fire shot to Kitty's cheeks the minute their eyes met. He seemed as uncomfortable as she did, looking at everything and everywhere except at her.

"Hi," Josh said, running his hands through his hair.

"Shit, sorry, I didn't see you there. I mean, I'm not avoiding you. I really didn't see you."

A touch of a smile played on Josh's lips, and Kitty cursed the return of her verbal diarrhoea. It spilt out whenever she was nervous around him.

Josh smiled at her. "It's really nice to see you," he said. "Wendy's been missing your ear tickles."

Kitty swallowed. Was he talking in riddles? Trying to tell her that it was *him* who missed her? And why was he smiling? He was supposed to be *devilstated* or, at the very least, furious with her. Why couldn't he play fair instead of being all cute and sexy looking? Reasonable. She'd built him into a villain in her musings, but his warmth disarmed her, one chiselled ab at a time.

Okay, she could talk in riddles too.

"I've missed Wendy too. I'm surprised she hasn't come to find me if she really wanted to see me." Kitty only hoped he read the subtext in her words.

Josh's smile grew a little bigger. "She's had a lot to think about. How are the plans for your move back to London going? Is everything okay?"

Was he trying to get rid of her now? Kitty sighed, berating herself for being so paranoid. He was making conversation, nothing more. Three minutes in his presence had sent her into a tailspin of confusion.

"It's good. I'm winding things down with Thea. Now that the sanctuary is running with the appropriate military precision, it's time to turn my hand to less demanding and less hairy clients."

Josh laughed. She'd missed his laugh so much.

"Don't talk about my sister like that," he said.

Kitty snickered. "I'll tell her you said that. Anyway, I better go. I need to get back home. I'll see you around?"

His blue eyes hung on hers, and he nodded, handing her the metal buckets Wendy knocked to the ground.

"I'll see you around," he said.

She turned, walking back to the house.

"Kitty?" Josh said behind her. She looked back. "Thanks for the pies."

Breath burned in her chest. Ammy must have told him about the mud pies. That they'd tried to make him feel better. Unsure what to say, she nodded and left, her head and heart in turmoil.

THAT EVENING, Kitty made her way through the better part of a tub of ice cream. She'd spent the day trying to convince herself that now they'd spoken, she and Josh could get through the next week without awkwardness. But no matter how many times she tried the notion on for size, she couldn't escape the fact that she was just as much in love with him as she ever was.

The thought of leaving Josh, Tottenbridge, and the happiness she'd found there was unbearable.

Devilstating.

She'd grappled with all the thoughts and emotions churned up from seeing him again and had decided her values were all wrong. She'd been so obsessed with success. But despite working like a trojan to build her career, all she'd really achieved was to make herself miserable.

She needed to talk to someone who wasn't involved or

invested in her disastrous love life or her work. Kitty picked up her phone and dialled Ronnie's number.

"Hello, Sis." The warm, familiar voice greeted Kitty like a soft hug, and she crumbled into a blithering mess.

"Ron, I've got something I need to tell you. Promise you'll hear me out."

By the time Kitty had finished, she was exhausted. Ronnie had been wonderful, listening to every minute detail of Kitty's story quietly and without judgement.

"Everything else aside, Kitty, what would make you happy? If everyone else disappeared, what do you really need?" Ronnie asked.

"I need to do something that fills my heart with joy. I feel that way when I'm with the animals. I make a difference in their lives. It's meaningful."

"Then that's what you need to do, Sis."

Her sister made it sound so easy. But Kitty could honestly say that even if Josh didn't exist, she'd choose her new life in Tottenbridge in a heartbeat. Living in this small village full of beautiful, caring people was the happiest she'd ever been. Why would she walk away?

After saying goodnight to Ronnie, Kitty turned to the laptop next to her. Her finger hovered over the touchpad. She took a deep breath and clicked the word 'SEND.' There was no turning back now.

Cross-legged on her bed, Kitty waited for the panic, the gut-wrenching plunge of deep regret, but she felt nothing. Quite the contrary, a sense of calm settled over her, and a smile grew on her lips. It was her first genuine smile in days.

Kitty had turned down her dream job, and she was smiling. For the first time in her life, she had no fixed plans and nothing, or nobody, to live up to. The feeling was exhilarating.

55

KITTY

THE NEXT MORNING, Kitty stopped off at the river on the way to Small Oaks. She wasn't sure what she hoped to find there, but as she plunged into the cool green waters where she and Josh had swum together, a strange comfort filled her.

She missed him desperately and thought of him constantly, but she couldn't and shouldn't rely on him to make her happy. She had to make a life for herself.

Later that day, huddled around a laptop, Kitty walked Thea through the business plan details. She talked her through the intricacies of an annual calendar of fundraising activities, a social media strategy, animal sponsorship programs, local corporate sponsorship initiatives, and even an educational partnership program to run with local schools.

"With the income we generate, you can afford to build the new cat adoption centre," Kitty said.

An adoption centre for cats and kittens had been Phil's dream.

"This is incredible!" said Thea, scanning the details on the screen. "You're amazing, Kitty. I could never have done this on my own."

Thea leaned over and gave her a massive hug. It felt so good to be held by another person. Maybe the ice queen had melted.

Kitty swallowed, nervous about her final proposal for Thea.

"There's one more thing," she said. "I want to be your Development Manager."

Kitty bit her bottom lip as she scanned Thea's face, waiting for a reaction. She was either going to love or hate the idea. The sanctuary had been Thea's personal project—and Phil's. She jealously guarded his memory and what they'd achieved together. Was she ready to take a chance on a failed corporate lawyer who'd got mixed up with her brother?

Thea sat still in her chair, blinking rapidly.

"You don't need to pay me a massive salary," continued Kitty. "Just enough so I can pay Julia some rent and support my Snickers habit."

The corners of Thea's lips twitched.

"I'd still do all the practical stuff for the animals, but I'll make sure everything else stays on the rails. You can even promote me to chief poo shoveler. I don't mind."

Thea's face cracked, and she dissolved in a fit of giggles.

Kitty's shoulders relaxed. "I promise you, I can turn Small Oaks around."

"But what about your real job? Aren't you due to chain yourself to a desk any day now?"

"I turned it down," Kitty said. The gravity of what she'd done finally hit her, and Thea's mouth gaped open. "If you're worried, this has nothing to do with Josh. I love working with *you*. I love all the animals, and I want to help them. I really think we can make Small Oaks a huge success. And if, as a side effect, Josh wants to be friends again one day, then I'll take that as a bonus."

Thea ran her fingers through her hair. It was one of Josh's mannerisms too. Could she honestly say her feelings toward him had no bearing on her decision? Thea leaned back and twisted her office chair from side to side.

"You say this has nothing to do with Josh, but I'm not sure I believe that."

Busted. Kitty looked down at her hands as they lay in her lap.

Thea continued. "This is his home too. But at least he'd be happy that there was a plan for us—for Ammy and me. He's been worried about us for so long. If you can keep whatever is going on with you and Josh separate, I say yes. I'd love you to work with me."

A warm glow spread in Kitty's chest, and she reached out and hugged Thea.

"Bloody hell! I'm so excited! Kitty, we're going to make a great team," Thea said, wiping tears from her eyes.

"Thank goodness for that," Kitty said. "We have an appointment with the bank on Friday."

56

JOSH

JOSH WAS RIDING Madonna across the fields when his phone vibrated in his pocket. He'd worked the whole weekend, not even seeing Thea, and was now taking some time off from trying not to think about Kitty. He'd promised himself he could obsess about her for the entirety of his ride, but after that, he'd go back to pretending there wasn't a gaping hole in his heart.

He'd only spoken to her once last week, but it'd been enough to send him into a tailspin. He'd been such an idiot, accusing her of kissing Daniel. He'd analysed every millisecond of that painful memory. He couldn't honestly tell if she'd kissed him back, but that hadn't stopped his insecure rant in the middle of the lane.

Josh pulled up under the shade of a tree and pulled out his phone. The text message was from Thea.

Thea: SOS

It was their agreed call sign in case either was in trouble. Within seconds Josh was on the phone.

"What's happened?" he asked.

"I have an emergency."

"What is it?" Josh said, hands trembling and urgency in his voice.

"I have a lovesick friend and an idiot brother on my hands," she said. "Do you think I need Fire, Police, or Ambulance?"

Josh exhaled. "That's not funny, T. I was worried."

"What's not funny is that I can't pin you down to talk some sense into you. This was all I could think of."

"Is there something specific you want to talk about?"

"Yes, there is. I want to understand how two people, who obviously care about each other, can't sit down and have a grown-up conversation about it. I want to know why they think it's okay to waste their chance at happiness."

Josh sighed and patted the side of Madonna's neck, the moisture from her sweat evidence of how hard they'd ridden.

"It's not that simple, Thea. I know I've messed things up, but I'm still losing Kitty even if the Daniel thing hadn't happened. She still goes back to London and leaves me here, miserable. Why would I do it to myself?"

"When did you last speak to her?"

Josh was ashamed to admit the truth to Thea.

"We spoke last week."

"Right, and what did you talk about? Her job plans? Your inability to commit to a relationship? Her inability to put you out of your misery?"

Irritation nibbled at Josh's gut.

"Mudpies."

Thea cackled on the other end. "Based on that, you deserve each other. Both of you are bloody miserable. It makes no sense. Look, I'm only going to say this one more time. You've shut yourself away for too long. You can't be on your own your whole life, and you can't run to the hills every time things go a bit curly. You need to take a chance."

"But—"

"But nothing. If you get hurt, you get hurt. It won't be any worse than you feel right now. What have you really got to lose?"

57

KITTY

"IT'S OFFICIAL!" Kitty grinned as she put the phone down on its cradle. "We got the money!"

"*You* got us the money!" squealed Thea as she pumped the air and jumped around the office in ecstasy.

She rushed over to give her a big hug. Kitty was so happy she could almost cry. With the financing locked in, Thea could afford to keep her on as Development Manager. She could stay in Tottenbridge and see Josh, be near him. Perhaps one day soon, they could sit down and have a proper talk.

"Phil would be so proud of you," Kitty said.

Thea unwound herself and looked at her, eyes full of tears. "*I* didn't have to do *anything*!"

Kitty wiggled her eyebrows. "Are you kidding? It was all down to you. The bank manager was like putty in your hands."

Thea rolled her eyes. "Only because you pummelled him into submission first! You're a bloody warrior. I can see why you were such a good lawyer."

She huffed a laugh. Her old life seemed like a distant memory now. After her email, the new firm returned with a better offer, but she had no problem turning them down a second time.

"We should have a glass of something to celebrate! I'll grab a bottle while I'm out," Thea said as she nipped to the kitchen to grab her keys. "I'm going to see the feed supplier, then I'm going to pick Ammy up from school." Thea walked back into the office. "The forecast said it would rain. Finally! The sky looks grim. Can you make sure the animals are all in?"

"Will do," said Kitty.

"Can you imagine what Josh will say when he hears?" Thea's smile dropped as soon as the words came out. "Sorry, Kitty."

"You can still talk about him. It's okay." In fact, she preferred it. Hearing news from Thea was the only connection she had to him.

"As long as it's not too weird for you," Thea said, touching her arm.

"It's fine. I'm a tough cookie, I promise. Now go! But negotiate us a good deal on the feed." Kitty rolled her eyes internally. A tough cookie? She was more like a soggy mush where Josh was concerned.

Once Thea had left, quiet descended on the farmhouse. Kitty sat, staring at the same spreadsheet she'd been looking at all morning. She'd already made an early start and completed most of the outdoor jobs on her list.

The office was a welcome relief from the thick, muggy air outside. As she glanced out of the window, dark, angry clouds hung on the horizon, promising relief. But their ominous colour meant Kitty needed to get all the animals inside.

The nerves at the end of Kitty's fingers prickled under her skin. 'All of the animals' included the horses. She still relied heavily on Thea to look after them. She and Simon, the copper-coloured gelding, had developed a kind of mutual tolerance.

Still, Madonna, the piebald mare, was another story. She

shied away from Kitty whenever she was near, her large eyes bulging and her thick tail swishing as she reared and stamped.

Distant thunder rumbled as Kitty worked in the yard to bring the residents of Small Oaks inside. Its booms echoed like distant cannon fire. As she secured the animals, leaving them with feed and water, lightning cracked above and around her, streaking a vivid pattern across the sooty sky. Just as she had as a child, she counted the seconds between the lightning and the thunderclap, the methodical action calming her nerves.

She was down at the meadow, encouraging a trembling Simon to follow her to the stables. He seemed to understand she was trying to help him, and once Kitty had him inside, she threw a blanket over him and tenderly stroked his nose.

With Simon safely tucked away, Kitty returned outside to retrieve Madonna. She stepped out into the yard as a huge boom of thunder echoed overhead. Her skin tingled at the electricity in the air, and large, icy raindrops began to fall. Slow, plodding beads gave way to a relentless onslaught, and it wasn't long before Kitty's clothes and hair were saturated.

With her wet hair threatening to blind her, Kitty ran, sloshing along in her polka dot gumboots to the paddock. There was no sign of Madonna at the gate where she'd last seen her. Kitty squinted her eyes tightly, trying to see through the thick curtain of rain across the field. It was no use. She couldn't see more than ten meters in front of her.

Her heart sank. She'd have to go in.

Kitty's fingers were too wet and slippery to grip the locking mechanism, so she clambered up and over the gate, dropping into the mud on the other side. The ground was a quagmire already, and the water was pooling in areas where the rain had been unable to penetrate the crusted, parched earth.

Not knowing what else to do, Kitty began to shout for Madonna. A voice nagged in her head. Madonna wasn't going to come running to her just because she called. She wasn't

Thea, and she wasn't Josh. The horse hated her. Nevertheless, Kitty continued to wade across the paddock, calling out over the thunderous deluge. She neared the end of the field, and Madonna's bold black and white markings stood out in the rain by the fence line.

The horse frantically paced up and down the wooden pickets, kicking against the rain and bucking each time the thunder rolled around them. What the hell could she do? She couldn't catch her, and she wouldn't come to her.

Trying to remember the Horse Whisperer videos she'd seen as a teenager, Kitty moved slowly toward Madonna, carefully using non-threatening body language. She managed to get within five meters of the panicky mare, but every time she tried to close the gap, she reared away and resumed her laps of the fence. Kitty wiped more water out of her eyes. There was no choice. She *had* to catch her.

As if the storm had other ideas, Kitty felt the air around her jolt as a blinding flash split a nearby tree in half, and a deafening crack of thunder rocked the field. It proved too much for Madonna. She turned on a penny, completed a tearaway dash around the field and flew over the fence to disappear in the haze of rain.

"Shit, shit, shit," screamed Kitty. She had no choice but to follow her. Madonna was Josh's favourite, and there was no way she would lose her. Kitty was determined to keep her safe for Josh.

58

JOSH

JOSH DROVE into the village just as the storm broke, the relentless rain slashing the desiccated streets of Tottenbridge. Negotiating deep puddles, he reached Small Oaks and parked outside his cottage. A feeling of nausea bubbled in his gut.

After Thea's call yesterday and a lot of soul-searching, he'd come home to see Kitty. To apologise for being such a fool. He couldn't bear the thought of her last week at the sanctuary being spent upset. He desperately needed to see her face. To look into her eyes and find the answers to the questions burning in his heart. It was too much to hope she'd give them a chance, but he had to try.

The noise of the rain hammering on the roof of his truck threatened to burst his eardrums. So, he sprinted out of the door, followed by an anxious Wendy, and ran towards the farmhouse. The front door was wide open, and as Josh entered, he headed straight for the office.

There was no sign of Thea. Or of Kitty. Josh scanned the scribblings on the jobs board for a clue. Where would they be? A thunderclap to end all thunderclaps ripped the air, and grimacing against the sound, he took the phone out of his pocket and called Thea.

Within three rings, she picked up.

"Joshie! Where are you?"

"I'm at the house, but where are you? Are you and Ammy safe?"

"Yes, we're stuck just outside the village. I got Ammy from school okay, but a tree has come down across the road, and all the traffic has built up behind us. We're stuck. Someone is on the way to move it, but we'll be here for a while."

"Okay, keep me posted, and stay safe," Josh said.

"Josh, I left Kitty to get the animals in before the storm hit. Is she there?"

Josh's heart lurched. There'd been no sign of Kitty in the yard.

"I haven't seen her. Which animals?"

"The sheep and the horses. All the others were safely inside."

Josh groaned to himself. The horses. Getting two spooked horses inside would be Kitty's worst nightmare. "I'll find her. Keep in touch," he said, hanging up the phone. Josh settled a trembling Wendy under a blanket on the couch and headed back into the tempest.

After checking the sheep and finding them all safely penned, Josh headed over to the stables. Simon was happily munching on some fresh hay, apparently oblivious to the chaos going on outside, but there was no sign of Madonna or Kitty.

Josh ran down to the paddock with the air vibrating around him and his boots sinking into the earth. The enclosure was empty. The gate was closed, but there was nowhere else Kitty could've taken Madonna. A sick feeling crept over him, and something elemental drove him to jump the gate and navigate his way across the boggy field.

Josh fought a losing battle against the mud. Though the thunder and lightning had lessened, the rain was still relentless. He finally reached the fence, but there was no sign of them. Absolutely exhausted, Josh leaned against the sodden wood and scanned the tree line ahead. Where the hell could they be?

His eyes raked the fields beyond, and as the sky lit up momentarily, he spotted something in the distance. Squinting against the sting of the rain, Josh saw something so hearteningly familiar but so out of place that he had to blink a few times to ensure he didn't imagine it. Sure now, he sucked in a breath and ducked through the fence, heading down towards the culvert running between their field and the next farm's.

As he'd thought, Kitty's pink polka-dot boots lay abandoned in the grass. They were coated in mud and spewing water, but she couldn't have gotten far if she'd left them here. Josh shielded his eyes and headed down through the trees towards the ditch at the bottom.

"Kitty! Kitty!" he shouted, his desperation growing with every reply of silence. God, he hoped she was okay. That nothing had happened to her. The thought of her getting hurt sent dread through his body. He needed to tell her what an idiot he'd been.

The ground fell away from his feet, and it was then that Josh saw them. Kitty was standing thigh-deep in a torrent of muddy water at the mouth of the culvert, clinging to a wild-eyed Madonna. Josh's breath caught, and his only thought was to get to them.

He ran the short distance to the edge of what was usually a gentle stream, coming to a slithering stop before he joined them in the water.

"Kitty!"

Her head flipped towards the sound of his voice, and her eyes found his. His heart clenched at the fear in them.

"She jumped the fence," Kitty shouted as if on autopilot. "I couldn't stop her, and now she's stuck here. I can't move her. I'm not strong enough."

Josh wiped his eyes. "It's too dangerous to move her yourself," he shouted, resisting the urge to jump in and touch Kitty. To run his hands over her and make sure she was okay. She heard him and nodded.

"The water's rising. I'm struggling to keep upright." The desperation in her voice sprung Josh into action.

"The edge is shallower over there." Josh pointed to where the culvert edge was lower and met the grass at a gentler angle. "I'll get a halter and rope."

"There's one hanging on the gate," Kitty shouted above the rush of the water. Josh nodded. He'd noticed it as he'd jumped over. Kitty must have brought it down with her when she came to get Madonna.

"I'll be right back."

59

KITTY

KITTY HAD NEVER BEEN SO pleased to see anyone in her life. She heard Josh before she saw him. With effort, she turned towards his voice. Was he really there? An urgency filled her chest as she stared at his beautiful face, rivulets of water racing down its planes. Every time she saw it, her heart lost a few beats.

Now, as Josh scrambled up the muddy bank to get the halter, Kitty turned her face into Madonna's coarse coat and gave in to her racking sobs.

The horse's slide down into the culvert was terrifying. But without hesitation, Kitty had followed her into the water. She immediately realised her mistake, though. The current was too strong, and the horse was too frightened for either of them to get out.

Now Josh had found them. Kitty's heart hammered as she clutched Madonna's mane and cried into her neck, the shield of it a respite from the cold water battering her face. Though still scared, the horse calmed under her touch and stood perfectly still as if stoically accepting their fate in the flood.

Josh returned far quicker than she thought physically possible. There was no way he could get the halter over Madonna's head from where he stood, so he threw it over to Kitty. She caught it in one hand, its sodden leather threatening to slither through her fingers.

"Do you think you can put it on her?" he shouted.

Kitty nodded, teeth chattering uncontrollably. She stood up on her tiptoes. Sharp stones and gravel gouged into her bare skin and turned into projectiles in the coursing water. Terrified to lose her balance and be swept away, Kitty laced the fingers of one hand through Madonna's mane while putting the halter over her muzzle with the other. When she was happy it was on properly and fastened securely, Kitty looked to Josh.

He moved towards Madonna's head and, hanging onto a thin tree trunk, leaned out over the water, taking the leading rope in his hand. They both tried encouraging Madonna to move, but she was steadfastly holding her position in the rising torrent around her.

"She's too spooked!" Kitty shouted, trying desperately to push her.

"You can't push, Kitty. It'll freak her out, and she'll panic. Can you help me lead her by the head? Once she gets going and realises we're trying to help, she has a chance."

Kitty nodded, brushing her hair out of her face. Despite her heart hammering in her chest, she moved closer to Madonna's mouth. The horse's big, yellow teeth loomed close to her face. Kitty looked into her rolling eye, and as if something silently passed between them, Madonna moved slightly.

"That's it, darling," Kitty whispered into her neck, even though the horse had no chance of hearing her over the sounds of water all around them. "It's only a short way. I know you're cold, but we need to get out now. It's time to go home."

With lurching steps, Madonna began to move and allowed herself to be led out of the water. It was slow progress, but Josh and Kitty managed to get her to the side, and he guided her to the muddy bank. Kitty stumbled after the horse and collapsed to her knees, all her adrenalin exhausted. Josh checked Madonna carefully. He ran his hands over her legs and body, and when he was sure she was okay, he tied her loosely to a tree.

The thunderstorm had blown itself out, and all that remained was relentless rain. Josh scrambled down the bank and held out a hand to Kitty. She took it gratefully and submitted to his strength as he pulled her through the slippery mud.

When they arrived on level land, Kitty stood inches away from Josh, breathing hard. His eyes travelled over her face and her body. He'd done the same with the horse, but for Madonna, he'd used his hands, not his eyes. An ache burned in her core. She wanted him to touch her too.

"Are you okay? You're not injured?" he asked, breaking her thoughts.

She shook her head. "I'm fine."

Kitty stared at him, counting the raindrops that hung on his eyelashes. Anything to distract her from reaching out for him. And yet, Josh seemed to have no such problem. His hand brushed strands of hair away from her face, his eyes taking her in.

"What were you thinking? Anything could have happened to you," he said a little too harshly for Kitty's liking.

"I know, but I couldn't leave her. She's your horse. She needed my help. Did you see how brave she was?"

A smile tickled at the edges of Josh's lips. Kitty's blood sang in her ears at the intensity of his blue eyes.

"But if anything had happened to you...the thought of something happening to you. I couldn't bear it," Josh said, his voice tight.

His eyes dropped, and the hand at her face drifted down the bare skin of her arm. Whether she was cold and wet or it was Josh's touch, all Kitty's nerve endings jumped to attention.

Fighting to control her breath, her eyes rested on his chest. His wet T-shirt was plastered against his body, outlining every muscle underneath. Kitty bit down hard on her bottom lip and, riding a wave of desire lost all inhibitions.

Before she knew it, she weaved her arms around Josh's neck, and her lips were on his. They were soft and warm against her own. For a terrifying moment, they didn't give. She pressed tighter, silently urging some sort of response from him. What would she do if he didn't want her, too?

But it was as if his mouth was on pause because he gave a small groan as his lips opened, and he kissed her back. The fire of Josh's mouth took her breath away. She'd waited so long. It was as if their lips and tongues were made for each other.

His strong hands reached around her back, pulling her to him, his hardness pressing against her thigh. As she ground her hips against his body, all Kitty could think about was the feel of him on top of her, under her, and inside her. She'd never wanted anything so much in her life.

Under her hands, though, his body tensed, and he pulled away, struggling to capture his breath.

"We can't. We have to get Madonna back. She's cold and tired. If she goes into shock, she'll go downhill fast."

What about *her* being cold and tired? Irritation sprung in Kitty's chest, and Daniel's words slunk, uninvited, into her brain. *He's always going to find something more important than you.* Kitty exhaled slowly. That he put his animals before everything else is why she loved him.

"That's why I love you," she said, her brain on autopilot.

As she spoke, her eyes widened, but they were quickly overshadowed by the size of his.

"I'm sorry," she mumbled. "I didn't mean that to actually come out. My head thought it, but my mouth didn't follow instructions to stay shut." Kitty babbled. She couldn't seem to turn the switch off. "Josh, please don't think...."

Before she could finish, his lips reclaimed hers, and he kissed her tenderly as if savouring the taste and feel of her. The hungry need was replaced by a softness that melted Kitty's body. Eventually, Josh pulled away and rested his lips against her forehead.

"I promise we'll revisit this. You need to take a hot shower when we get back, and then we'll talk."

"I don't have a towel or any other clothes," she said.

"I have a drawer full of T-shirts just waiting for you."

60

KITTY

After an arduous and slippery journey through the mud, Josh and Kitty made it back to the farm with Madonna. Kitty said nothing, but Josh held her hand all the way back. A quick call to Thea confirmed she was still stuck in the traffic jam but that the downed tree was almost cleared.

"I'll need to dry Madonna off," Josh said. "Why don't you grab a shower at my place. There're fresh towels in the bathroom and T-shirts in the top drawer, next to the bed." Kitty's eyes darted to his, the thought of his bed sending heat to her cheeks. For goodness' sake! She was nearly thirty. She had to get a grip!

Josh reached down into his soaked pocket and handed his keys to her.

"I won't be long," he said, pulling her into his body and kissing the top of her head. Kitty's arms snaked around him, and she rested her head on his chest.

"Don't be," she said before peeling herself from his arms and turning to walk the short distance to his cottage.

Halfway across the yard, Kitty stopped to drain her gumboots, putting one upside down on an upturned shovel, the other on a broom handle. She'd make it the rest of the way in her sodden socks alone.

She glanced over her shoulder to check Josh was really there, and her heart sang when he was staring after her, a contented smile on his lips.

Kitty entered Josh's cottage after pulling off her dripping socks outside the door. She'd never been inside before, had never dared to call around on the off chance that he'd be there. Her hand drifted along the kitchen countertop that ran under the window. There was an old coffee cup there and a spoon. The everyday normality of it grounded her.

Putting the keys on the side, Kitty walked across the room towards a door that stood ajar. She nudged it, and it swung open to reveal a small, tidy bathroom. There was a pile of thick, fluffy towels on the dresser, and as she took one off the top, the smell of his laundry liquid hit her nose. Kitty smiled. She'd smelled it on him countless times.

Shutting the door behind her, she turned on the hot tap in the stall. She stopped for a moment and studied her reflection in the mirror. Dark hair hung around her shoulders in heavy strands, and her cheeks were a rosy red. Steam reached her from the shower, and after peeling off her wet shorts and knickers, she glanced up to see her nipples, dark and hard against her top.

Damn, Josh would have seen that. He'd have seen her boobs in all their glory. She wasn't sure if she was more mortified or deliciously excited by the thought. Cursing the tingle between her thigh, Kitty decided it was the latter and flung off her top, jumping into the shower.

After attempting to scrub her wicked thoughts away, Kitty stepped out onto the mat and wrapped herself in the towel. If her cheeks had been flushed before, they were florid now. Looking for some talcum powder to temper their glow, she opened the bathroom cabinet and ran her hand along the line of bottles and tubes. Thankfully, there was nothing embarrassing in there. But she couldn't help but sniff the bottle of cologne. As she inhaled, its fresh, spicy scent assaulted her, so familiar and sweet. Wanting nothing more than to cover herself in the smell of Josh, she dabbed a little at her neck and wrists.

After carefully putting everything back, Kitty picked up her clothes and padded back to the sitting room. Thankfully Josh hadn't returned. She at least wanted *some* clothes on before she spoke to him.

Kitty dragged her fingers through her hair and headed to the door on the other side of the room. She found his bedroom and the chest of drawers he'd mentioned there. The room was neutral and bright, and she sang the hallelujah chorus in her head at the neatly made bed. She'd never have to grapple with the urge to do it for him.

Kitty sat on the edge of the crisp white duvet and pulled open the top drawer, selecting a pale blue T-shirt that drowned her. It skirted just below her crotch, which was far from ideal, but the thought of putting her wet knickers back on wasn't appealing. There was nothing else for it but to put on a pair of Josh's undies. She pulled on the handle of the second drawer, tentatively revealing its contents.

The drawer was full of trunks, and Kitty took out a pair and pulled them on. They looked ridiculous, slipping off her hips, so she searched the drawer for something smaller. Instead, she found a shiny rectangular packet tucked at the back. Without thought, she picked it up and examined it. The familiar logo and the words Durex, large and real feel, screamed out at her from the box. Kitty's eyes widened. Well, at least he was locked and loaded... and from the claim on the box, packing something bigger than average.

The front door banged next door, and Kitty threw the condoms back into the drawer, closing it hurriedly. Her heart thumped, and she prayed that he wouldn't see the glow in her cheeks and the guilt written on her face. Jumping up, she turned as Josh knocked cautiously on the bedroom door.

"Are you decent?" he asked.

Well, technically, no, not really. She'd just been rummaging around in his drawers uninvited, and all she could think about now was the size of his penis.

"Yes," she said instead, steeling herself for their *talk*.

Josh opened the door and stood, leaning against the frame. Kitty's heart thundered in her chest. He looked as perfect as he always did, his blond hair wet and in its usual disarray. Even from across the room, faint dark circles under his eyes were evident, but their striking blue still shone through. A muscle jumped in his jaw as if he held all the tension in the world, but his eyes burned with hunger. Kitty tugged down on her borrowed T-shirt and opened her mouth to speak.

"Josh, I…."

Kitty's voice hitched in her throat as he slowly walked towards her. His eyes stayed glued on hers as he stripped off his wet clothing with each step. First to go was his T-shirt. At the sight of him, Kitty's breath threatened to leave her body altogether, the knit-together muscles of his chest leaving her mouth dry. Next, he kicked off his boots and peeled down his jeans in a tantalising display of rock-hard thigh muscles. By the time he reached her, the only thing left on his body was a pair of tight black boxers. The second he was close enough, Josh took the top of her arms in his hands, looking into her eyes.

"What? I was a bit wet," he said with a cheeky grin. Kitty's mouth opened to speak, but Josh shook his head.

"Don't say anything. I don't want to talk. We can do that later."

"But I need to tell you—"

"You don't. There's nothing you could possibly say that would change how much I want you right now."

With those words dying on his lips, Josh leaned down and

kissed Kitty. He was tender at first, but soon, the blood rushing in her ears competed with the sound of the rain outside as his kiss turned more insistent and greedier. She gripped onto him, matching the rhythm of her tongue with his.

Josh ran his hands up and across her shoulders, dragging his fingers on the cotton of her T-shirt, the friction against her skin increasing her ache for more. Desperate to quell the feeling, she pressed her body into his, yearning to feel him against her. He was still damp and smelled delicious, like the outdoors.

Kitty circled her arms around his broad back, her fingertips on his muscles, trying to pull him into her body, to join the two of them together. In unison, Josh traced his hands down her back and found her buttocks, his large hands spreading across them. His hard length nudged against her, and the heat building between her legs thrummed in anticipation.

Releasing her slightly, one of his hands tangled into her hair, and he pulled it aside gently, exposing her neck. He snaked his tongue in a trail of slow and steady kisses down her shoulder, pulling the neck of her T-shirt aside so he could continue along her collarbone.

With a moan, Kitty urged him silently to just rip it off and consume her. Under his lips her skin had become a galaxy map of goosebumps, and as she tipped her head back, she reached down to take him into her hand.

Josh growled, a low guttural sound, as she touched him. His blond lashes did nothing to shield the desire lying within his eyes. He lifted his lips to meet hers, speaking soft words against them.

"If we do this, I'm all in. Are you sure?"

"I've never been more sure," Kitty murmured.

She bit her bottom lip and touched his chest, savouring every hard muscle. Dragging her fingers down his hard abs, she found the scar below his waist, and she traced it slowly, enjoying how his skin jumped beneath her touch. She'd waited so long to do it.

"Why do I find this scar so sexy," Kitty murmured, meeting his eyes.

"Goats aren't all bad, then?" he asked, returning her gaze with a scorching one of his own.

"Not all bad," Kitty whispered, smiling languorously.

With an intake of breath, Josh picked Kitty up and tipped her back on the bed. He hovered over her, the bronzed muscles in his arms and shoulders firing hard.

"That was sudden," she giggled.

"I need to make sure you're unhurt. As the closest thing to a doctor in the room, I'll have to perform a thorough examination."

Kitty grinned. "Go ahead," she said, wondering where her boldness was coming from.

Josh leaned down and gently kissed her nose, then her lips, then her neck, inching up her T-shirt with every brush of his lips at her skin. When it skimmed her ribs, he looked down, and one of his eyebrows lifted.

"Interesting," he said as he tugged lightly at the undies she wore.

"It was either that or go commando. I thought that might send the wrong message." Kitty smiled up at him.

"Or just the right one," Josh said as he moved down to kiss where the waistband met the concave of her hips. It was *her* skin's turn to jump at his touch, and as he slowly drew the material down, stopping just above the junction of her thighs, Kitty thought she was going to explode.

"Josh," she panted.

"Too soon?" he asked, teasing her skin with his tongue.

"No." Kitty struggled to catch her breath. "Shit, I didn't mean no to you, to this. I meant no, it's not too soon. Oh crap, I'm babbling again, aren't I?"

"Babble away. It's gorgeous," he said as he joined her on the crisp white pillow. "I'm almost ready to give you a clean bill of health, but I just need to check another couple of points before I can." His eyebrow cocked and brought his lips to her neck again, but this time he slowly worked the pale blue T-shirt up to her ribs and over her head in one slick manoeuvre.

"You've done that before," Kitty giggled, cursing her brain for resorting to humour in all the wrong places.

He looked at her, practically peeling her skin off with his intense gaze. "Not for a long time, and never to such a rich reward. You're beautiful, Kitty. You're everything."

As Kitty fought to control her shallow breath, Josh's eyes slid across her skin, taking in every curve. He leaned over and took one of her nipples into his mouth, his tongue brushing over its tip, sucking and flicking against its hardness, over and over. Kitty moaned and stretched under his lips.

Stroking an insistent path down her body, Josh's returned his hand to the undies that lay crumpled at her hips. This time though, he didn't stop. With his mouth still teasing at her nipple, he pushed them down gently, easing them lower, inch by inch, until he gave them one final tug. He lifted his foot and tucked it into the material, removing them completely.

Without a pause, Josh moved his hand to the top of her thighs and gently nudged her legs apart with the same foot, his thumb hovering over the aching bundle of nerves at her core. Kitty's breath hitched in anticipation of his touch, and sweet torture overwhelmed her as he trailed a thumb across her clit and down to her centre.

"I'm not the only one who's still wet," he murmured at her breast, a smile of appreciation on his lips.

Josh dipped two soft fingers inside her, his skin sliding deliciously against hers, luxuriating in the feel of her. "So warm," he whispered.

Kitty groaned at the friction—at his words. But she wanted

more. She wanted more of him inside of her. Moving her hand to grip his wrist, she pushed his fingers further into her, rocking onto them. She shut her eyes as she ground against him, and Josh moved his mouth from her breast to rest his lips against hers, his breath coming hot and hard.

Slowly, he pulled his fingers out, circled her clit with his thumb, and then slid them back inside. Each time Kitty pulled him into her, her body was on fire with need. Again and again, Josh repeated the motion, stroking and teasing, until Kitty became a squirming mess, waves of bliss overtaking her. She was going to explode.

"Please, Josh, please just... Oh, fuck!" And with those legendary words, Kitty came.

Hot breath reached her ear, his lips millimetres away as her body calmed.

"I've wanted to do that for the longest time," he whispered. "You don't know how incredible you are. How mad you've driven me."

Kitty recovered herself and looked into his eyes.

"Josh, I need to feel you inside me. I want to know I'm not dreaming. That this is actually happening."

A beautiful smile lit his face. "You're not dreaming, but I'm happy to provide you with all the proof you need."

Josh's voice trailed off as he leaned over, slipped off the side of the bed to take off his undies and put on a condom.

Hearing the noise of the drawer and then the wrapper, Kitty panicked.

"If you haven't done this in a while, are you sure those things are still in date?"

Josh laughed gently, joining her back on the bed, his hot skin against hers.

"That's the one thing about having a sister desperate to get you back on the dating scene. I found these at the bottom of my

Christmas stocking. I think we're good." He kissed her gently. "Now, stop ruining the mood."

Josh brought his lips down on Kitty's again, and her body came to life at his touch. This time though, she wanted him to know how much she desired *him*. She pressed against his pecs, pushing him gently over onto his back and straddled him, tracing his chest with her fingers. He watched her through heavy lids.

"You're everything I ever wanted," he said, reaching out to tangle his fingers in the hair that hung over her breasts. Kitty gave him a playful grin and bent over to kiss him, his cock jumping to attention beneath her. He brought his hands to her breasts, and a low moan escaped his lips as she ground into him. She quelled the sound with her mouth and moved against him harder, the sensation of pressure growing at her core, awakening her fire for him.

She needed him. Now. Reaching down between them, Kitty took his length in her hand. The condom packet had been accurate. With a smile, she lifted away from his body and, never taking her eyes off his, she lowered herself onto him. The slide was slow and delicious. Josh closed his eyes, and Kitty's mouth curled with relief at finally feeling complete.

With a glorious burn of power in her chest, Kitty began to ground on him, finding her own pleasure and giving him his. She moved on him slowly at first, but soon, her relentless rhythm brought Josh's breath to a ragged rasp. The throb in Kitty's core began to build, and she ached for her release.

Wordlessly, she took his hand and guided it between her legs. Needing no encouragement, Josh found her sweet spot, and her movements against him intensified. Undone by her pleasure, she clawed at Josh's chest, and he sat up to meet her, his lips locking with hers. Kitty wanted to drown in his mouth.

He held her hips and pulled her down onto him, driving

himself deeper and deeper into her. She broke their kiss, desperate to tell him how she felt and what she needed.

"I want you so much," she panted.

"You have me," he replied, his voice husky and tight against her neck. "I'm yours."

The pressure of him inside her, the friction of them together, sent Kitty over the edge, and she gasped, tipping her head back and giving in to the sensations wracking her body. She reached out to Josh, crushing her mouth against his, as waves of pleasure rolled relentlessly over her.

With his eyes on her the whole time, Josh went rigid below her, then with a low growl, he drove into her with slow, deliberate strokes until he was finished, and his body stilled. They were left clinging to each other, coated in perspiration, their breath heavy and fast.

Josh was the first to speak.

"You have no idea how good that felt," he said as he gently leaned back on the pillows and brought Kitty into his chest, stroking the hair off her face.

"Maybe I do," she smiled, kissing him just below the collarbone. "I have a confession," Kitty said quietly. "It's been quite a while since I've done that, too."

Josh snickered. "Well, if that was you out of practice, let me know when you're back in the saddle. I'll gladly take you for a ride."

"Oh, I will," she said with a giggle.

Josh brought the back of Kitty's hand to his lips, holding it there as if contemplating his next words.

"I suppose we need to talk," he said eventually.

Kitty looked at Josh, the smile falling from her lips. Was this the moment where it all went wrong? She had to tell him what she'd done with Daniel.

She nodded and slowly slid off him. Once he'd disposed of the condom in the waste bin next to the bed, Josh turned back over and pulled Kitty's body into his, spooning her from behind, one large hand holding onto hers.

Kitty took a deep breath. "Whatever this is, whatever happens, I have to tell you how much, how much—"

"I know," Josh said quietly, kissing the inside of her wrist. "I love you too."

Kitty felt as if her heart would explode with happiness. If he loved her, then she had a chance to make him understand.

"So, what now?" she asked.

"So, let's have that talk," he said, caressing her arm with his fingers. "One question each. You go first."

Kitty closed her eyes, trying to block the memory of the disastrous night at the party. "I didn't kiss Daniel back at Patricia's. Why didn't you believe me?" she asked.

Josh took a deep breath.

"Because I'm an idiot. I've been racing around, terrified at the thought of getting everything I want and then losing it. Perhaps it was easy for me to believe you wanted Daniel. That way, I wouldn't have to face my fears. But I've been so scared of being hurt that I only hurt myself. Hurt you."

"We all run away," Kitty said, stroking her thumb across his. "I've spent most of my adult life running away. From my feelings and my insecurities. But all I did was create my own prison."

"Your job?" Josh asked.

Kitty nodded.

"Well, it's time I stopped running," he said. "I need to let go of some old baggage and start living again."

"How are you going to do that?" asked Kitty.

"I'm going to give someone very special my heart and hope she looks after it."

Kitty smiled and squeezed his hand.

"She will."

Now was the moment of truth. Kitty owed him a question. And an explanation.

"Your turn," she said.

"Were you and Daniel ever seeing each other? He hinted that you were." The rigid tension in Josh's body pressed against her as he waited for her answer.

"Not in the way you think. Our hanging out might have looked like we were dating, but that's not what happened. If I'm honest, I used him. Strung him along. He charmed me and made me feel special, but I couldn't stop thinking about you." Josh's body relaxed a little behind her, and his feet entwined with hers. "But I did kiss him. Let him touch me. Not at the party, but before that."

Josh took a breath, held it down in his lungs, and slowly let it out.

"I have no excuses," said Kitty. "I could say that I was confused with how you were acting, blowing hot and cold. I could tell you how Daniel dazzled me. But, at the end of the day, I let my fears control me. What he offered was so easy, so convenient. What you offer is so much more."

Josh kissed the top of her shoulder, his warm lips sending a scattering of goosebumps over her skin.

"At the party, he told me you wouldn't put me first, that you'd never be there for me. You didn't come, and I was confused by his words, and then he kissed me. I knew you'd seen it when I saw the wildflowers you'd brought, but you wouldn't wait to hear me out."

Josh's lips found Kitty's neck, his warm breath tickling her skin as he turned her around in his arms.

"I'm so sorry," he whispered. "I've wanted you for the longest time. If I'd had the guts to show you, none of that would have happened."

Josh touched his lips to Kitty's, resting them there as their breath tuned into each other.

"Okay then. Is the confessional over?" Josh said, his face serious. Kitty nodded. "Then can we have a try at this? At an *us*? Even if we do this from miles apart, I still want to know you're with me. I'll visit when I can, and you can come here too if you can get away. I hear phone sex isn't bad."

Kitty's eyes widened. Josh didn't know about the job. Thea hadn't told him about her working at Small Oaks full-time!

"Josh, I turned it down," she blurted. He blinked at her. "I turned down the job. I said no."

"You said no? Are you serious?"

Kitty nodded. "I'm staying here in Tottenbridge. This is my home now," she said, finding and curling her hand into his.

Josh shook his head. "What happened?"

"Nothing happened. I just realised that everything I want is right here. You're looking at the Development Manager and chief poo shoveler for Small Oaks Animal Sanctuary."

Josh's soft blue eyes crinkled at the corners. "Really?"

"Why would I leave? I have a great new boss, and I'm even learning to love goats. Besides, I hear the local vet is pretty hot."

The enormous smile that grew on Josh's face was all that Kitty could've hoped for.

"And so," she said, looking up into his soft blue eyes. "You're *completely* stuck with me now. No escape."

Josh looked back at her, his smile turning mischievous as he gently traced his fingers along the side of her waist and down across her hip.

"I don't think it's going to be too much of a struggle."

THE END

EPILOGUE

Kitty sat at her desk in the office, re-finalising the run sheet for the day's activities. She'd poured her heart and soul into the Small Oaks re-launch day. Now that it was here, things were running like clockwork.

All the major donors had arrived and were being suitably schmoozed. They'd announced the results of the contest to name the new donkey, and next on her list was the photo op with Jeffrey, the pig. Thea was with him now, dressing him in a crimson bow tie and top hat. A large queue of kids had already formed by the sheds, ready and waiting for a snap with Small Oak's most popular resident.

A burst of cool air glanced Kitty's cheek, and smooth, warm softness brushed her bare skin. She reached her hand down to find Wendy weaving around her legs under the desk.

"Hey baby," she murmured, stroking the curls at the dog's back.

"Hello," a velvety voice sounded behind her.

Kitty closed her eyes and smiled. *Josh.*

He put a cup of coffee on the desk, then leaned down to

thread his arms around her, bringing his mouth to the side of her neck.

Kitty sighed, spun her chair around, and grasped his broad shoulders, their solid, taught muscles moving under her fingers. She smiled as he nuzzled into her, his sweet cologne tickling her nose and tempting her to claim a kiss. The feel of his lips on her skin would never get old.

She let out a low, throaty moan. "Can we just rewind a few hours?" she asked.

A few hours ago, they were locked in each other's arms, coming hard together, with Josh whispering into her ear how much he loved her.

"I think Thea might notice you've gone missing," he said.

Kitty giggled. Thea would kill her. Not known for her organisation skills, she was already charging around like a headless chicken in the yard. Her reliance on Kitty to manage the farm grew as the months passed.

"Well, if you're sure I can't convince you," she said.

Josh chuckled into her neck. "There'd be no problem convincing *me*, but I'd have to explain to Barry Johnson why I can't deliver his foal."

Kitty's head turned to Josh, and his arms around her loosened.

"You have to go?" she asked, standing up. Josh nodded and sucked a breath in through his teeth.

"I'm so sorry. I know how much this day means to you. If I could stay, I would, but nobody else is available to attend."

Kitty tipped her head to the side and studied his face. Josh's jaw clenched tight, accentuating his high cheekbones. His blue eyes searched hers for a sign that she understood.

Kitty knew Josh's insecurities well enough by now. He wanted confirmation that leaving her at the farm on such an important day was okay. That she accepted that his job left him little choice, and she wouldn't use it against him in the future. Like Tabitha had.

The same worry had come up in their thousands of conversations since that day in the storm. Slowly, she'd been able to calm his fears. She wasn't going anywhere and accepted him just as he was. The same way he did with her. Kitty would happily take as little or as much as he could give her each day.

"It's fine. I'm sure we can soldier on without you. And at least I won't have to fend off the ladies of the W.C. all afternoon. They can't seem to get enough of you," she smirked. Kitty often joked about hiring him out for their functions as an escort. Small Oaks would make a fortune.

Kitty pressed her body against Josh's and, with her palms on his chest, moved him gently against the wall. "I know *I* can't," she whispered against his lips. "And that's why you'll make it up to me later. I mean, *really* make it up to me," she said, gently grinding her hips into his.

Josh smiled that lazy, sexy grin she loved. "Anything," he said, meeting her lips in a long, deep kiss.

As blood pounded in Kitty's ears and her body came alive with desire, she considered handcuffing him to the desk. She could think of a few ways to while away the hours with him as her prisoner.

Reluctantly, she broke their kiss, and Josh weaved his arms around her waist.

"Are you staying tonight?"

Kitty's lips curled. "Try to stop me."

Technically, she still lived at Julia's but spent most nights at Josh's cottage. Her aunt's hip had mended now, and she'd added golf to her list of hobbies, not to mention her younger golf instructor. Julia was officially a cougar and never failed to remind Kitty that she still had 'it.'

The noise of giggling children filtered in from the yard, and Kitty sighed, moving away from Josh. "Duty calls."

"For both of us. How's it going out there?" Josh asked, checking his watch.

"It's good. Busier than I expected, though."

"Well, at least Ammy is running a tight ship. She's put bows on all the kittens, strong-armed the face painter into letting her have a go, and I may or may not have busted her feeding Jeffrey candyfloss."

Kitty snickered. "She'll run the country one day."

Josh grasped Kitty's hand.

"Has you-know-who showed up?" he asked, a muscle pulsing in his jaw.

Kitty sighed. He meant Daniel. They didn't talk of him often, but she'd hoped he'd make it to the opening today. Hoped that one day they could be on friendlier terms. Life in a small village made holding grudges awkward.

"No. And I'm not sure he'll come. Jonty told me he's hardly seen him at the pub."

Josh shrugged. "It's not as if you haven't tried. I don't think I'd be as forgiving if I were you. He lied, hid your phone, then kissed you without permission, and all because of jealousy." The furrow at Josh's brow deepened.

"Well, I am irresistible," she quipped, desperate to lighten the mood with humour. They'd talked a lot about what Daniel did, about what Kitty did, and what Josh didn't do. She'd been prepared to draw a line under it and had offered an olive branch to Daniel. He, in turn, had donated a small fortune to Small Oaks. Blood money, Josh called it. Insanely protective of Kitty's feelings, it would take way longer for him to bury any hatchet.

Kitty grinned. "We'll see if he has the balls to put in an appearance. But even if he stays away, he's practically funded the whole adoption centre. I should have organised a marching band and a VIP section just for him."

Josh huffed a laugh. "Well, as long as something good came

out of the whole mess. I can't feel sorry for him, though.

"Why exactly?" Kitty weaved her fingers through Josh's. "Do you think he had a lucky escape? Am I really that bad?"

"If he had the lucky escape, then I'll gladly take the punishment." With a mischievous grin, he pulled Kitty into his body. "Although it means you're totally stuck with me now."

Kitty gazed back into his soft blue eyes. "I think I can cope," she said, planting a soft kiss on his lips.

"You're perfect," he whispered against her mouth.

Kitty looked up into his eyes. "You said nothing needed to be perfect."

Josh's lips curled slowly. "You're right. But *you* are. Perfect for me."

GET A FREE E-BOOK AND EXCLUSIVE CONTENT

Building a relationship with my readers is one of the best things about writing, and I'd love to keep you up to date with what I'm up to and any new releases.

In return for trusting me with your email address I'll send you a **FREE** copy of the starter book for the Tales from Tottenbridge Series – Power Moves.

If you like laugh-out-loud humour, sizzling banter, and scorching hot romance, you'll love this steamy slow-burn story that introduces the village of Tottenbridge, along with some of its best loved characters.

To get your **FREE** copy, sign up at:

vickihilton.com

ENJOYED THIS BOOK? YOU CAN MAKE A BIG DIFFERENCE.

Reviews are the most powerful tool an author has when it comes to getting attention for our books, and committed, loyal readers, like you, are incredibly important.

Honest reviews of my books help bring them to the attention of other readers, sharing the love all round.

If you enjoyed this book, I'd be very grateful if you could spend just five minutes leaving a review. It doesn't have to be very long, but you'll make my day.

Visit: https://books2read.com/u/bWp50W

Thank you very much.

ACKNOWLEDGMENTS

First, to my family and friends who have put up with lack-lustre dinners, a lack of availability for coffee catch-ups, and the incessant tapping of my keyboard for hours on end. You guys rock!

Second, to my accountability partners, my amazing team of beta readers and my critique group. I couldn't have a better team of brutally honest but wonderful folk guiding me in my writing adventures. You know who you are, and I thank you from the bottom of my heart.

Last, but certainly not least, thank you to my amazing editor, Heather at Write On Studios. You make me look good!

ABOUT THE AUTHOR

Writing about love, passion and all things tingly has always been a dream for me.

Originally from rural England, I now live in Sydney's glorious Northern Beaches, where I'm steadily gathering freckles and dipping my toes into the ocean for inspiration.

With a focus on smart, quirky heroines and sensitive, sexy heroes, I create steamy, slow burn, contemporary romance. Always on the funny side, with a nice touch of spice.

I'm a devoted wife, mother of one beautiful daughter, a wrangler of assorted animals, and a lover of Skittles.

It's a mix made in heaven.

I love to hear from my readers, so why not give me a shout-out on social media, send me an email or send your romance loving friends to my website.

Come and find me at:

https://Vickihilton.com

All the characters in this book are fictitious, and any resemblance to actual persons living or dead is entirely coincidental.

Chowstr Studios Pty Limited

Suite 701, 88 Foveaux Street

Surry Hills NSW 2010 Australia

Created with Vellum

Printed in Great Britain
by Amazon